Best Wi

Feast of the Antlion

Also by this author

Breathless

Feast of the Antlion

A novel

Caro Ayre

Greenham Hall
TA21 0JJ

The Feast of the Antlion

This is a work of fiction. Names, characters and incidents are the product of the author's imagination or are used fictitiously. Any resemblance to actual persons, living or dead is entirely coincidental.

ISBN **978-0-9572224-0-3**

Greenham Hall
Greenham
Wellington,
Somerset TA21 0JJ

The writing journey has been a long one, and I have to thank my family for bearing with me over the years when I lost track of time while engrossed in the lives of the characters I was creating.

My heartfelt thanks also goes to all the helpful writers I've met along the way. Without their support and encouragement, I might never have had the courage to continue

Chapter 1

The cockpit radio crackled with static. “Trouble at top camp. Repeat, trouble at top camp. Can you assist?”

Sandra shifted uncomfortably in the confined space, resenting the interruption to her first solo flight since Nick’s death, a hard-won moment of solitude to enjoy the sunset over Mount Kenya on her way home to Ol Essakut.

She flicked the switch to respond.

“What’s the problem, Simeon?” She wondered what her newly appointed manager wanted that couldn’t wait for her to land. She trusted his ability to deal with whatever crisis the demanding guests threw at him.

“An armed gang has hijacked one of our tours.”

“What?” Her hands tightened on the controls.

“They held up two vehicles, stole all their possessions, watches, cameras, phones, etc. then dumped the tourists in the bush before disappearing with both vehicles and our drivers.”

She shivered. A million questions filled her head. One couldn’t wait.

“Are the twins safe?”

“Yes. Amina’s taken them to Nanyuki.”

“What can I do?” She tried to sound calm.

“Locate the tourists. We think they’re somewhere north of Hyrax Rock. If you pinpoint them, it’ll save a lot of time.”

“I’ll head there now.” She was glad to have a

practical task. His decision to evacuate her step-children made the situation more real. The thought of Ol Essakut becoming a place where fear could thrive made her shiver. She brushed a strand of hair off her face and focused on the dials, checking her position in relation to the mountain as she altered course.

"What else have you done?" she asked.

"Alerted the police and implemented the emergency plan."

"Good," she muttered, too embarrassed to admit she had no idea such a thing existed.

"How many people am I looking for?"

"Eleven. It's the Americans who arrived two days ago."

Sandra remembered their chaotic arrival. The staggering quantity of luggage they came with took ages to distribute to the right tents. They struck her as an odd mix of people and she couldn't imagine how they'd gel as a group.

"I thought there were twelve..."

"One of the younger Americans hiked back to break the news."

"What about our drivers?"

"The gang forced the drivers to go with them. They headed north. I've sent all the available manpower to track them down. Unfortunately, we're short of vehicles. Rory's gone missing again."

The annoyance in his voice came as no surprise. The unexplained hostility between the two men was escalating rather than calming down. Rory Lyons' presence on the ranch was a mystery, complicated by the terms of Nick's will. She had hoped the simmering dispute would sort itself out. Rory still ran the workshop while Simeon did everything else.

"How short?" she asked.

"I've just enough roadworthy motors to get those tourists to safety once I find them."

"Don't worry. I'll locate them for you." She looked at the vast expanse of sun-baked Kenyan plains below, hoping that her confident reply wouldn't come back to haunt her.

"Check Camel-foot Gorge."

She was glad she'd paid attention when Nick showed her the landmarks he used to pin-point the numerous camp sites and look-out posts on Ol Essakut.

The sun was sinking fast. The light wouldn't last much longer. The shadows of the landscape cast great dark patches on the ground below making it hard to pick out details, let alone spot a bunch of people who had probably taken cover under a tree.

She wiggled her fingers to release the cramp caused by her tight grip on the controls. Nothing in her twenty six years had prepared her for a situation like this. She regretted not asking Simeon for the names of the missing drivers. The ranch staff had been so kind and supportive since Nick died and she hated to think of any of them being in danger.

Gradually reducing her altitude, she scanned the countryside, automatically converting the image into paint colours, raw sienna for the most part, an overlay of cedar green where the last rays caught the tops of the bushes, and pink madder lake for the sky. She pointed her nose cone to follow the rocky gorge that snaked through the landscape. A small herd of zebra scattered as the plane passed overhead. She was close to giving up hope when a flash of white in the shadows caught her attention. Quickly she veered round and swooped down, skimming over the flat-topped acacias lining the sides of the dry riverbed. At last she spotted a group of waving figures emerge from under the canopy of trees. There were at least five people. A second sweep raised the number to ten. All were standing, a good sign. Only one unaccounted for.

She flicked the switch on the radio.

"Simeon, I've spotted ten people. They're down-river, roughly a mile below the bridge. I've buzzed them twice. I'll go round again and check for the last one."

"No, leave it. Head home, it's getting late," he answered.

His protective behaviour annoyed her. Men had a habit of thinking because she was blonde and only five foot tall she was incapable of taking care of herself. She'd never quit whilst there was even the faintest chance of her being useful, even if she had to land in the dark.

"I'll make another circle. Hang on … There's a vehicle on its side, on the road to the look-out hut. Not one of ours. I'll fly over Hyrax Camp before I come back to base. Can you arrange for landing lights on the strip?"

Doubt crept in with the deepening shadows. Perhaps she should head home. Her limited experience didn't include night flying, Nick had talked her through the rudimentary rules, but she'd never had the opportunity to put them into practice.

"I'm approaching Hyrax camp. The light is bad. Hold on. I see movement. It's one of the rangers. He's about half a mile away from the main tent, trying to signal. I'm going lower. There are two people lying on the ground. I'll..."

A clang of metal on metal made her yank the controls, pulling the plane upwards.

"What was that?"
"Shit! I'm being fired at!"
"Get out of there!"
"I'm pulling out. Three guys are waving guns..."
Another clang set up a reverberation that almost wrenched the stick from her hands.
"The plane's been hit," she shouted as she struggled to steady the plane. A third shot twanged through the cockpit. Searing pain ripped up the side of her leg. She almost let go of the controls, but managed to hang on, forcing herself to take deep breaths. She had to stay strong. She could do this. Then she heard a loud crackle from the instrument panel, all the needles on the dials dropped to zero. She looked down. There was blood trickling down her leg into her shoe. She tested moving her toes. They still worked, she must not give up.
"Sandra, what happened? Are you hurt?" Simeon yelled.
"No… no. I'm fine… but the controls are dead."
"Give me your bearings."
The dials were blank. "Dropping altitude... Take care of the twins."
"Don't worry about them. Concentrate on yourself."
She pulled, tugged and shoved every available lever and switch... nothing responded. "I can't turn her. I'm heading away from you over the river onto Chui Farm, towards the flat ridge where the aloes grow." Of all the places to land, Martin Owen's neglected ranch was the last place in the world she wanted to go.
"Don't... too many rocks. Find somewhere better."
"No choice..."
"You'll be fine." Simeon's voice was calm, almost

convincing, but she guessed he'd never been in a plane crash. She'd survived one, to live through two was asking for a miracle. Giving in to fear was not going to help. She had to live. Too many people depended on her.

Could she jettison the fuel? The luminous dots on the dials glowed in the half-light, giving no information. The engine cut out. She tried to remember what her flying instructor had told her about crash landing. One thing she remembered was to be careful not to overcompensate. Keep everything steady. She fumbled with the switches hoping to get the engine to restart. Nothing happened. She prayed her wheels were intact.

"I'm going down fast."

"Good luck," he shouted. She fiddled with the switches. The engine stuttered, fired. Blood pounded in her head. Feelings somewhere between elation and terror overwhelmed her. The engine died again, this time for good, leaving her with a rudderless glider. Her heart skipped a few beats, but her hands continued to fight with the array of levers, trying to coax the tiniest movement that would help her to gain some control. No response. The little plane drifted lower, skimming over the bush hurrying to land. For a moment she remembered the terror of her first landing. This was faster, bumpier, scarier with no slowing down. The plane ploughed on at speed over the rough terrain, straight at a warthog sized boulder sticking out in her path. She braced herself for impact.

One wheel smashed into the rock. The force blasted the air out of her lungs. The strut crumpled and a huge hole appeared in the floor beneath her feet, letting in a cloud of powdery choking dust. The lowered wing snagged on another rock and crumpled like tissue paper. The crippled machine spun in a circle. The clatter of sand, stone, gravel, and branches hitting the sides and the force of rushing air deafened her. The metal screeched as the guts of the plane disappeared from under her, almost drowning his voice.

"Talk to me." The plane juddered to a standstill. An unnerving silence followed. Simeon persisted. "Sandra, talk to me."

There was no time to check if the radio still worked. All she worried about was the smell of fuel and the danger of fire.

"I'm down. The fuel tank ruptured... I'm out of here…" She flung off her head-set and struggled to escape the tangled wreck.

Chapter 2

Habit made Martin Owen turn into the driveway that led to the Harriman's Ol Essakut Ranch. The imposing new rhino-shaped gates and an approaching uniformed askari reminded him that this short cut home was off limits. He'd never met Nick Harriman's widow, and he wasn't in the mood to face Rory Lyons either.

He hastily reversed back onto the main road. The official entrance to his property was a good hour further on. The extra hour on top of the twenty four he had already travelled by train, plane and car, didn't bother him. He'd rather avoid people and awkward questions.

He drove on until he came to the paint-flaked board for "Chui Farm". Leaning gateposts flanked the rough track, the missing gates replaced by a single strand of wire. He stopped, unhooked the barrier and drove through, stopping again to replace the flimsy barrier.

As he crossed the boundary of his childhood home the impact of ownership hit him. His mother's death, so quickly followed by Nick Harriman's attempt to kill him had forced a hurried departure two years ago. He rubbed his shoulder, briefly reliving the painful moment.

He had no idea how many people knew about the shooting incident. Simeon Mugo had helped him leave the country without alerting the authorities. The right choice at the time, but now he'd returned to Kenya he needed to know what story had circulated.

There was enough daylight left to make a detour to the highest point on the farm worthwhile, and delay his having to face the empty house a little longer. He sped through the parched, dusty landscape leaving a billowing cloud of red dust in his wake. Half a dozen white-bellied Thomson gazelle skittered into sight then fled into the dry bush, providing proof that some animals had survived the drought. A pair of zebras and a small herd of impala followed.

On reaching his destination he switched off the engine and automatically reached across to the passenger seat to rummage in his battered camera box for his favourite. His father's Leica. So good to have this trusty old friend back in his grasp. He slipped the strap over his head, flipped off the lens cap, and panned the view. Mount Kenya's massive base loomed up out of the deceptively flat plain laid out before him, its jagged snowy peak hiding behind a narrow bank of clouds. He twisted round in his seat, and through the open window settled his sights on the glory of the sunset. This was a better cure for his shattered nerves than any amount of Prozac or the mind-numbing drugs his fellow war correspondents in Baghdad had offered him.

The sun appeared to grow as it sank, changing from a dazzling glare to a fiery molten orange orb. Puffball clouds dotted the purple sky. He fiddled with the light meter, wondering if he could get the true colours to transfer to print. He took a picture, revelling in the pleasure of taking time over a photo. Working in a war zone forced him to use high powered digital cameras on Auto Focus to leave him free to duck for cover. More difficult had been recording the aftermath, to keep his sanity he worked fast, trying not to let the smell of blood or rotting flesh invade his psyche. Not that it worked. Horrific events etched themselves into his memory, along with the sound of gunfire, grenades, bomb-blasts, screams of the wounded and the wails of the grief-stricken onlookers. Haunting images invaded his dreams and made sleep an unwelcome state. Perhaps in this haven of peace he'd find a way to cope, or push the memories deep into the recesses of his mind.

The chattering, and twittering of birds would continue until darkness fell, the only other sound, the distant buzz of a plane. As his eyes adjusted to the light, he picked out the little Cessna over the western tip of Ol Essakut, instinct made him frame it and click.

The plane turned sharply and not long after turned again, swooping down, very low, circling over the same spot close to one of the Ol Essakut camps, going even lower. Dangerously low, he thought. No sensible pilot would take such risks in an area without a landing strip.

He reached for the ignition key when a change in the tone of the distant engine made him seek out the plane again. Now it rose steeply, too steeply for safety. Martin froze, holding his breath as he waited for it to level off. He'd seen some crazy stunts but none as scary as this. The light was going fast. The pilot ought to land soon, but now the aircraft headed towards his property, Chui Farm.

The plane dropped a few feet then jerkily recovered. Although still far away, he made out the splutter of the engine, as it lurched forward. The engine died.

"Get up," he yelled. "Get up." But the little plane kept descending, heading for Aloe Ridge, the most inhospitable stretch of land on his property and vanished from view. He didn't have long to wait. A fireball erupted behind the lip of the ridge marking the spot. He whispered a quiet prayer, turned the key, slammed into gear and headed towards the plume of smoke.

He raced down long forgotten tracks until the terrain forced him to complete the search on foot. He cursed at the absence of a first aid box, or any other useful equipment on board, and ran empty handed along an animal track up the side of the ridge. The swift onset of darkness deprived him of the half light the sunset had earlier provided. Sweat poured off him as he scrambled over the lip of the ridge. By the time he reached the crash site the flames had died down to a dull glow that radiated heat, the scant vegetation reduced to ash with the odd smouldering bush.

Martin stopped and stared at the wreck, wondering how many people had been on board. Habit made him record the scene with the camera that hung round his neck. He circled the debris, the light from his flash illuminating his way. A cough and a faint groan made him change direction towards the sound. He hadn't expected survivors.

He clicked the camera again. His eyes smarted from the cloud of acrid smoke that hung over the scene. He pushed forward to a shadowy outcrop of rocks and flashed again. This time, in the split second of brightness, he found the source of the sound. A figure lay tucked away behind the boulders. Another groan reassured him he wasn't too late. He clicked again, this time registering the details. A young woman with badly singed hair, her face covered with blood and dust, lay propped up against the stone with both her legs stretched out in front of her. She appeared to have a belt looped around her wrist and was trying to wrap the rest around her foot and was concentrating so hard on the task he didn't think she noticed the flash.

"Need some help?" he asked quietly, not wanting to scare her. His vision slowly adjusted to the darkness.

Her head jerked upwards, her startled face screwed up in pain. "I've got to get this arm straight."

He hunkered down to take a closer look. She was right. Even in this dim light, without an x-ray he could tell her arm was broken, but he didn't fancy attempting to manipulate it right here, without painkillers.

"Got to do it now… before it swells up…" Every word needed super-human effort.

"Are you sure?" Her assumption he'd know what to do surprised him. "Can't it wait until you get to a doctor?"

"No. Just do what I say... And don't stop even if I scream."

"I promise," he answered, though he had strong reservations, his rudimentary first aid, necessary for all war correspondents was rather inadequate when put to the test. "What's the belt for?"

"I was trying to get it round my foot to provide tension to pull my arm, now I won't need it."

Martin admired her confidence.

"Can I touch you? I'd like to check if anything is going on that should be dealt with first."

She nodded.

His hands felt huge as he ran his fingertips over her tiny frame, talking as he worked to distract her.

"Who are you?" he detected sticky blood on her silk shirt which came from a cut on her forehead. More blood on her leg drew his attention to a gash that ran from her ankle to her knee. The wound appeared to be drying out. Best left alone.

"Sandra Harriman," she answered.

This young girl was Nick's widow. He knew Nick married an English artist, but always imagined her to be more flamboyant, nothing like this petite figure stretched out in front of him.

"Who was flying?" he asked.

"Me."

Her answer surprised him, not many women took up flying. In England the weather made it hard, but here in Kenya flying was a useful skill.

"Passengers?"

"No... Skip the questions. I have to find the others."

He checked her torso and shoulders. "What others, you said no passengers?"

"Stranded tourists... down near Camel Foot Gorge." Her voice broke slightly.

He was impressed that anyone this badly injured could spare a thought for anyone else. He ran his hands over her head. Her hair was straight and silky, except where singeing had left stubby ends. Then his fingers touched a large swelling on her forehead just under the hairline. She let out a soft moan.

"Were you knocked out?"

"I'm not sure, maybe for a little while. I fell when the fuel tank exploded. That's when I hurt my arm. Can we get on?"

"Tell me what to do?" He felt odd about letting her take charge, but she seemed confident with her plan.

"Get a firm grip on my hand. When I say pull, put all your weight behind it. And whatever you do, don't stop. Not even if I scream my head off."

"How long for?"

"Until the bones have lined up."

"Tell me when you're ready." He grasped her

delicate, slightly sweating hand, undecided as to whether she was brave or foolish.

"On the count of three. One. Two. Three."

Martin concentrated on the angle of the break. He had her arm fully stretched to the point where he thought he'd lift her off the ground. She kept her heels firmly dug into the sand, pushing herself back against the boulder. He sneaked a quick look at her face. Her eyes were shut and her jaw clenched.

Something gave. She screamed.

The sound tore through him. He wanted to scoop her into his arms to comfort her. But he held fast. The displaced bones were still not in line. He exerted another burst of pressure, and another movement. Something had shifted. Her body sagged as she fainted.

He gently lowered the straightened arm onto her lap. He'd attempt to splint it while she was out cold. He found a reasonably straight stick, tore a sleeve off his shirt, ripped it into strips and set to work.

Chapter 3

Sandra woke to darkness, disorientated by the throbbing in her arm. Her first thought was for the twins, amazed at how quickly Nick's children had become part of her life. She recalled that Simeon sent them to Nanyuki with Amina, most likely to Nick's Aunt Jenny.

She ran her good hand over the bindings and the belt that acted as a sling bringing her predicament into focus. Better to think about the next move than the pain.

"We must go."

"Calm down. We'll go in a moment. First, let me adjust your sling."

She slumped back against her rock support and prayed for the agony to subside. Her attempt at movement took her near to screaming. The suggestion to wait had merit.

"I'll get you to the hospital as quickly as I can."

"I need to know the twins are safe," she pleaded.

"Who was minding them?"

She told him about Simeon's call, evacuating the children, the stranded tourists. Something held her back from telling him about the cause of her plane crash. She hoped that Simeon would have the sense to keep quiet.

"You can trust Simeon. If he sent the twins to safety, he'd have picked up those stranded tourists. They'd have been top priority. Simeon's good in a crisis. You must think so too or you wouldn't have appointed him as manager. And Rory's still around, surely he would help?"

"No chance, he's off on a rally driving weekend. He's always missing when he's needed."

"Nothing new," Martin muttered, as he fiddled with her sling.

She wanted to ask him for background information about Rory to help her understand why Nick gave him the right to live on the estate. No one else wanted to tell her, perhaps they genuinely didn't have an answer. His adjustments intensified the pain and she had to concentrate on hiding her agony.

"Let's do a deal. I'll take you to hospital and after that I'll go check what Simeon has done."

She let him help her up. His tall, lean frame towered over her as he wrapped his arms round her shoulders. His hand slid under her armpit locking her to his side. Once upright she realized she was too weak to stand without his support.

"Where are we heading?"

"I got here by climbing up onto the ridge using an old game track." He led her round the dying embers of the plane. "To be honest I'm not looking forward to going down in the dark, but we don't have a choice."

The pain increased with every step. She bit her lip, determined not to show the effort needed to put one foot in front of the other. She focussed on the pressure of his hand against her ribs. When she'd first caught sight of him hovering over her she'd assumed he was Martin Owen. His comments about Simeon convinced her. But he was so thin, borderline anorexic sprang to mind. She looked up, trying to make out his face again. Darkness obscured it. From what she remembered of the photos hanging on Nick's study wall, Martin had been the more muscular, athletic one, making Nick look almost scrawny by comparison. She couldn't believe this was the same man.

The intensity of the night made her reliant on him to lead the way. The lack of light didn't seem to bother him. The track narrowed, her legs brushed against thorny bushes and his grip tightened whenever she stumbled over a rock, his physical presence strangely reassuring.

"We'll stop in a minute for a rest," he said.

"No, carry on," she begged, afraid of giving in to pain.

"You might not need a break, but I do." He came to a standstill. "If we're lucky the moon will rise and give us better visibility. The next stretch won't be so easy."

Disheartened, she slumped against him making her acutely aware of his bony frame. Could she cope if the path got worse? It took a moment to figure out what he was doing. He was standing on one leg testing the ground in front of them with the other.

"This spot's clear. We'll rest here." He eased his hand out from under her arm, and placed it on top of her shoulder, pushing gently. "Sit down." An order, not an option, and she hadn't the energy to argue. She sank to the ground. He eased himself down beside her, putting his arm round her shoulder to support her.

The lack of motion intensified the throbbing in her arm. Perhaps the stabbing pain caused by each step had dulled the throb, now she couldn't decide which was worse. She took deep breaths in an attempt to ease the agony.

The stillness surrounding them was soothing. Neither spoke. The void filled with African bush noises. A useful distraction as she tried to identify the grunts, shrill calls, high pitched whistles and squeaks of the nocturnal creatures that surrounded them. The temperature plummeted, making her more aware of the warmth of his body against her skin. His proximity made her uncomfortable, but at the same time safe.

"I never introduced myself. I'm Martin Owen," he said softly, as if he were unwilling to interrupt the night chorus.

She had been right in her assumption, but puzzled, because gaunt or not, Martin Owen was supposed to be in some distant war-torn country.

"I heard you'd sworn never to return," she answered keeping her voice low wondering what reaction he would expect from her. If he expected a warm welcome, he was out of luck, especially if he'd come back to finalize the sale of his property to Beverley Wyatt. Could she talk him out of it? Or at least persuade him to sell to someone else. He must know the impact her ownership would have on the Ol Essakut consortium. Life was complicated enough without that woman having a part in the management.

"I didn't expect to. I wasn't sure I'd be welcome at Ol Essakut. I was sorry to hear about Nick." The sincerity in his voice surprised her. "You must miss him."

"We hadn't been married long - three weeks to be precise." She clamped her jaw shut, wondering what he would make of her response. She hoped he hadn't picked up her bitterness. No, Martin was only making polite conversation. All he wanted to do was make her forget her injury. He didn't care about her or anyone else. Once he'd sold his land he'd vanish out of their lives for good.

"That doesn't make it any less painful. Had you known him for long?"

She wished he'd shut-up. She didn't want to talk about Nick, but found herself compelled to answer.

"Three months," she whispered, her voice breaking with emotion, "and three weeks." His arm tightened round her shoulder, his kindness made matters worse. "I was so happy. I thought he was too…" A stifled sob stopped her saying more.

"It's okay, you don't have to talk." He pulled her into his chest and held her firmly. She fought to regain control of her emotions and shifted her position slightly. The movement bumped her injured arm, the throbbing pain turned to one of heart-stopping intensity. She pulled away from him, embarrassed by her near loss of control and shocked that she had come close to revealing the truth about Nick to him of all people. He lowered his arm, while she wiped her eyes with the back of her good hand.

The huge, blood red moon crept up on the horizon, the size and colour awesome. As it rose, it became smaller but brighter. The shape of the landscape emerged from the gloom. Maybe now Martin would move on.

"Can we go?" she begged. Martin helped her up clasped her to his side and led onwards in silence. She tried to ignore the pulsing ache and the bouts of dizziness that made her want to beg to stop.

Little clouds scudded by, obscuring the moon, plunging them into momentary darkness. Martin's vision seemed to adjust faster than hers as he propelled her forward.

After what felt like hours, he halted.

"We have to go single file from here," he said. "The track goes down the face of the ridge. It'll be steep and narrow, and the surface loose and slippery. Can you manage?"

"Lead on."

"Grab my belt tight with your good hand." He adjusted his stance, "I'll lead. I'll take it slowly. Tug if you want to stop."

With one hand firmly on hers, he inched forward, allowing her to get used to the change of pace and the gritty terrain. Gradually he picked up speed and she adapted to his stride. She liked that he didn't pester her for updates on her condition. Keeping upright sapped her energy. Time and distance lost their significance. Dizziness returned, her grip slackened and her knees wobbled. She tried to steady herself but Martin spun round and clamped her against him with her splinted arm sandwiched against his chest, lifting her feet of the ground and squeezing the air out of her lungs, making screaming impossible.

He stumbled. The path crumbled. He jumped sideways, setting off at a run with her in his arms. With each step he took, the pressure on her injured arm became more unbearable. Her moans drowned by the avalanche of sand and stones that cascaded down the slope into the dark void below.

His grip never eased. Thorny bushes tugged at her clothes and flesh on the way down. The tangled roots of an old tree stump halted the descent. The momentum ceased and Sandra found herself lying on a bed of choking dusty soil, trapped under the weight of Martin's body, his camera digging into her ribs. Clouds of debris piled down on top of them. She spat out some dirt, and was drawing breath into her lungs to bellow to him to move, when his hand clamped over her mouth. She thought for a moment he was trying to suffocate her.

"Shush," he hissed, with such urgency she froze.

His tension transmitted itself, heightening her sense

of awareness. The rustling noises surrounding them had nothing to do with their fall. The crackling of branches a couple of feet from where they lay filled her with dread. A snort, a swish of a tail, and a deep rumbling stomach. What was it? A bull bellowed. Another more distant one answered. Buffalo. As the dust settled, she could make out the shape of the huge boss and long tapered curving horns of the one nearest them. The head so close his hot moist breath warmed her face as he snorted and pawed at the disturbed earth on the edge of the dry river bed. Others came and nosed their way into his scrap, quickly losing interest. A few feet away, a tussle began between two of the younger males. They sparred and parried, one reversed to within six inches of Martin's head, and another kicked his elbow. Martin didn't flinch, nor did she, because Martin's sprawling body effectively immobilized her, making her arm numb. She lost all sense of time. Even her hearing seemed dulled as she waited for a signal it was safe to move.

The numbness wore off faster than she had expected. First a slight tingling which built up to a sharp pin-sticking sensation, reaching the point where she felt as if every nerve ending had a six inch nail hammered through it. Screaming wasn't an option. She clenched her teeth together to prevent sound escaping. Blood drained from her head leaving her clammy and weak, and without control of her body.

She made no protest when Martin scooped her up and said in a whisper, "Nearly there. Don't worry, I'll get you home."

She was aware of being put into his vehicle. For her it was one step closer to knowing whether the children had reached safety.

Chapter 4

Martin pulled up at the wrought iron gates of Jenny Copeland's house with trepidation. He hadn't been in touch since his hasty departure after his mother's funeral nearly two years ago. Not even to thank her for all she had done for his mother before her death.

The night-watchman, wearing an ankle length army greatcoat with a woolly hat pulled down over his eyebrows, eventually loomed out of the darkness and peered through the window, shining a torch on Martin's face. Martin couldn't be sure if the watchman recognized him or if the colour of his skin made him acceptable, but without any fuss the man unlocked the gates and waved him through. At the main entrance of the house a pack of barking and snarling dogs stood guard. Martin cautiously eased the door open, letting them sniff his legs and calm down before venturing further.

One he recognized as his old friend Bonzo, a wonderful multi-breed, who had belonged to his mother. Bonzo, always in the thick of any scraps, had gained a few new scars and gone white around his muzzle which made him appear less ferocious than his companions. Martin called his name, put out his hand, and soon the tail wagged furiously. Martin fondled Bonzo's ears while the other dogs familiarized themselves with his scent. Once they stopped treating him like an enemy Martin stepped out of the car and knocked on the door.

An elegant young Somali woman greeted him. Martin shook his head thinking how foolish of him not to check if Jenny still lived in the same place. In the half shadows of the porch the woman's amazing bone structure made him wish he had his camera with him.

"Can I help?" she asked, her posh English accent somewhat unexpected.

"I'm looking for Jenny Copeland," he explained. "Has she moved?"

"No, she's out."

"Will she be back soon? I've an urgent message for her from Sandra Harriman."

"Sandra? Oh my God," she said putting her hand to her mouth, "you don't know... Sandra's plane crashed."

He reached out and touched her. "It's okay. She's at the hospital."

"Is she hurt?"

"A broken arm, a few bad cuts and a lot of bruises and possible concussion," he said. "They're giving her a thorough going over to make sure there's nothing more serious."

"We've all been so worried. Simeon and the others are out searching. I must tell them she's been found." She pulled the door open wider. "Come on in. Sorry I didn't introduce myself." She stretched out her hand. "I'm Amina Ishmail, a friend of Jenny's."

"Martin Owen," he answered, taking her hand. So this was Simeon's new girlfriend, the one mentioned in his last letter.

"He'll be so pleased you're home."

Home, what a nice thought.

She led him into the sitting room and pointed to a chair by the fire, "Take a seat. Help yourself to a drink while I call Jenny."

He shook his head. "Sorry, I can't stay. Sandra wants me to find some stranded American tourists," he said, ignoring her invitation to sit down. The chair looked tempting, but he was afraid if he sat down, he'd never move again.

"Oh, no panic, they've been rescued and are safe at the Safari Club. Jenny's taking care of them."

"And the twins? Sandra's stressing about them, too."

"They're fine, tucked up in the spare room down the passage. That's why I'm here – I'm baby-sitting."

Martin's relief at not having to drive back to Ol Essakut to round up a crowd of disgruntled tourists allowed him to sink into the offered armchair. With everyone safe, he could relax.

"I'll go and make those calls, and I'll ring the hospital and get a message to Sandra."

"Thanks. She'll appreciate that."

Amina left the room and headed to Jenny's study.

Afraid sleep would overtake him Martin rubbed his face with his hands and surveyed the room. Not much had changed since his last visit. The ancient Persian rugs more threadbare, the spines of the old classic tomes that lined the bookshelves faded to a paler shade of khaki. Time stood still in this haven, and he was grateful.

Amina's half-drunk cup sat next to an open book on the low, brass-studded Arab chest. He turned the book over, it appeared to be a study of chemicals in the environment, heavy stuff, not Jenny's choice of reading matter, a thriller, or a romance would be more her taste. Any reader of a book like that was a perfect match for Simeon.

Amina returned looking thoughtful. "Simeon's pleased you're back. He's keen to talk, but has things to sort first."

Much as he wanted to, he couldn't tell her he didn't want to speak to anyone. Trying to explain the need for time alone before renewing old friendships would be harder than going with the flow. Coming back to Kenya had been an impulsive move. He'd hoped one last visit to Chui Farm, his family home, might help him find tranquillity and restore his shattered nerves and make sense of his life. Rescuing Sandra forced him straight back into the fold.

Amina continued, "Jenny gave me strict instructions to feed you and keep you here until she returns."

"Trust Jenny to think of food," he said, trying to recall when he had last eaten. Breakfast on the plane? No, he'd pretended to sleep to avoid the plastic food, as he had with the dinner offering. Half a dried up sandwich at the airport before his flight was the last meal he remembered. He found eating hard these days. He'd hated hotel food even before his first front line assignment. Watching his colleagues tucking into black market luxury dinners after a gruesome day of filming had made hotel cuisine more repulsive, especially when they washed it all down with copious quantities of alcohol. For some it was a coping mechanism, maybe better than his. Time would tell. To avoid making excuses for not joining in with their nightly feasts, he'd return to the hotel too late for dinner, but early enough for a drink and to catch up with the latest news. Then he'd slip away and head for his room. Away from the war zone he found cooking for one depressing.

"What would you like?" she asked.

Martin glanced at his watch, almost eleven o'clock. "I'm fine," he muttered with a tiny pang of regret. He didn't want her to drag the cook out of his bed at this time of night.

"There's soup in the fridge, let me heat it up."

It sounded tempting, but he couldn't ask her to wait on him.

"No, don't bother."

She smiled showing a perfect row of teeth. "Bother! If Jenny comes back and finds out I haven't fed you, then there will be bother."

Martin laughed, "Okay, you win, let me help."

He followed her to the kitchen, noting the graceful way she moved. She instructed him to sit down on the only chair in the room and set about heating up the soup. Her familiarity with the old fashioned, functional kitchen fascinated him. She filled and switched on the kettle, went to the fridge and pulled out a bowl, tipped the contents into a pan that had been hanging on a rack over the table, and quickly had a gas flame licking the bottom of the pan. Then she found a large wooden tray, a bowl, spoon, and some bread, butter and cheese, and finally a pot for tea, milk, and a couple of mugs.

"Do you take sugar?"

He shook his head.

"Good, I wouldn't know where to find it." This lack of knowledge puzzled him as she seemed so at home in Jenny's house.

"Have you known Jenny for long?" he asked, hoping for clarification.

"About a year. Simeon introduced us. I'm here because he asked me to drop the Harriman children off earlier today." She poured the soup into the bowl, plopped the teapot on the tray. "Let's take this through. You can eat by the fire."

He struggled to keep his eyes open. The thick

vegetable soup, the tastiest food he'd eaten for months, combined with the warmth from the fire and the tranquil atmosphere had him fighting not to drop off in the chair. It was past midnight when Jenny came through the door and gave him a warmer welcome than he deserved. He stooped to hug her. She seemed to have shrunk, and her hair was greyer than he remembered, but her smile hadn't changed, even though she was both worried and tired.

"My God, have you been ill?" she blurted out, her hand squeezing his arm. "You're just skin and bone. You must have lost several stone. When did you last see a doctor?"

"I'm fine. Nothing that a little tender loving care won't put right."

"Are you sure?" she said with genuine concern, stepping back to take a long, hard look at him.

He smiled. She reminded him of his mother fussing and showing genuine concern. He'd cope as long as she didn't overdo it.

"I visited Sandra on my way home. She's most grateful for your help."

"Least I could do."

"Simeon wanted me to ask you a favour."

"Fire away," he answered nervously, not sure he wanted to commit to anything.

"When Sandra told you about the stranded tourists, did she give any details?"

He shook his head and Jenny filled him in with the full story of an armed gang attack and their being hi-jacked and then abandoned.

"That explains her anxiety," he answered. Curious that Sandra had omitted to tell him any of this. Had she guessed his identity? He tried to recall how she had reacted when he told her his name. People behaved in strange ways when they found out he was a journalist, they either poured out their whole life story whether he wanted to hear it or not, or they became secretive. Sandra fitted the latter.

"Simeon's gone after the gang and needs your help."

Martin shivered. He stuffed his shaking hand into his pocket to hide the tremble. To refuse would sound pathetic. He'd come home to get away from gunfire and the senseless loss of life. He wasn't ready to admit to anyone he was too stressed to function properly, not until he'd come to terms with the problem himself.

"I… I can't," he mumbled. He wouldn't dare go after anyone the way he was feeling.

Amina who had been sitting quietly on the other side of the room since Jenny's return, stood up, and reached for the tray. She smiled at Jenny, and said, "I'm off to bed. I can see you two have a lot to talk about." Her dark eyes focussed on him as she added, "Goodnight," and before he had a chance to say anything left the room.

Jenny stayed quiet for a while then spoke softly, "It's okay, Martin. They only want you to write an article."

Had she guessed his dilemma? Was his fear so transparent, that someone who hadn't set eyes on him for two years could read it?

"Simeon was worried you'd refuse. He asked me to remind you that you owed him a favour."

Martin swallowed. He hadn't expected to be returning favours this quickly. Friends or not, there were limits. Limits he was learning about the hard way.

"Hank agreed you were perfect for the job," she added.

“No pressure then,” he muttered.

Hank Bradley, his one time mentor, had supposedly retired from running the biggest news syndicate to concentrate on his passion, African wildlife conservation. Retired or not, no self-respecting journalist would risk turning down an assignment from the master himself. Another consequence of Hank knowing he’d returned was that he’d tell Beverley Wyatt. Once she knew the hounding would begin. She was desperate to get the contract for the sale of Chui Farm signed. Right now he wasn’t sure he wanted to complete. All he wanted was solitude.

“What am I expected to do?” he asked, hoping to get any surprises over quickly.

“Write the story of the attack. Handled sensitively it’s possible to minimize the damage. Bad coverage would destroy the future of the Ol Essakut Conservation Project. Nick might have taken credit for making it happen. But no one’s forgotten how passionate you are or that the original idea was yours.”

“How am I supposed to keep the lid on this?”

“We’ve isolated the rescued tourists. Hank has offered them substantial deals for the exclusive rights to their story, giving him complete control of all the coverage. Thankfully they’ve all signed the contract.”

“Must have cost a lot.”

“Yes, but worth every cent. Tourism can’t survive another sensational round of media frenzy. It took years to recover from the hotel bombing in Mombasa.

“My readers expect blood and guts from me,” he pointed out, “Hank knows that. And I’ll bet that’s why Sandra kept the attack secret from me, she thought I’d write a tabloid terror story.”

Jenny gave him a scolding glare. “High time you proved you’re capable of something different.”

"I'll only do it if everyone is completely open with me with every detail. I don't want to write my story and then find out I was kept in the dark."

Jenny looked indignant. "There's nothing to hide. One of the American tourists, Bill Huxter, was badly beaten. But he's such a keen conservationist he's already promised to play his injuries down. He's the only one of the group who knows about the men who died and the injured staff or that our drivers are still missing."

Martin understood the problem. Ideas of how he would handle the story to Ol Essakut's advantage were flashing through his head, but he wouldn't do anything without a specific request from Sandra.

"I'll think about it," he said, not wishing to elaborate.

Jenny looked across at him and nodded. "Sorry, you must be shattered. Let's talk tomorrow. Had you made plans for tonight, or do you need a bed?"

Martin checked his watch, wondering if it was set for the right time zone. "A bed would be good."

Jenny showed him to a room, but sleep eluded him. The image of Sandra captured in the light of his flash, struggling to straighten her arm, kept coming back to him. He tried to think of words to describe her. Vulnerable, determined and brave sprang to mind. Harder to describe was the memory of her body lying crushed beneath his weight after the landslip while the dust settled. Her intoxicating perfume, a hint of lavender, roses, and other fresh blooms filled his nostrils and lingered on his clothes and skin.

When he woke he lay on his back and started his daily ritual of first remembering which town he was in, trying to visualize the room and finally the layout of the hotel. He heard whispering, close to his pillow.

Someone was in his room. He flung a hand out blindly, sweeping the lamp off the bedside table.

There was a cry, “Run,” followed by a scurry of feet, and the door banging behind the intruders

He remembered where he was and worked out who his early morning visitors had been. He had to get help. His reflex actions could so easily have hurt a child. And that terrified him.

Chapter 5

Rory Lyons was pleased with their training run. The car sounded sweet and Harry Dawson's navigation skills were spot on as usual, though spoilt by his unexpected need to make conversation.

Harry's wife was pushing him to quit the rally circuit. Harry, the stammering, overweight, insurance company number-cruncher bore no resemblance to Harry the navigator. In the car he was confident and the stammer disappeared.

The two of them had similarities. Rory relaxed more behind the wheel of a car than he did anywhere else. He'd always been a loner, and made few friends, Harry being the exception, and he resented Harry's wife for trying to ruin that friendship.

"You really should consider Balbinder Singh's offer of a car and a co-driver," Harry said once more.

Rory wanted to end the conversation. He didn't want to swap Harry for one of Balbinder's rookie nephews. Not now when their rally trials were going so well.

"No," Rory answered. "If you give in to your wife your life will be a misery."

"You're just jealous," Harry answered. "You fancy Sandra Harriman. I bet if she asked you to stop driving, you'd quit."

The suggestion he fancied Sandra or that he'd quit driving for her was outrageous. Harry was so far off the mark along with his concentration.

The distraction put them in trouble.

He touched the brakes, wrong move. He tried to accelerate, wrong again. The camber of the road on the bend worked against him, forcing the motor towards the steep drop to the left.

The car took off, flying off the loose surface of the road and heading into the wide open air beyond. Rory was left powerless, unable to save them or the car.

Harry dropped his clip board and grabbed the handle on the dash board.

Rory braced himself for impact. Two wheels touched down first, bouncing the car up into the air then bouncing it back onto the other pair. And over onto the roof, back onto its wheels and over again. The windows shattered into a mesh of tiny shapes preventing him from seeing how far down the slope they were travelling. Loose tools rattled about their heads, clattering like stones in a cement mixer. A final bone-shaking crash brought them to a halt. An immovable object had ended their downhill tumble.

Rory dangled upside down, his head spinning as the adrenalin coursed through his system. Harry let out a loud moan beside him.

"I quit."

Rory laughed. Harry threatening to quit was a good sign.

"Resignation not accepted. Come on, let's get out."

He groped around and found a spanner to bash out the remainder of the crazed glass and eased himself out of the car. Harry needed help to escape. He'd twisted his knee badly so Rory acted as his crutch and led him away from the wreck. He found a rock to sit on. Both of them sat and silently assessed the damage.

There was nothing fine about the car. The chassis had buckled beyond repair, the engine block firmly embedded in the huge baobab tree that saved their lives. The drop below the tree would have resulted in certain death.

They didn't have to wait too long to be rescued. One of their rival's support vehicles offered them a lift to the hospital. Rory persuaded the driver to drop him off at the hotel afterwards. He didn't fancy facing Harry's wife and being accused of trying to kill him.

He had a couple of beers at the bar, and tried to contact Simeon at the ranch to send someone to fetch him. He couldn't get through, not to the office, or the mobile. He even tried to call Sandra. He left a few irate messages on Simeon's machine before his mobile battery died. He didn't have a charger so gave up.

When he got up there was no sign of any driver in the carpark. He tried to ring Simeon again from reception. Still nothing.

He ordered breakfast, with a beer to wash it down. He sat contemplating the drips of condensation running down the bottle when Balbinder Singh appeared and sat in the chair right beside him, crowding him into the corner.

Balbinder's immaculate suit and slickly-tied turban made Rory feel scruffy in the oil-stained clothes he had been wearing the day before. Rory tried to edge away, but the wall hemmed him in.

"Sorry about your car. I'm surprised you're not back at Ol Essakut dealing with their crisis. Have they caught the bastards?"

Rory had no idea what Balbinder referred to, but that didn't surprise him. Balbinder Singh had a reputation for knowing about everything, his widespread interests meant he was likely to pop up in the most unexpected places.

"Crisis?"

"You haven't heard?"

Rory shook his head. "Phone's dead."

"An armed gang robbed a bunch of tourists. I believe they dumped them in the bush, and your boss has crashed her plane."

Rory thought he was joking, but dismissed the idea. Balbinder and humour didn't mix.

"Seeing as you have no car after your crash, I'll call Parjit, he can drive you up to Ol Essakut. Be a good chance for you to spend time with him and see him drive. I'm sure Mrs Harriman needs your support at a time like this." With a wry smile he added "Good chance to get closer to her, not that you'd need encouragement, I've been told she's a lovely lady."

Rory wanted to turn down the offer, but Simeon would be short of transport and he would rather be up there and involved than stuck in Nairobi.

"Thanks."

Balbinder made the call and reported. "He's on his way."

"Try the car, my sponsorship offer is still on the table."

Balbinder clicked his fingers and a waiter appeared with another beer and a cup of coffee.

Rory wondered what Balbinder wanted from him. Until he figured that out he didn't want to agree to any deal. The man unnerved him. But he couldn't figure out what made him so unsettling. By all accounts he was a ruthless businessman, who drove a hard bargain and always honoured his debts. Nothing wrong with that. He'd done just about everything there was to do in Kenya, from mechanic, to builder, and even big game hunter until the hunting ban came in. Rory couldn't picture him in the bush or doing physical work. Lately, he'd become a property developer and had a transport business and a string of garages up and down the country, bearing his name.

Chapter 6

Martin put his hand over his glass when the waiter came round offering a top up. The wine, the best the Mount Kenya Safari Club had to offer, failed to tempt him. He managed to eat a little of the sumptuous feast Jenny arranged, the atmosphere such that no one commented on what he left on his plate.

Jenny excelled herself. Since taking charge of the hijacked tourists the previous day, she'd isolated them from the other guests at the Safari Club by sequestering them in the beautiful cottages edging the lawns looking down on the gardens and ponds, towards the majestic snow capped mountain. In this carefully chosen location Martin had interviewed each victim individually to record their version of the attack. He made sure to remind them of the terms of contract they'd agreed to, and got them to sign a second document confirming they understood the exclusivity clause.

Jenny didn't believe in taking chances. She'd arranged a private tour of the animal orphanage and game ranch to fill the morning; a round of golf for the men and beauty treatments for the women took care of the afternoon. All this followed by a cocktail party in one of the privately-owned cottages. The impressive guest list had been hand-picked and well-briefed by Jenny and Amina. Jenny must have called in a huge number of favours to get such an interesting group together so quickly. A couple of film stars who were involved with conservation headed the list. They in turn had persuaded three more actors from film shoots nearby to turn up, along with three diplomats, two Counts, two Barons, three famous hunters, two authors, and half a dozen well-known artists, all of whom effortlessly mingled with the shell-shocked tourists.

His fear that her strategy would fail vanished the minute the eclectic mix of celebrities met Jenny's nervous mob. They treated her charges like long lost friends, chatting about their own homes, their children, their hobbies, even work, in fact every topic possible, other than the recent traumatic incident.

The chatter got louder and louder and then the whole party moved on for champagne on the terrace to watch the Chuka drummers give their regular evening performance on the main lawn. Jenny looked like a double for the queen and Amina like a glossy magazine model. Both stayed watchful, making sure the guests had full glasses and someone interesting to talk to. Half an hour later the whole party was ushered into the private dining room for a seven course dinner.

"Jenny's worked a miracle with her table plan, everyone's smiling," Bill Huxter commented, as he peered over his shoulder to study the layout of the tables behind him. "She's matched the guests well. Clever move to put me down here near the kitchen with my back to the room. I guess she wanted to stop people from seeing my battered face."

Bill guessed right. Jenny had agonized over seating, especially over his placing. Eventually she'd decided to seat Bill with fellow conservation enthusiasts, a flying instructor, Jim Standish, and Martin himself.

"Oh don't get me wrong. I'm happy with the

company. Meeting film stars doesn't excite me." Bill nodded towards Jim Standish. "This man here has promised to teach me to fly."

"They say he's the best teacher in the country." Martin said.

Jim looked embarrassed and changed the subject. "I'm surprised neither Hank Bradley nor Simeon Mugo came tonight."

Martin decided the truth wouldn't hurt on this table. "They're still at the ranch, helping to track down the gang."

"What news of Nick Harriman's widow?" Bill said as he topped up his wine glass. "I gather you rescued her from her crashed plane."

Jim, who had been busy buttering his bread roll, put down the knife. "Sandra? Is she okay? What happened?" His brows almost met in the middle with concern as he spoke.

"Her engine cut out," Martin answered. "She crash-landed in a rocky area and was bloody lucky to get out with only a broken arm and mild concussion."

"I can't believe she's been in another accident. I hope it doesn't put her off aeroplanes forever. She was nervous enough about flying again when I first met her," Jim said. "Nick applied a lot of pressure to get her to agree to go up. He had no idea how scared she was or the courage needed to overcome her fear. I had to promise not to tell him."

"I gather he was good at pressuring people." Bill chipped in before Martin had time to query what Jim meant by his comment about Sandra's fear of planes. And what did Bill mean about Nick being good at pressuring people? He wanted to ask more but the place and time were wrong for such inquiries.

"Yes I suppose he was. But in that instance it was a

good thing, as it got her on board a plane again." Jim added thoughtfully. "Shame she won't have him to give her a shove again. Flying is a skill she'll need if she hopes to keep running Ol Essakut."

"Yes, but not much use if she doesn't have a plane. It caught fire and the fuel tanks exploded." Martin said, wondering why he was telling Jim and Bill this, but it seemed right for them to know.

Jim picked up his glass and drained it. "The insurance might cover a replacement. I hope so, because she's a natural up there, and she might find it hard to raise enough cash otherwise. That is assuming she has the guts to have another go."

"Cash shortage.... what makes you say that?" Martin asked.

"Nick left everything in trust to his children," Jim answered.

"Tell her if she needs funds, to come to me," Bill muttered. Martin saw Jim was taken aback with the offer too. Bill seemed genuine enough and followed it with questions to Jim about planes currently on the market, which were most reliable and best suited for hopping from estate to estate, how many passengers they carried and even the cost of hiring a pilot.

Martin found himself distracted by activity across the room as Jenny and some of the party moved towards the door. A waiter came over to the table and informed them that coffee and after dinner drinks were being served in the lounge. More people stood up to go, along with four from their table.

As they departed, Jim checked with Bill if he wanted to join them.

Bill shook his head. "I'd hate to ruin all Jenny's hard work by reminding the others of their ordeal by showing my face."

Martin declined too, saying he'd rather stay and keep Bill company. He signalled to a waiter and asked him to bring two coffees to the table. Bill was quite a character, and proving to be a more sensitive man than one might have expected, willingly playing down his part in the attack. He'd made light of his heroic hike back to camp to alert the staff, making it sound like a stroll in the park. His efforts had spared the assembled tour party from being stuck out in the bush for the night. Bill could have sought praise from the others, but instead he shrugged it off claiming his military experience made him the natural volunteer to go for help.

As soon as the others had departed Bill seemed to relax. "I didn't think Jenny could pull it off, but I was wrong. This party was an inspired idea. She sure has a load of impressive friends. How long have you known her?"

"All my life. She was my mother's closest friend." Martin answered.

"Lucky you. She told me you're thinking of selling your land. I got the impression she's not keen on your potential purchaser, but I might be wrong. Maybe she just wants you to stick around."

Martin was surprised on two counts. Firstly to hear Jenny had talked to a relative stranger about his affairs, and secondly that she disapproved of the buyer.

"What did she say?" he asked, baffled as to why Jenny would disapprove of Beverley. He had assumed Beverley, with her connection to Hank and her existing stake in Ol Essakut, not to mention her unlimited finance, was perfect.

"Jenny seemed to be worried about it being turned into a playground for the mega wealthy, rather than a conservation area." Bill answered.

"You surprise me," he said. He should have guessed Jenny's morals and Beverley's lack of them might create friction. The trouble was everyone loved Beverley, sometimes too well. Maybe Jenny was right to be concerned. He needed to think it through more carefully.

Bill spooned sugar into his coffee. "I gather you had a tough year."

Now Martin was annoyed, Jenny had no right to discuss him, or his work. She had no idea how tough it had been. His life, private or otherwise, was off limits.

Martin responded with diversionary tactics. "When do you fly back to the States?"

Bill drained his cup, folded his linen napkin and placed it neatly on the table in front of him. "I haven't decided. The others fly out late tomorrow. I might just stick around for a week or two. I'd like to go back and see the guys at the camp, especially the men who were injured. Jenny was evasive when I asked about them. Can you tell me more? Or are you sworn to secrecy too?"

"Honestly, I don't know much but I will pass on any information as soon as I know something."

"Thank you," he answered, rising to his feet. "The party is in full swing in there. Are you going to join them for a night cap?"

"No. I'm done for the day."

"Me too."

Martin signalled to Jenny from the doorway that he was leaving. She waved back. No doubt she would stay until the last guest retired. She should be proud of her achievement in giving the traumatised guests an exciting set of memories to blot out the horrors of the attack. If only the horrors dominating his memory could be dismissed so easily.

Jenny had booked him a room for the night at the Club. He was glad not to have to drive anywhere. He wasted no time climbing into his bed. Sleep came quickly, as did the predictable nightmare which woke him. Knowing he would not sleep again, he pulled back the curtains and watched the blue-black sky, dotted with stars, take on a purple then orange hue as dawn crept in, exposing the broad based silhouette of Mount Kenya that rose to a jagged summit devoid of cloud.

Unable to bear being cooped up any longer, Martin dressed and left his room, making his way down to the river. A security guard dozed in the sentry hut by the gate. Martin rattled the padlock and chain. The man leapt to attention and ran over with the key. A string of colobus monkeys clattered in the branches overhead, their long white tails flashing as they flung themselves from tree to tree. The guard quietly shadowed him down to the water's edge. The temptation to slip across the river on the rounded boulder stepping stones and follow the animal tracks on the opposite bank was great. The times spent in the forest with Simeon and Nick had been among the best days of his life, now impossible to recreate. The presence of the guard made him realize 'bundu-bashing', as they used to call it, was not an option. Martin had more pressing commitments to face.

Chapter 7

The enthusiastic greeting from Bonzo made Martin stop to fondle the old dog's ears. Sandra's raised voice carried through the open window.

"The police said I can go home. If you won't take me I'll find somebody who will."

"Not with the children." Jenny's tone left no room for argument.

The last thing Martin wanted was to gate-crash a row between the two women, but awkward or not, he needed them to be aware of his presence. He gave Bonzo a final pat on the head, and knocked on the door. The heated debate ceased, replaced by footsteps. Jenny opened the door and greeted him warmly. Sandra looked put out by his intrusion.

He had only seen her once at the hospital, when he faced her to ask if she wanted him to take on the job, and promise to be open about everything. Her facial injury was far less noticeable than it had been.

Sandra's expression changed. "Can you drive me to Ol Essakut?" she asked.

Jenny's smile evaporated. He wished he'd stayed outside with the dogs. Driving Sandra out to the ranch was no problem - making an enemy of Jenny was.

"Are you sure you're ready?" He regretted the query which made him sound as if he was afraid of taking her home.

"Of course I am... will you both stop treating me like an invalid."

"Sorry," he said, "I didn't mean it like that."

"Jenny doesn't understand. I need to see the damage for myself." Sandra winced as she adjusted the sling the hospital had provided. "The police forensic team finished gathering evidence, though what use their effort will serve is anyone's guess."

Martin didn't like to confirm her fears that no amount of forensic material would put matters right.

"Any news from Simeon or Hank?" Martin asked, hoping to break the intensity of the clash of wills.

"They've found the gang's den," Jenny answered. "They're waiting for reinforcements, and will probably flush them out under cover of darkness tonight."

"So will you take me or not?" Sandra asked.

He admired her determination. The only thing on his agenda had been to visit his parents' graves and to spend time with Sandra, learning more about Ol Essakut to do his article justice. He glanced in Jenny's direction to check her reaction.

Jenny sighed. "If Martin's prepared to take you, he must agree to stay with you the whole time and bring you back tomorrow for your appointment at the hospital."

Her ultimatum sounded reasonable to Martin.

"That's ridiculous. I don't need a minder or your permission." Sandra protested. "I'm not a child. I'm only asking for a lift. He can go home from there, if he wants."

Jenny shrugged and turned to Martin. "I give up. She's impossible. Do what you can."

Martin sympathised with Jenny, who obviously cared for Sandra to be making such a fuss. "Don't worry I'll take care of her. We can use the time to catch up on Ol Essakut news." He decided not to react to the suggestion about his going home. He liked having an excuse to delay that for another day. "When shall we leave?"

"As soon as possible, as long as Jenny or Amina are prepared to mind the children." She touched her plaster cast.

"Of course I'll look after them," Jenny said. "I wouldn't expect you to take them with you. Amina's going to town to see the guests off. She doesn't need me there."

Sandra gave Jenny a spontaneous hug. "Thanks." Then she turned back towards him and said, "I'll go and say goodbye to the rascals. Are you sure you can spare the time?"

"Ready whenever you are," he assured her.

His answer was rewarded with a beautiful transforming smile. Not even the black eyes, scratched cheeks, grazed chin and the straggly hair, scraped back off her face and stuffed under a baseball cap could detract from her beauty. No wonder Nick had snapped her up. He took a more detailed inventory. The baggy clothes weren't flattering. So different from the tailored trousers and silk shirt she had been wearing when he rescued her.

Sandra seemed to read his thoughts.

"I need a change of clothes. I don't always look such a mess," she explained.

At that moment the children hurtled through the door, scattering papers and rucking the rugs as they crossed the room. Sandra braced herself for impact. She managed to keep her balance as she knelt down to give them both a hug. Once she had their full attention she quietly explained her plans. "I'm going home. You're staying here with Jenny, until I get back."

"I want to come," Emma wailed.

"I'm sorry." Her voice was gentle but firm. "I'm going to be very busy. If you're good Jenny will take you to Clare's party this afternoon and to the pool tomorrow."

"When will you come back?" Sam demanded.

"In time to read you a bedtime story tomorrow night," she said as she ruffled his hair.

The children looked at each other, in unison they said, "Promise…"

"I promise." She gave them both a kiss then stood up and headed to the door. "Can we go now?"

Martin, sensing a speedy exit was required, followed her out to his borrowed Land Cruiser.

He opened the passenger door and helped her up and fixed her seat belt then hurried round to the driver's seat.

"Great kids," he said giving the send-off party a wave as he pulled away. "Last time I saw them apart from the other morning when I scared the wits out of them, they weren't even crawling. How old are they now?"

"Three," Sandra smiled as she answered. "Nick deserves all the credit. He was a wonderful father."

Martin wound down his window and greeted the watchman, glad the distraction made commenting on Nick's capabilities unnecessary. Sandra fidgeted in the seat beside him. He wondered if having an askari on duty, day and night, bothered her. He had grown up with it, but after time away from the country he found the need for watchmen made him strangely unsettled. The man fumbled with the lock making a ritual of opening the gate, saluting them as they passed by.

"I'm sorry I commandeered you like that," she said as she tugged at the seat belt, trying to free a corner of her sling caught up in the strap. "What plans did you have that I mucked up?"

"I had thought about visiting my parents' graves," he answered honestly. "Another day or two won't make a difference."

"Nonsense," she said. "We can stop on the way. I wouldn't mind going into the cemetery. I haven't been since Nick's funeral. Too difficult with the children in tow, they don't quite understand the finality of death."

"They're not alone."

"No."

"Well, if you're sure?"

"Martin, we'll get on much better if you accept I always say what I mean. It makes life less complicated in the long run."

"Suits me." He turned out of the driveway, heading towards the little cemetery half a mile down the road.

A vigorous Kai-apple hedge marked the boundary. He pulled onto the verge outside the gates, regretting his lack of flowers. He went round to open the passenger door for Sandra. The sun was still trying to burn through the early morning mist. Sandra shivered when he opened the door. Her action had nothing to do with the cool breeze coming off the mountain. It was obvious the cemetery visit was a mistake, best to cut it short and pretend not to notice her discomfort.

He stretched over to undo her seatbelt, but she put her good hand out to stop him. "I think I'll wait here." He picked up a catch in her voice.

He backed off. She had a good view through the gap in the hedge so he pointed to the far corner. "My family's graves are over there. I won't be long."

"No need to hurry," she answered without conviction.

He went on alone, eyes fixed on what he assumed was Nick's grave, a mass of wilted floral tributes on a newly raised mound without a headstone. His guess was confirmed when he read Helen Harriman on the cross next to the mound. Seeing her name carved in stone made him want to stop and pay his respects. He glanced back. Sandra hadn't moved. He forced himself forward. Best leave that for a more private visit another day.

His family plot was better tended than the others nearby which were overrun with grass and weeds, with tilting headstones. On previous visits to his father's grave, his mother always took a single bloom from the bunch she carried and placed it on one side, in memory of his little sister who died. He barely remembered her, but if he'd had flowers he'd have copied his mother's gesture.

What would his parents make of his plans? His father would probably have been okay with him moving on, but his mother would have fought against the sale. Her passion for the family home, which his great grandfather had built, caused rows between her parents, mainly over the cost of maintenance. Maybe Jenny was right, he should give the matter more thought. He bowed his head then and turned back thinking he must remember to thank Jenny for organizing the care of his parents' graves. One more responsibility he had so carelessly neglected.

He stopped for a minute beside Nick and Helen's graves wondering about Sandra's change of heart. Something she said when he rescued her made him think the short marriage was not a happy one, as if he touched a raw nerve. Maybe she was not as tough as she pretended to be.

As he climbed back into the driver's seat, he noticed tears in her eyes. He made no comment. Grief hit people in different ways. The trip to the cemetery had been a mistake, making her withdrawn and pensive.

He navigated out of town, wondered how to draw her out. "Why the hurry to get home?" he asked.

"I need to visit the families of the men who were killed and injured and of the missing men." She glanced towards him with an expression that silenced him.

"I don't care if you think I'm crazy, it's important. I'm the only person who can reassure them they'll be looked after and not thrown out of their homes."

"A generous offer. I'm sure they'll appreciate your concern." He swerved to dodge a huge pothole in the road. When he checked if Sandra was all right, she didn't seem to have noticed.

"You're like everybody else. You think I'm an idiot straight out from the UK, who doesn't understand how things work in Africa. That I should let them fend for themselves." Her tone had an unexpected spiky edge.

"No way! I don't think that at all."

"So what would you do?"

Her question exposed his personal failure as an employer. When he left Kenya two years ago he hadn't considered the effect on the staff at Chui Farm. His guilt deepened. Ensuring they had jobs was one thing, but jobs weren't enough. The staff had come to rely on his mother for help whenever they faced a crisis.

"I'm not sure I am the right person to advise you," he said. "I haven't set a good example. I'd try to figure out a way of giving at least one member of each family employment."

"I realise I can't just hand out charity. No one can afford that. I'm working on an idea of setting up a community and school meals project. Do you think that might fit the bill?"

"It's an interesting idea." He was impressed she'd come up with a potential solution so fast and with such enthusiasm.

"I'd provide a plot of land and supply seeds, they would grow the vegetables, the mothers could prepare the food. Cash generated by the sale of surplus produce could buy things they can't grow, and possibly provide an income to pay the mothers for their work. They could serve meals all year round, no need to restrict it to term time. Simeon's father is a great organizer and might be willing to be involved."

Martin was amazed how her infectious genuine concern for others transmitted itself. No wonder Nick had been captivated.

"What a brilliant idea. I take it Mr. Mugo still runs the school?"

"You know him."

"Of course I do. He can be quite scary. We got Simeon into a lot of trouble as kids. He was always fair, never took sides, and certainly never afraid to reprimand us as if we were his pupils, which of course we weren't."

"I've never seen that side of him." She smiled as if remembering some private memory, then added. "He's so proud of Simeon."

"With every right. He gave Simeon a fantastic start in life. His coaching got Simeon the scholarship that transformed his life. I often wonder what he'd have achieved given the opportunities Simeon had."

"He's so well-read."

"Yes, but things were different then. I was so pleased you made Simeon manager. Did you meet much opposition?"

"No, should I?"

"No," he answered, relieved attitudes had changed. Years ago appointing an African manager would have been unthinkable, even if they were better qualified for the job than all the Europeans in the area. But he doubted Rory had been pleased.

"How well do you know Simeon?" Martin asked.

"Amina introduced us. He's the reason I came to Ol Essakut and met Nick."

"I gather you're illustrating a wild flower guide book for Amina."

"Yes. We shared a flat in London when she was at University studying botany. I simply paint whatever she puts in front of me. Half the time I can't spell, let alone pronounce the names of the specimens she finds."

Her passion was evident. A surge of envy hit him. Few people were fortunate enough to love their work and get paid for the privilege. He knew from experience the importance of passion. He loved his work, or he had until recently. He'd pushed his luck too far. Maybe one day the magic would return… he didn't hold out much hope.

Recognition of his loss overwhelmed him, and he lapsed into a quiet thoughtful mood, jolted out of his reveries by an unavoidable array of holes in the road. He heard her gasp as he hit the brakes, but when he turned to check she pretended to be fine.

"Sorry." He hated causing her pain.

"Don't worry. I'm okay."

He concentrated harder on navigating round the craters in the tarmac.

"Tell me the most difficult part of taking control of the ranch." He hoped his query would distract her and provide information about Ol Essakut to add to his article.

After a moment of hesitation she said, “Not fully understanding everyone’s role.”

“Can you be more specific?”

“Rory Lyons for example. No one will explain his relationship to Nick? I don’t even know how long he’s lived on the ranch, or why Nick decided to let him move into the Lander’s house. They hardly spoke to each other before Nick died.”

“No change there. I believe old man Lander was his Uncle, and he had no other family.”

“So that’s the connection. He’s trying to claim ownership of half the ranch.”

“I didn’t know, but it doesn’t surprise me.”

“What I can’t understand is why no one warned me. Usually people are happy to gossip, but as far as Rory is concerned there’s complete silence.”

“Perhaps they don’t know anything.”

“I find that hard to believe.”

“He never talked much,” Martin explained. “When he first came his Swahili was better than his English. He’d lived with his grandfather somewhere up near Eldoret, and spoke Afrikaans all the time. When his grandfather died Rory had nowhere to go.”

“How old was he?”

“About eleven, I think.” Martin remembered how hostile he and Nick had been towards the newcomer. They didn’t need or want a stranger tagging along spoiling their adventures, especially one barely able to speak English.

“How awful,” Sandra said.

Martin wanted to say it had been awful for them too. Rory was a bully. A racist bully, though at the time no one called it racism. Simeon became his target. Back then Martin had assumed Rory’s treatment of Simeon stemmed from jealousy. Simeon was far better educated than Rory. He'd just won a scholarship to a top school in Nairobi which led to a place at an English university.

"Rory thought he'd live with his Uncle, Tom Lander, but Tom's wife refused to have Rory in the house."

"The Landers? Helen's parents?"

"Yes," Martin continued. "Anyway he ended up living with the farm manager Mr. Munroe and his wife. They didn't have children of their own, and did their best to cope with a wild eleven year old. Rory didn't make it easy for them. Then one day, Dennis Munroe, who was a brilliant mechanic, took Rory to the workshop and handed him a spanner. From then on they had a job to get him out of the workshop. Nick and I went to boarding school, Rory did lessons at home. He learned the basics but he never took to books."

"I wonder why Mrs. Lander refused to have him in the house."

"That wasn't the sort of question one could ask back then."

"Do you think he minded?" There was real concern in her voice.

"Who can tell? But one thing for sure, appointing Simeon as manager will have made him mad. Rory's Afrikaans upbringing would make taking orders from any African difficult. Added to which Rory probably expected to land the job himself."

"I never even considered him."

"I'm not surprised. If it's any consolation, Rory would have made a lousy manager." Perhaps now was a good time to warn her. "Rory won't be pleased to see me back at Ol Essakut."

Sandra shot him a sideways glance. “You’re not going to explain why.”

He didn’t answer. It was not his story to tell.

“You’re just like the rest, clamming up when I’m around.” Her disappointment was clear.

Noticing the cloud cover that had been shrouding the peak of the mountain during the day had lifted, he pulled over to the side of the road, grateful for a distraction. “Beautiful, isn’t it?”

“Have you ever climbed to the top?” she asked.

“Never to the highest peak, my climbing skills don’t extend that far. What about you?”

“No, Nick promised me one day we’d go up. But…”

“Want to stretch your legs?”

“No, my arm’s in a less painful position, and I don’t dare move. Have you any water handy? I’d love a sip.”

Martin reached back behind his seat, retrieved a bottle and handed it to her. She struggled to hold the big plastic bottle, spilling a little as she lifted it to her lips. When he thought she’d drunk enough he took the bottle back and had a swig himself. The way she held herself was enough for him to know the pain was bad.

“Take some pain killers.”

“I don’t like taking them.”

“It’s better to take more for the first couple of days to stop your whole body from stiffening to protect your arm.”

“I didn’t know you had medical training.”

“I don’t. I speak from personal experience.”

“Can you pass me some then?” she asked, looking towards a plastic bag on the floor by her feet. Martin popped a couple of pills from their foil blisters, gave them to her and passed back the water bottle, glad she'd taken his advice.

Time to move on. The road changed from tarmac to recently graded murram. Regular grading left the surface of the road looking smooth, but beneath the powdery layer was a coarser layer of loose material that made sudden braking a dangerous manoeuvre. He drove cautiously, conscious of the fine rust coloured dust seeping into the vehicle. Even with the windows tightly closed, the particles filtered through minute gaps in the floor and the dried out door seals, steadily filling the cab with a choking, eye-watering cloud. Sandra never complained.

Eventually they approached Ol Essakut gates. This time he took more interest in the research and education centre complex that had sprung up in the last two years. The smart new stone buildings were impressive, all with properly laid out lawns and gardens and tarmac parking areas, neatly enclosed by a seriously forbidding electric fence. He hated the need for fences in Kenya, but theft was rife. The contrast between the rich and poor was heartbreaking. Even in this rural location the number of new jobs in tourism would never keep up with population growth and the demand for work.

"Do you want to stop and look around?" Sandra asked as the ranch gates were opened by a welcoming askari.

"Not unless you'd like me to. I've read all the latest press releases and have enough to be going on with."

"Good," she sighed, "I'd rather get home." She waved to the gatekeeper and managed a strained smile. As soon as they moved ahead she closed her eyes and leaned back against the headrest. Martin kept silent, and drove carefully down the familiar track leading to the Harriman's house and his family home.

Chapter 8

Rory couldn't stay a moment longer in the workshop. The incessant chatter of the Singh boys drove him mental. Balbinder's original proposal never mentioned Parjit's two cousins, Vejay and Lalji would tag along as support crew. He must leave before he killed one of them. He set them to work on a dilapidated old Land-Rover to test their mechanical abilities, and made his escape.

Freedom from watching eyes became his greatest desire. With Simeon and all the rangers off tracking the armed gang, Sandra away and no tourists on the property he had the perfect opportunity to test his grandfather's gun. He extracted his treasure from the gun cabinet and stroked the butt. He loved the weight in his hand though in his memory the gun had seemed heavier on the day his grandfather died.

The touch of the smooth curves of walnut drew the long submerged details of the day that everything changed back to the surface. He recalled his grandfather's struggle for breath, as he told him he'd be going to live with his uncle, a man he'd never heard of, and start school.

Rory didn't fancy living with someone else or going to school, so decided to run away. He needed a gun and ammunition to survive. He pinched the key to the gun cupboard and slipped into the study to fetch his gun. He'd intended taking the light gun his grandfather had taught him to use. But the old man's best gun was too tempting to resist. He pulled it out of the rack, stuffed his pockets with ammunition and snuck out of the house.

His grandfather always complained the gun shot six inches out of true. Rory decided to test the accuracy by firing at a goat. The goat bleated and leapt sideways into the bush, but the herd-boy who had been standing to one side collapsed to the ground, his goats scattering in every direction. Rory didn't dare go closer to find out how badly he'd wounded his accidental victim. He feared his grandfather's punishment more than anything. If he returned the gun and said he'd never left the house, his grandfather would never find out. The servants took no notice of his activities and wouldn't know if he had been out or not. Anyway who'd believe their word against his? He crouched out of sight and carefully erased his tracks the way his grandfather's tracker had taught him. Nothing must lead to the farm. He stopped briefly to clean the gun.

When he got home, he nipped round the side of the house, away from the servants' prying eyes and crawled through an open window. He wiped his prints off the gun and the door of the cabinet and went to sit with his grandfather. The old man was dead in his chair. Rory sat beside him and waited for someone to come.

Tom Lander turned up a couple of hours later and took charge. He announced that after the burial Rory would be leaving to live with him. He sent Rory to pack his belongings, while they dug the grave. A few neighbours appeared. One lady brought a cake, and instructed Rory to eat as there'd be nothing to eat on the journey. Then, loaded up with an odd assortment of things, ranging from his grandfather's guns, the tin trunk that he kept his papers in and a pile of pictures of nameless old folk, Rory was driven away.

His uncle drove in silence. Darkness had fallen when they arrived at the Lander's ranch. Rory wondered what sort of welcome he'd get from his aunt. He'd never had much to do with women. His grandfather's cook had taken care of him since his fifth birthday after his mother died.

The aunt didn't make a good impression. First she insisted he had a bath and then threw his clothes on a fire and made him wear someone else's cast offs, and finally announced he'd eat his meals in the kitchen. The room where he slept had flowery paper and lacy curtains.

Two days later the police came. They talked to Uncle Tom in his study for a long time before Rory was called in.

Some of his grandfather's guns were lying on the desk along with one he'd never seen before. His uncle pointed at them. "Have you fired any of these?"

Rory touched the lightweight one he normally used. "This one." It was the truth. He was glad his grandfather's favourite was not part of the selection.

Later his aunt and uncle argued. Everyone in the house heard her yelling that she didn't care who his father was, he couldn't stay in her house. His uncle stormed out and later that day Rory moved into the Munroe's house. The farm manager and his wife gave him a warmer welcome than his aunt had. And no one ever mentioned his grandfather's guns again until the reading of Nick's will.

Now with hindsight, Rory understood. The incident with the goatherd, all those years ago had cost him his birthright. His uncle had known all along what he did.

He put the gun to his shoulder. He'd put three

targets up earlier, he aimed six inches to the left of the first. Parjit, he thought as he squeezed the trigger. Bull's eye. He reloaded and aimed again. Lalji. A perfect shot. Finally,Vejay. How he'd love to do that for real. The trio made his life a misery.

He laid the gun across his lap and lit a cigarette and sat back on the creaking chair, when an unfamiliar Land Cruiser pulled up in front of the Harriman's house. He recognized Martin Owen's long, distinctive gait the moment he stepped from the vehicle.

"What the hell is he doing back here?" Rory muttered to himself.

Sandra emerged from the passenger seat, one arm in a sling, her stiff walk indicating pain. Serve her right.

Bad enough having her on Ol Essakut, but Martin wheedling his way in could only lead to trouble. Martin would tell her lies to stir things up.

For the first time he regretted moving to the Lander's House. He'd originally enjoyed watching what went on across the vlei, but now felt he was the one in the goldfish bowl. Everyone could witness what he did and when he did it. His old place, tucked away down a little track completely screened by trees and rocks, had been more private and suited him better. Nick knew that. Maybe that was the reason for leaving him the use of the house in his will. Spite... it had to be behind Nick's legacy.

Being so visible created a dilemma. Sandra would have spotted him sitting on the verandah and expect him to go over to discuss the situation on the ranch. To keep up the pretence of accepting her new role as guardian of Ol Essakut he'd have to go, even if it meant facing Martin.

He took one last drag on his cigarette, dropped the

butt on the wooden floor and stubbed it out with the heel of his safari boot. Then he levered himself from the comfort of his cane chair, went inside to lock his gun away, then strolled over.

Sandra stood on the porch, getting the red carpet treatment from Juma, the cook and Wanjiru, the house girl. Fine, he couldn't begrudge her receiving some respect. But Martin was getting it too. Africans had short memories. They'd forgotten about Martin's dramatic departure two years ago, when he'd been lucky not to leave in a body bag. Now they greeted him like a long lost friend. Well, they might have forgotten, but he hadn't. Hard to believe Sandra didn't know the story, and odder still she'd invite him in.

Rory climbed the steps, "Glad you're back. It must have been pretty scary, being shot down like that."

Martin's eyes widened, and Sandra stiffened.

"I was lucky," Sandra answered quickly.

Rory guessed there was a lack of honesty between them. She was more interested in Martin's reaction than in him. Something was going on, shame he couldn't work out what.

"I came back to see the staff." She waved her good hand towards Martin. "Martin kindly drove. I gather you know each other."

"Yes." Rory faced Martin and forced a smile. "Back for long?" he queried, hoping Martin would say he was off the next day.

"Not sure." Martin stared him straight in the eye.

"Martin's staying tonight so he can take me back tomorrow. The children are with Jenny. I don't want to bring them home until Simeon and Hank have rounded up the gang. Any word yet about the two drivers?"

"Yeah, about an hour ago. They're dead. Shot in

the head."

Sandra grabbed the door jamb. "Did you tell their families?"

"Not yet." Her tightening lips showed she wasn't happy with his answer. He excused his failure as he followed her inside, "I'm still trying to get more vehicles back on the road. Simeon's orders," he added, happy to lay the blame elsewhere. He even had written proof.

After a nerve-wracking drive with Parjit behind the wheel, Rory had found the place deserted. A note had been pinned to his door telling him about the armed gang up on the northern part of the ranch, with strict instructions not to venture further than the village compound or the main house.

Rory's specific instructions were to make as many vehicles road worthy as possible. A sick joke, as the only vehicles left in the workshop were a rusty Land-Rover and a clapped out minibus.

Parjit Singh, Vejay and Lalji had to be kept occupied. The only part of the deal with Balbinder which made sense. Fixing the decrepit Land-Rover would test their mechanical skills and right now they were stripping the vehicle back to the chassis, trying to impress him. That done he would get behind the wheel of Balbinder's Subaru and do some practice runs on the ranch roads. The northern circuit was the best route, but the danger of being shot by Simeon and his Army mates put the area out of bounds.

"How are the injured men?"

"Don't know, I'll go and ask if you like?"

"No, don't bother," she said. "I'll go myself as soon as I've changed into clean clothes."

He wanted to say it was too late to do anything for them, better to warn her how mercenary the families might become.

"Don't let them think they can get money out of you or you'll be pestered for life. These people are best left to deal with grief on their own."

"You've made that obvious," she answered. This time he detected an icy edge to her tone.

Well, if she wants to mollycoddle them, let her. When he took control things would be different. For now he must be patient, especially with Martin hanging around, pretending to share Sandra's concern for the natives. Martin had always been a native lover. They made a good pair. Shit, he'd lay a bet Martin's only interest in Sandra was the ranch and the reason for his unexpected return.

"Is there anything else I need to know?" she asked, bringing him back to the present.

"I've got some rally driving friends staying. I've put them in the guest cottage behind my place. Parjit Singh is a driver, and his two cousins, Vejay and Lalji, are mechanics. They're giving me a hand in the workshop," Rory said, trying to sound casual, as if he frequently entertained friends.

"No problem, not many people will want to stay once the news gets out about the attack," she answered.

"I thought extra people about would be a good thing," Rory said, wanting her to think he had invited them rather than him being lumbered with them.

"That cottage was in a mess. Did someone clean it out?

She was incredible, standing there battered to hell, and still bothered about cottage cleanliness. "Yes, all under control."

"Good. Just make sure they have everything they need."

He nodded, hardly able to believe she had accepted his unexpected visitors without resistance. Simeon would have reacted differently.

Martin said nothing. He seemed preoccupied with taking in his surroundings. From the moment he entered the house, his eyes had been sweeping over the rooms absorbing every detail. Rory watched with interest, especially his reaction to the photos on the mantelpiece. The stunning picture of Helen Harriman halted Martin in his tracks. For a second Rory thought he would touch it, instead he shoved his hand in his pocket and stepped backwards, feigning indifference to the impact of the image. He was glad to see Martin still suffered. The bloke who swore time healed needed his head checked.

Rory made an excuse about being needed at the workshop. Martin's presence put him in a bad mood. He'd really love to take a spin alone in Parjit's vehicle. Instead he had to inspect greasy engine parts and put up with three leech-like characters hanging on his every word. He much preferred to work alone with his tools in his own particular somewhat disorderly order, preferably in silence, or at most listening to the radio. Not being subjected to the three stooges and their endless chatter.

He couldn't handle them right now. Once he was out of sight of the Harriman house, he ducked through the bushes and slipped inside his own house through the kitchen door.

He took a cold Tusker beer out of the fridge and sat on the doorstep, to drink it. A waft of curry from the guest cottage hit him, tainting the taste of his hard earned beer, then, to add insult to injury, the wail of sitar music shattered the normally peaceful atmosphere. That's it, getting rid of the trio had become top priority. First he had to discover the real reason why Balbinder wanted them out of town. Then he'd look for a new sponsor.

Chapter 9

A prickle of apprehension made Martin shiver as he pulled up outside the Harriman house. He'd never be here if Nick were alive.

The sight of Rory Lyons crossing the wide open grass vlei that separated the Lander Farm buildings from the Harriman's made him nervous. Rory's long, sun-bleached hair, gave him a mane-like appearance to match his name.

Rory's lack of eye contact felt deliberate. His greeting, a slight nod his only acknowledgement of Martin's existence. Martin returned the gesture, relieved the vitriolic outburst he expected from Rory never came. Had Rory changed? He seemed more confident. No, confident was the wrong word, the way he blocked Sandra's path to the door to her home bordered on arrogant.

Whatever happened between Rory and Nick must have been dramatic. Why else would Nick leave Rory the right to live in the Lander's House? Simeon might know, but he'd have to wait to find out.

"You okay?" Rory said to Sandra with a distinct lack of genuine concern. "Pretty scary, being shot down."

Martin thought for a second he had misheard Rory's comment, but the way Sandra's back straightened and her cheeks turned red, signalled she was uncomfortable with the revelation. She glanced in his direction and changed the subject. Martin pretended to be interested in a weird, scrap-metal, bird sculpture on the verandah rather than in their conversation.

"Any word from Simeon? Have they found the two drivers?" she eventually asked.

Neat evasion to avoid the topic of her plane being shot down. At least Rory had solved one mystery. He'd been sure Sandra had been hiding something. But he'd never give Rory the satisfaction of knowing he'd let her secret out.

"Yeah," Rory answered casually. "Dead. Shot in the head."

The colour drained from Sandra's face. Rory's blunt delivery hit her hard.

"Did anyone tell the families?" she asked as she blinked back tears.

"Not yet," he answered, before launching into some garbled excuse about being too busy.

Martin knew he was lying. He'd caught a glimpse of Rory sitting on his verandah when they arrived. He hadn't looked like a man with anything urgent going on. He kept quiet. He wasn't here to stir up trouble.

Instead he listened, fascinated at how polite and formal Sandra sounded when speaking to Rory, so different to the relaxed tone he associated with her. Rory sounded different too, somewhere between aggressive and completely uncaring. He wondered if Rory's behaviour and the strained atmosphere had anything to do with his presence.

While they spoke he peered through the open front door. From this angle, little had changed, except for the heap of toys on the floor in the corner of the sitting room. This had been a no-go area for children when Nick and he were young. Good to see life here was now more relaxed. The dining room had lost its high days and holidays stuffiness too. The long polished table now littered with pots of brushes, tubes of paint, piles of books and untidy heaps of paper showing signs of everyday use.

Sandra edged round Rory to go inside. Rory sauntered in after her and Martin followed.

Nostalgia overwhelmed him as he scanned the sitting room. To avoid engaging in conversation with Rory, he studied the selection of framed photos on the mantle-shelf. A particularly beautiful photo of Helen on her wedding day caught him off guard with a surge of conflicting emotions. He'd lived next door to Helen all his life. Living next door didn't equate with understanding her. Helen made a career out of breaking hearts, his amongst them. Thinking he'd cracked it, and sure she was ready to commit and go public regarding their relationship he'd bought a ring. She turned him down and married Nick instead.

He became aware of Rory's intent gaze. The strength of the animosity forced him to look away, waiting for a snide remark. None came.

He concentrated on the other photos but couldn't help thinking about Nick and Helen's marriage. Ol Essakut had benefited from having the two adjoining twenty thousand acre properties merge under one owner. Helen soon got over the honeymoon period. Marriage wasn't going to change her ideas regarding free love. Martin shuddered, not sure how he'd have coped with her infidelity.

Sandra walked Rory to the door, arranging to meet at the office for Simeon's next call at six.

Juma reappeared with coffee and biscuits. Sandra took a cup, and went to change, giving Martin a few minutes alone to wonder if his revelation to Nick had somehow led to Helen's death.

Sandra returned with impressive speed, her hair hidden under a scarf instead of a cap. Her neat fitted trousers and shirt made her look more petite than before. Only the scratches and bruises and the sling remained as reminders of her recent ordeal.

Her impatience to visit the dead men's families to break the news was genuine. She wouldn't settle to do anything else until she had done her duty, which included speaking to the wounded men and their relatives.

It wasn't far, but he suggested driving across the vlei to avoid the heat, and she eagerly accepted. A clear indication her arm was more painful than she'd admit to.

He hadn't been down to the farm village for years. The village had doubled in size, but what impressed him most was the unexpected cleanliness. The original style of round thatched labourers huts were all smartly painted, and there were at least twice as many as he remembered. Behind them stood ten new, much larger, square houses with decent-sized windows and guttering, a rare sight in Africa, especially guttering with pipes leading to large black plastic water butts. Hardcore paths led to each door, and plants grew where previously the ground would have been barren, grazed bare by goats, and squawking chickens. Beyond, further evidence of building work in progress.

"Wow, what a transformation." He was like an eager tourist soaking up the sights.

"I'm glad you approve. Nick had problems recruiting new staff. I convinced him the run-down conditions the families had to cope with were unacceptable, and got him to set up a community project, with a committee, financed by the estate. The more they do to improve things themselves, the more money the fund gets. The plan is to get the employees who have families into the new houses, and to revamp the old ones for the single men and women." She pointed to an unfinished building, "They're rebuilding the school, and putting in a shop, a sort of co-op, to help save money by buying in bulk."

"Sounds like a big investment."

"A small price to pay to keep everyone happy. If I don't make the effort, I'll lose them. Without good staff, getting Nick's project off the ground will be impossible. Apart from which, they've earned the right to a decent home."

His admiration for Sandra grew. Her enthusiasm was refreshing, and inspiring. And then he witnessed her interaction with the families of the dead and wounded. Her empathy so genuine, and heartfelt, no play acting on her part, every word, every tear shed showed the sincerity of her condolences. The grief stricken families invited her into their homes. She hugged their children and spoke to them in their own language, with surprising fluency. Newcomers rarely bothered to make the effort, assuming everyone understood English.

Several of the older men greeted Martin warmly, and said they were glad he was there to help Sandra.

Jacob, one of the rangers, with his face still swollen from the beating received during the attack, singled Martin out. Sensing the man wanted to talk to him privately, Martin moved away from the throng, to listen to his tale.

"Those men who attacked. Someone sent them."

"What do you mean?"

"They stole things. But they had orders to break the radios and damage the water tanks."

"How do you know?" Martin asked. Jacob wouldn't make up something as odd as this. He'd worked at Ol Essakut since before Martin was born.

"I thought they only want to steal. Then one man give order to smash the radio. He very angry and say, the Singh wouldn't give money if they not do it. Then he shoot holes in the water tank."

"The Singh? Who do they mean?"

"We too frightened, taking cover, to understand. When we get back and talk, all say same thing." Jacob shook his head. "No one understand... why anyone want to damage camp?"

"Did you tell the police?"

Jacob's shrug told him the police didn't rank high in Jacob's estimation. "No, everyone say tell Simeon first."

"Are there any Singhs in the area?"

"Not before, but now three come to work in the workshop with Mr. Rory."

"When did they come?"

"When Rory come back." His disdainful look said it all. "Mbaya sana," he muttered while shaking his head.

Martin trusted Jacob's judgement. If he thought they were "very bad" Martin had to take him seriously. "You watch them. Tell Simeon or me what they do."

Jacob seemed happy to accept the task. He stuck out his hand to confirm the deal. Sandra was coming out of one of the huts, so he moved back towards her.

She looked worn out, the reassurance of the families complete.

Martin took her elbow and edged her back to the car and drove her home. He insisted she took some painkillers, and sent her to rest, promising to wake her for the radio call.

Just before six they entered the office, half way between the Lander's house and the village. The stone building had a tin roof which needed a coat of paint. Its shabby exterior made the smart modern interior complete with computers, printers, fax machines and shelves full of neatly labelled files lining the walls of the room a surprise. No doubt Simeon was responsible for the regimented paperwork.

Rory sat in front of the radio, fiddling with the dials, waiting for Simeon to make contact.

To Martin's relief the call came through on time, avoiding the need for polite conversation with Rory.

The radio hissed into life and Simeon identified himself.

"Hello Simeon, yes, we can hear you." Sandra said over the static. "What's happening?"

"It's over!" There was a mixture of sadness and relief in his voice. "We tracked them all the way up to the northernmost tip of the ranch. They'd cut through the fence, but we found their den and surrounded it, making sure the whole gang were there. Then the troops moved in. The gang refused to surrender, and started firing. They had no idea what they were up against."

Sandra signalled to Rory to move, and sat herself down in front of the controls. "Did anyone get hurt?"

"Not on our side, but five of the gang died, the other two are seriously wounded. To be honest, I don't hold out much hope for them." Simeon said. "I have to go back to Nairobi with them. I don't know how long I'll have to stay."

"Don't worry. Martin is here with me."

"Great, get him to take you up to the camps, as soon as the police give you clearance. There is a lot to sort out before we can open up again."

"I will."

"Did Rory get any of the vehicles back on the road?"

Martin noticed how Rory's jaw clenched at the query. He obviously hated having Simeon as his boss.

Sandra answered, "He's working on it."

"Good, I'll contact you tomorrow. Is Amina with you?"

"No, she's in Nairobi. I'll tell her you're coming."

The call ended and they sat in silence relieved that the threat was over, but shocked at the death toll.

"The families of the dead men will be happy," Rory said. "Pity about the survivors. Let's hope they don't make it. Who wants the bother of a court case?"

Sandra's jaw went tight. She didn't need Rory's callous reaction right now. Martin had to get her away.

"Shall we go back? You look like you could do with more painkillers." She gave him a nod, and got up to go.

"Jacob is outside, let me pass on the news then he can tell the others," Martin said, knowing she'd promised to let the staff know the latest news.

His tactic worked. She probably wouldn't resort to more pills but accepted his lift home.

He waited until after their evening meal, when Juma and Wanjiru had cleared the table and taken away the empty coffee cups to ask the question that troubled him all day.

"When were you going to tell me your plane had been shot down?"

Sandra fidgeted in her chair.

"No denial then?"

"What's the point? You'll print anyway."

"Possibly, but I don't have to make a big thing out

of it."

"Who are you trying to kid. No journalist is likely to skip over a shot down plane. Or are you expecting to be paid to leave it out?"

Martin clenched his fists under the table. He resented the suggestion he was open to a bribe. Anyone else would have been in danger of having a fist in their face. He studied her across the polished surface of the table. She had no idea how deeply insulting her suggestion was.

"I'm not an irresponsible tabloid hack. I always try to give an honest account of what's going on and try not to harm innocent people. And I never have and never will, accept money to kill a story."

She raised her eyebrow. "But I understood that's what Hank employed you to do."

"Covering things up was never part of the deal. He wants me to write the story, but to emphasize the importance of the conservation work rather than the attack. The bulk of his budget was spent paying the Americans involved for the exclusive rights to their version of events to reduce the risk of a high drama scoop."

"I didn't realize."

"I've written the first draft. Read it and see how much I've toned down the attack. Trust me there will be worse publicity if I don't put something in about your plane being shot and someone else finds out. Now the gang are no longer a threat, the sensation would be the cover up, rather than the deed."

"Won't Hank edit it out?"

"Trust me, he won't. He knows as well as I do another journalist is bound to hear the story and publish it. You need all the positive publicity I can muster. I will describe in detail the conservation work, the plans for the future, which is why I want to meet the people working with you. See the paperwork. See everything. No more secrets."

She didn't answer, and he didn't want to push her.

"Sleep on it. Just, let me drive you around while you're making up your mind, otherwise Jenny will kill me."

"I never had you down as the sort to be terrorized by little old ladies," she said with a smile.

"Don't ever let her hear you call her an old lady."

"Don't worry, I won't." She waved her hand towards the sideboard. "Would you like a drink?"

An array of cut glass decanters with silver labels stood alongside a selection of glasses. Martin shook his head. His nightmares were bad enough without alcohol stimulation. "Glad you're afraid of Jenny, too," he said, thinking maybe he should have accepted her offer of a drink, if only to prolong the evening.

She stood up. "I'm exhausted, I think I'll head off to bed now."

He'd missed his chance, the evening over. She banished him to the luxurious guest cottage set away from the house which under different circumstances would have been a wonderful haven to withdraw to. The cosy atmosphere and relaxed companionship Sandra provided was a treat he hadn't experienced for a long time and one he didn't want to end.

"Sure you'll be all right on your own?" he asked, half hoping she would suggest he stay in a room in the main house. She ignored his hint and walked him to the door, bolting it firmly behind him.

Chapter 10

The next day, before six o'clock, Martin wandered over to the main house and settled on the verandah to watch the rising sun. Sandra soon joined him. A colourful scarf replaced the hospital sling.

Juma brought out a heavily laden tray. Martin was surprised at how good the breakfast tasted. His appetite was starting to improve.

"What time is Rory coming over?" he asked, as he spread homemade jam on the last slice of toast.

"I don't know. We needn't wait for him. Juma can tell him to follow later."

"Sounds good, I'm ready whenever you are," he answered, eager to leave before she changed her mind.

"Great, let's go." She gave Juma the message for Rory, as he loaded the cool box of food he'd prepared into the Land Cruiser.

"I'm dreading this," she confessed as they set off, "Hearing about the damage is different to seeing it. You never told me what Jacob had to say."

Martin hadn't wanted to bother her with Jacob's fears until he had more to go on, but perhaps better to tell her now as he couldn't protect her forever.

"He was at Bushbaby Camp loading stuff into the store when the gang pitched up. He saw their guns, but didn't connect them with trouble. He thought they were new rangers who hadn't got uniforms. As soon as he realized they were thieves, he shouted a warning to the other staff. That's when the gang turned on him and beat him up. The others ran away, and shots were fired, and they got hit. Luckily neither suffered critical injuries and successfully hid.

Jacob pretended to be dead hoping the gang would leave him alone. He lay still for a long time while they looted the camp.

They fought about what to take. Some only interested in cigarettes, booze and food. Their leader didn't appear to have much control, but shouted instructions that the generator, the water supply and the radio system must be destroyed."

"Why would he do that?"

"Jacob heard him say the Singh wouldn't pay them if they didn't do the job properly."

"The police never said anything."

"No, Jacob didn't tell them, he hasn't much faith in them."

"Why would anyone give that instruction?"

"Trashing the radio would stop the other camps being alerted."

"I'm dreading this," she said, her fist balled, her knuckles white.

First impressions were deceptive, not much seemed to be out of place. He helped Sandra out of the vehicle and walked with her round the camp. The store was empty. Martin wondered if the police had cleared out what the gang missed.

In the little office, the smashed radio lay on the ground, a tyre wrench nearby. The ground below the water butt was still damp along the little rivulets caused by water pouring out of the bullet holes. The generator was missing.

The camp had only been in the early stages of preparation so not much to steal.

Satisfied with the inspection, they moved on.

“I was expecting much worse,” Sandra said as he helped fasten her seat belt.

Martin didn’t like to say she’d probably find worse at their next stop, Hyrax camp.

As he halted by the dining area, a hyena shot out in front of them. Martin put out a hand to prevent Sandra from getting out of the car. He blasted the horn. Two more hyenas darted out from behind the main banda. Jacob had warned him what the men who survived had reported. When the attackers reached the second camp they were drunk. Because the camp was in use there was more to interest them.

The kitchen staff had been preparing the evening meal. All the left out food would attract scavengers. He wanted to go ahead without her, but Sandra insisted on following him.

The dining area consisted of a high semi-circular wall at the back with a low one at the front to complete the circle. Rough hewn posts supported the thatched roof. Visitors had a clear view of the salt lick on the other side of the river.

At first glance everything looked normal, but close inspection showed the evidence of animal activity. The serving tables and floor were littered with fruit debris, broken china and animal droppings. The buzz of flies and the chattering of monkeys got louder as they approached the wide open door of the kitchen.

Martin picked up a bucket and stick, and made a loud clatter. Animals scurried for cover. He peered in at the devastation. Overturned pots, including what looked like a huge pot of curry, had left a congealed stinking mass on the floor. Animal paw prints radiated outwards spreading the mess onto every surface foraging animals could reach. Bags of sugar, flour, rice, salt and custard powder had been knocked over and torn apart, adding to the carnage.

None of the mess disguised the huge blood stain in the doorway.

Sandra froze next to him. Nothing would induce her to go further. After a minute, she turned away with tears in her eyes. She didn't need telling the cook died there.

By the communication hut they found another dark stain on the ground marking the spot where Wanjiru's son, Kamau died. Bullet holes from a burst of automatic gunfire peppered the painted mud and wattle walls. Sandra stood silently for a few minutes, then with a shudder walked away to examine the tents. The guests belongings were strewn over the beds and floor. Animal droppings littered the surfaces, clear evidence of their unrestricted access to the campsite.

"They've wrecked everything," she whispered. He wasn't sure if she was referring to the animals or the armed gang. "We must close the camp. I can't ask anyone to come here. The atmosphere has been wrecked, no one will ever feel safe here again."

"Don't make hasty a decision. Get Jacob and a couple of men out to clear up, then find out what the staff think."

"Can you do something about the blood?"

"I'll try," he answered, wondering if his efforts would make a difference.

"Thanks." She blinked back a threatening tear. "I feel useless, I wish I could do something."

"Go and sit down. The last thing I need is for you to collapse with heat stroke." He dusted off a folding chair and placed it under a tree.

"I'm fine."

"Your fingers are swollen." He left the bucket and stick with her and went off in search of a spade and an area with light dusty soil. Taking a shovelful he covered the dark stain by the office doorway. In the kitchen he found a bottle of bleach which he liberally poured onto the stain on the concrete. He filled a bucket with water, poured a little onto the stain and brushed the pool he had created out of the door, taking the worst of the blood with it. He eked a second bucketful of water out of the tap before the supply dried up. He'd made an improvement and wished he could do more, but Sandra's health took priority now. He had to persuade her a trip back to the hospital was more important than giving the staff instructions about cleaning up the camps.

"But my appointment isn't until later."

"I know, but the swelling is too bad to leave. Don't do it for me, do it for the children." That argument won. She'd do anything for the twins. Mentioning them made her eyes sparkle

On the drive back she was subdued. The painkiller made her sleepy and resulted in companionable silence. By the time they reached the house, she admitted the pain was intense. Martin put his foot down and headed to the hospital. After lengthy discussions, more x-rays, and a fresh plaster in place, Sandra was released.

The whole process took longer than expected, and Martin found himself in danger of missing Jenny's deadline to get back to read the children a bedtime story.

Outside the hospital he told her to hang on tight. "I promised Jenny I'd get you back for bedtime, and I don't intend to fail. Brace yourself for a bumpy ride.

"Jenny has you under her thumb," she joked.

"Only because I've known her most of my life," he replied. "It was a tragedy she never had children of her own. She'd have been a great mother."

"I know what you mean. Since Nick died, she's practically adopted me, and taken on the role of grandmother to the twins."

"Bet she's a star," he said, putting his foot down.

Sandra sat rigid, teeth firmly clenched, no hint of complaint.

The welcome from the children surpassed expectation. The two freshly bathed, pyjama-clad children, smelling of talc and mint toothpaste, flung their arms round Sandra in a suffocating clinch. Martin wished he had his camera handy, though no camera would be able to capture the emotion of those hugs. He envied Sandra, unconditional love was rare. Something to be treasured.

Jenny watched silently until Sandra left the room to put the children to bed. Then she scolded him for returning Sandra later than her stipulated time. He explained about the swollen fingers and the delay at the hospital, which made Jenny suitably contrite. "I worry about her. She has so much to contend with."

"She's tougher than you think. She did an impressive job dealing with the grieving families."

"Was Rory back?"

"Yes, along with three motor-mad Singhs, who are staying in one of the cottages."

"Balbinder Singh's nephews, I heard a rumour they were around."

"They're giving Rory a hand in the workshop. But I'm worried."

"Why?"

"Jacob doesn't think much of them. I need you to tell me more about Balbinder Singh. Is he the bloke who used to run a shenzi tour company, and got into trouble for shooting without a licence?"

"Yes, a real wheeler and dealer," Jenny said. "I believe he's been doing rather well recently. I can't believe he'd let his family work for nothing."

"I thought that was odd too. Jacob's promised to keep an eye on them."

Jenny nodded. "What does Sandra think?"

"I didn't tell her, I figured she has enough worries for now."

"Well if you find out more about them, you must let me know."

He raised his hand. "I'm not sure Sandra will want me hanging around."

"Rubbish, she needs the help. You should stay and talk to Simeon before you head off home. I assume you are going back there before you sign your inheritance away."

"Of course I am, but I doubt I'll change my plans."

"Plans?" she asked. "I got the impression you were on indefinite vacation, or whichever term you prefer for unemployed."

He looked her in the eye. "You think I'm mad to sell, don't you?"

"Not entirely," she answered, with an air of sadness that was infectious. "The old place can't mean much to you, to have let it get so neglected. I know you've had a lot going on in your life. But why sell to Beverley Wyatt?"

"I thought with the commitment Beverley has invested in the Ol Essakut project already, she was the perfect purchaser."

"Perfect because she has the cash, or perfect because it will benefit the project? It's not too late to change your mind."

"You'll need to convince me."

"I gather Beverley's returning in the next few days

which gives you time to consider the consequences."

He wanted to ask what she meant, but Sandra reappeared and asked, "What consequences?"

"Oh Martin and I were talking about the long term consequences of the attack," Jenny said quickly, throwing a glare in his direction to silence him. "Best to close the camps for a month and let the dust settle. The staff will need time to adjust. I know the loss of income isn't ideal, but it's the sensible option."

Martin wondered why Jenny had lied and so neatly changed the subject.

"I wondered if we should relocate Hyrax camp."

Jenny ignored the comment and said, "Several neighbouring estates have offered alternative accommodation for our bookings matching the rates. The clients can choose which alternative they'd prefer. All you need tell them is that you have a problem with the water supply on Ol Essakut. The thought of no baths or showers will ensure no complaints about the change of venue."

Sandra didn't look convinced. Martin decided not to get embroiled in the debate. Jenny's alternative arrangements for the next party of guests were meticulous to the last detail. Her comments about his plans needed more consideration.

"I'll head off now."

"Where are you going?" Jenny asked.

"The Sports Club. I have a few things to do in the morning, but I'll pick Sandra up at twelve and take her back to Ol Essakut."

"I can get someone else," Sandra said. He caught Jenny's eye across the room. He had been right, Sandra didn't want him around.

"No need," he said, "I'm more than happy to help. Will you take the children back with you?"

Jenny looked horrified at the suggestion.

"No," Sandra answered, before Jenny managed to get a word in. "Wanjiru needs more time off." She looked at him and added, "Wanjiru who minds them is the mother of one of the men who died. She insisted on coming back to work to help me, but she needs to take time off, and the children won't understand if she's not around. I was going to ask Amina and Jenny to mind them, while I concentrate on getting Ol Essakut back in order."

"Of course they can stay with me," Jenny said.

"Thank you." She turned to Martin. "See you tomorrow then, if you're sure."

He nodded, and left them chatting.

When he got back in the morning to collect Sandra, Amina greeted him, and whispered. "Please say something nice about her hair. I don't think she likes her new style."

He expected a disaster, but the singed hair, kept hidden from view for the last couple of days had been dramatically restyled. Only one comment came to mind. "Wow!"

Sandra blushed.

"Stunning isn't it?" Amina said enthusiastically. "She had to get something done before the book launch. I couldn't let her appear in public looking like a scarecrow. You will make sure she comes?" Amina added. "She's likely to make some excuse to miss the event."

"What event?" he asked. He'd been so busy staring at Sandra he'd lost he thread of the conversation.

Amina turned and glared at her friend. "Sandra, you told me you'd invited him." She turned to the table behind her and picked up a blank envelope which she handed to him. "Never mind Martin, here's an official invitation, complete with all the details. Just get her there. Use whatever tactics are necessary, and make sure she wears the new dress I bought her. The turquoise one. Nothing else will do."

"Something I should know about this dress?" he queried.

Amina winked at him and answered, "For a start, it's not black. This girl needs reminding the book launch is about her and her paintings, her future, not her past."

The expression on Sandra's face showed this was a battle between two exceptionally close friends and Amina meant business. Sandra caught his eye and raised her eyebrows, goading him into the fray.

"So if she appears in any dress that isn't turquoise, I have permission to rip it off?"

Amina opened her mouth as if to reply then realized this was what he hoped she'd do. "Oh, not another joker, get out of here."

"I'll make sure she gets there, don't worry," he said, trying to keep a straight face.

Sandra kissed the children goodbye, and got in the car. Amina put a bag on the back seat. As he drove out the gates, he commented on the parcel. "The dress, I presume? Afraid you'd forget it?"

"Dead right."

"Can't be that bad?" he said, enjoying her discomfort.

"Don't you believe it."

"I can't wait," he said chuckling.

Chapter 11

Sandra barely recognized the face in the mirror as her own. The short, sharp, hairstyle was so different from her normal cut.

She put her lipstick down. Gripping things with her right hand was a struggle and painful, but she had to persevere. She needed to get back to painting. Drawings done with her left hand were not good enough for Amina's book.

With the dress on, she'd be ready.

As she slipped the dress off the hanger she decided friends were sometimes a liability. The excitement in Amina's voice when she presented her with the tissue wrapped gift was difficult to forget. "You haven't had time to go shopping, so I got you a dress to wear," Amina had said. "Try it for size."

Jenny and Amina cajoled her into putting the dress on. The size, the fabric, the colour, her favourite shade of turquoise was perfect. The style was not. She'd never have bought something so daring or extravagant for herself.

The ecstatic response from Amina, "Magnificent," made the situation more difficult, especially with Jenny echoing Amina's enthusiasm.

"Gorgeous," Jenny said.

Sandra accepted. She couldn't offend her friend by refusing the gift, thinking that on the night she'd find an excuse not to wear the dress. But that was before Amina went to work on Martin.

She held the dress up against herself. What possessed Amina? It bordered on indecent. Martin would most likely stick to his promise and insist she wore it.

The sheer luxury of the fabric falling into place made her gasp. The zip was impossible to manage with her hand in plaster. Wanjiru would help but asking her felt heartless. Wanjiru insisted on returning to work to help her because of her arm, even though her son's funeral still hadn't taken place. Going to a party seemed frivolous under such circumstances. She nearly said something. But Wanjiru got in first.

"Don't be sad. Good for you to get on with life," she said as she pulled up the zip.

Sandra stepped backwards and checked her reflection in the mirror.

The drastic haircut, the dress, everything struck her as familiar, scarily familiar.

Sandra dashed downstairs to the dining room, yanked a briefcase out from under the table, lifted the lid and clumsily sifted through the contents until she came to a well thumbed manila envelope. Using her teeth she opened the flap and scattered photos onto the table, spreading them out to search for a particular photo - a photo of her mother.

People often said they looked alike, but she hadn't believed them until now. With identical hair styles, and identical necklines to their dresses, no mistaking the similarities. The only thing missing was the necklace her mother wore, an omission easily remedied. Sandra dropped the photo and hurried back to the bedroom to her jewellery box.

While she searched, she heard voices in the hall. Wanjiru would fuss over Martin making sure he had a drink while he waited for her to come down. In fact

Wanjiru would be disappointed if Sandra came down too soon and deprived her of the chance of looking after a guest. As for Martin, he'd happily make himself at home anywhere. He was such an easy person to be with. When Jenny foisted him on her, she had thought he'd crowd her, but in all the time spent ferrying her around he never had.

The oddest thing was his reluctance to go back to his own property. He'd had plenty of opportunity, but he stuck by her side, using the excuse that he promised Jenny he'd stay with her, proving he kept his promises.

At last she found the correct box with the antique gold and turquoise necklace which her mother wore in the photo. A perfect match for the dress. She checked the colour briefly in the mirror before heading back downstairs.

"Sorry to keep you waiting," she said to Martin who was looking at her pictures on the table. "Can you help with this? The plaster cast makes it rather difficult."

Martin took the necklace from her. His fingers brushed the skin on the back of her neck triggering a shiver. He stepped back and said under his breath, "Perfect."

All the worries about the indecency of the dress, which vanished while she searched for the photo and the necklace, returned.

Martin standing there in his ill-fitting dark grey suit made her feel like a gawky teenager. Her senses awakened to the fact he was tall, good looking, and had extremely sexy eyes. The thought plunged her into guilt mode. She hated that she found him attractive. She still hurt from her trauma with Nick. The feelings of awkwardness had little to do with the skimpiness of her dress.

Martin broke the train of thought. “Your mother?” he asked, pointing to the photo abandoned on the table. “She’s beautiful. You’re so like her.”

Sandra, embarrassed by the compliment, had to say something. “Must be the hair cut, looking in the mirror this evening I remembered the photo and the necklace. That’s what held me up.”

“You didn’t deliberately try to recreate this look?”

“No. I told the hairdresser to do what she wanted, and Amina chose the dress. All rather weird, even the neckline of the dress is similar. I’m not sure I dare wear it.”

Martin laughed. “Now I understand why Amina was afraid you’d chicken out. Shame the plaster cast doesn’t do the dress justice. Never mind, if your mother wore something similar, I don’t see why you can’t.”

“You men are so lucky, put on a jacket and tie, and you conform to the regulation dress code. For me fitting in is harder, I’ve no idea what sort of party Amina planned, or who she invited.”

“Don’t fret, if Jenny is involved, it will be great. Your dress is perfect, and I’m proud to escort you. What’s more, I promise I’ll protect you from lecherous old men.”

“Dressed like this I’ll probably need you.”

“How’s the arm?”

“Itchy and driving me mad, but I’m getting a better grip with my fingers. I can’t wait for the plaster to come off and start painting again.”

“You should frame your mother’s picture and put it on display,” he said as he picked up one of the photos of Helen Harriman from the sideboard.

Sandra noticed sadness in his eyes as he held the

photo. Of course he'd known Helen well, perhaps he'd tell her more about her predecessor.

With a wistful sigh he put it down. "You should put these away. You can't keep living with other people's memories."

"Not so simple. She's the children's mother. I have a duty to keep her memory alive, plus I don't want to upset them."

"Yes, but those could go somewhere less intrusive, and the sooner you move them the better for all of you. Remember it's your home too."

"I'm not used to the idea yet."

"It shows."

"Is that bad?"

"Only if you feel you can't make changes. From what I've seen so far you are more of a mother to Sam and Emma than Helen ever was or would have been."

"Sounds as if you didn't like her. Everyone else either wants to make a saint of her, or rapidly changes the subject. You knew her. Could you tell me what she was like?"

"Yes," he answered quietly, "but not right now."

The sadness in his voice made her decide to be patient.

"Thanks. We'd better get moving, Amina will throttle us if we're late."

"I thought you didn't want to go?" he said.

"I don't. I'll be honest, this is my first function since Nick's funeral. I'm dreading every minute."

Martin took her hand. "Don't worry, I'll fend off morbid souls as well as the lechers, as long as you protect me from loud Americans. Are you sure you want to drive all the way back tonight?"

"Yes. I can't miss the meeting with the Wildlife Fund delegates and risk losing funding because of a party. I'd rather miss the party." She picked up her silvery-grey pashmina and moved to the door. "I'm sorry to ask you to drive there and back in one evening."

"No problem. It's not as if you'd get time with the children."

"They'll be home in a couple of days, and hopefully some normality will return."

True to his word, when they arrived at the Safari Club, Martin stuck by her side. A few people stopped and offered her sympathy over Nick's death, most avoided the subject. Several greeted Martin like a long lost friend. Only one asked what he'd been doing for the last two years. He quickly steered the conversation away from himself and his work onto her book illustrations. As the evening progressed signs of tension appeared, Martin picked at the canapés as they came round and fiddled with a cocktail stick. His smile became more fixed, his jaw clenched, his eyes less focussed and his infrequent responses to the inane chatter got shorter, almost abrupt. Sandra sensed that at any moment he might be tempted to say what he thought, and she didn't think it would go down too well. Time to leave.

"I'm too hot in here," she said to him, "I need fresh air." Martin grabbed her arm and had her out of the room almost before she finished the sentence.

"Come, I want to show you something."

The earlier tension built up during the evening evaporated so quickly she wondered if she'd imagined it. His enthusiasm had a childlike quality making him look happy for the first time in hours as he guided her through the bar and out across the lawn towards the swimming pool. "I love this place at night."

Sandra stopped to remove her high-heeled shoes

which kept sinking into the soft lawn. The dew-drenched grass was freezing on her bare feet, but she didn't complain. Martin led her down the garden, past a small lake, over a wooden bridge, leading to another one. There were fewer lights as they got further from the club house, making the moonlight, reflected in the still water, more spectacular. In the middle of the lower pool rose a small island. All round the edge birds stood on one leg, sleeping with their heads tucked under their wings. Beyond was darkness and further beyond, the outline of the mountain. One small cloud softened the silhouette, hovering just below the main peak. A puff of cold air rustled the leaves. Africa's night time chorus of nocturnal birds, insects, and pond creatures was in full swing, with the occasional burst of activity from a couple of ducks and geese on sentinel duty. The faint tinkle of piano music, chattering voices and bursts of laughter drifted down from the clubhouse reminding her of her neglected duties. She shivered.

Without a word, Martin slipped his jacket round her shoulders. "Sorry I forgot you weren't dressed for outdoors."

The silky satin lining of his jacket warmed her. With a light touch of one hand on her back he guided her back. Just below the swimming pool he stopped and kissed her.

She responded, no hesitation, intoxicated by the moment. Then she lost her balance, sticking out her good arm to steady herself. Martin drew back. The magic of the moment vanished.

He put his arm back around her shoulder again and continued walking, as if nothing had passed between them. She didn't know whether to be pleased or disappointed.

At the door she slipped on her shoes, and handed his jacket back to him. He dropped it on a chair, and led her onto the dimly lit dance floor. The music was slow. The physical contact of his arm around her fired through her as if someone had pulled a switch. For nearly a week she had spent almost every minute of the day with this man and not thought twice about it. Now without warning, she found herself torn between an urge to run and a crazy hormone driven desire to give in to the unbelievable sexual craving raging within.

Get a grip, she told herself. A man's hand brushing the nape of her neck, a tender kiss in the moonlight and a smoochy dance hardly added up to a sound basis for a relationship. Her instincts told her to get off the dance floor before she did something she'd regret.

With extreme will power, she pulled away from him and said, "Please tell Amina I've a headache and take me home?" The moment she spoke she was afraid he'd get the wrong message.

"Headache?"

"Just make an excuse," she answered making the situation worse. "Sorry, I can't do this."

"What's the hurry?" he whispered pulling her back towards him. This was madness. She had to break away. She put up her good hand and pushed him away. "Martin, please... get me out of here."

He brushed her cheek with a kiss. "Sorry, my mistake?" and added softly, "Shame, I hoped you wanted me all to yourself."

His hand lingered on her back as he led her from the floor across the room towards Amina to make their apologies for departing so early.

"Come on. Let's find your wrap."

Martin insisted she wore his jacket for the drive

home. The night air was cold, and she was too tired to argue. He drove in silence, intent on watching the road, which gave her a chance to gather herself together to make sense of her confusion. Fear was stupid. Why should she care if the locals accused her of being unfaithful to Nick's memory? The fear went deeper. She was terrified of getting hurt again, and determined to avoid the risk. Would a day, a week, a year, or longer change the odds? The tricky part was deciding when to take a chance. So hard when her mind wanted one thing and her body screamed out to be held and loved.

She had just about made a decision when Martin stopped and switched off the motor. She looked round to see where they were. It was somewhere between the second farm gate and the house. The headlights still pointed down the road, lighting up the thorny bushes and reflecting the eyes of a small herd of Thomson's gazelle that were grazing on either side of the road. "Is there a problem?"

Martin, with both hands firmly gripping the steering wheel. turned towards her and answered, "Yes." The luminous dashboard dials gave off just enough light for her to see his tender, worried expression. "Whatever happened tonight, the occasion, the drink, the food, the company, even the moonlight, we can't let anything spoil the friendship we had before. If I behaved out of turn, please forgive me?"

She leaned forward, kissed him on the cheek, and said, "You did nothing wrong. I'm the one with the problem."

"Curable?"

If only she knew.

Chapter 12

Martin drove on wondering when, if ever, they would open up to each other. Trust worked two ways. He expected her honesty yet he avoided talking about himself, particularly regarding his reluctance to head home. Perhaps he'd tell her if he understood himself.

She was desperate for information about Rory, Helen and Nick. Should he tell her? What difference would it make? He had a crazy notion something went wrong before Nick's fatal accident to take the romance out of the marriage, and equally certain she'd never divulge what happened.

All too soon the lights of the house loomed out of the darkness. Sandra touched his arm. "Park outside your cottage."

He halted right outside the door as instructed. Before he had a chance to speak, she slid out of the vehicle and walked towards the door. "Coffee?"

Was he in danger of misreading her intentions? He couldn't risk a misunderstanding.

"If you only want coffee, you should know coffee won't satisfy my needs."

"Nor mine." She stepped backwards, pushing the door open and drew him across the threshold.

All evening he'd longed for this, now he was nervous. He wanted her so much he was prepared to forfeit the pleasure to avoid regrets. He had to slow the pace, give her time to be certain. Not that he wanted to resist.

He closed the door with his foot, and pulled her into his arms savouring the pressure of her body against his. Her figure moulded to his as one. He bent his head forward, breathed in her fresh delicate scent. He kissed her forehead, her eyes then her lips. Was it too late to back out? He wanted her so much, but had to give her a chance to change her mind.

He pulled away a fraction, and reached for the light switch. She caught his arm and held it.

He forced out the words, "Is this a good idea?"

She looked up at him, and even in the dim light from the outside lamp he could see she wasn't happy with his knock-back.

She shivered, throwing him into panic. She was freezing, he must do something. A second shiver spurred him into action. He made her sit on the sofa by the fire. He coaxed the few glowing embers in the grate into life, added fresh kindling and soon had flames dancing over crackling cedar logs.

An awkward silence existed between them as he waited for the answer. She hadn't left, which was encouraging. He held her hand and asked again, "Is this a good idea?" not daring to look into her eyes, for fear of adding pressure.

The delay resigned him to her going back to her house alone, when she whispered, "I'd like to stay."

Why argue? Instead he kissed her. The heat of the roaring blaze was nothing to the passion the kiss ignited. No need to rush. He savoured every move. Her plaster cast made undoing his shirt buttons hard. He solved the problem for her by doing them himself then dealt with the zip of her dress. His hands ran over the smooth silky contours of her back. The scratchy plaster cast pressed against him while her good hand lightly caressed his body. Her fingers danced all over his skin eventually reaching the scar caused by Nick's bullet. The contact made him shudder. He willed her not to break the spell of the moment by asking him about it. He kissed her again and her fingers moved on and continued to explore and excite.

When she was warm he lifted her up with ease and carried her to the bed. The intensity of emotion and physical passion she roused in him exceeded all his dreams and expectations.

In the aftermath of love making, words were unnecessary. A gentle stroke, a tender kiss, the rhythm of her breathing in time with his was enough. As she slept beside him he wondered how the evening would alter his plans.

His mobile phone woke him with a jolt. Sandra lay still, her naked body snugly curved alongside his, her broken arm propped up on his chest. He tried to pick up the phone from the bedside table without disturbing her.

"Hello," he said softly, hoping Sandra was still asleep.

"Morning, Martin, I hope I didn't wake you," the caller said.

Martin recognized the voice instantly and knew Beverley wouldn't care if she had. You did... but never mind," he replied sharply. "What can I do for you?"

"Rather a lot I hope." The innuendo inferred was not lost on him. He prayed Sandra couldn't hear the conversation, especially when she added, "When can we get together?" Every muscle in Sandra's body went rigid alongside him, she was listening.

The inviting tone rather than the actual words threw him into a panic. He responded with a brusque, "I'm not sure."

"Well I'd like it to be as soon as possible, I shall be checking into Mount Kenya Safari Club later today. How about dinner tonight?"

"I can't," he answered firmly, annoyed by her timing.

"Well sometime tomorrow might be better. There's a lot of paperwork to deal with."

"I'll call you later when I know my plans. Good bye." He snapped the phone shut and slid it back on to the bedside table. He already had an agenda for the day. It started with kissing Sandra, and hopefully would end the same way. An agenda he intended putting into action right away.

"Sorry, about that," he said, moving himself so he could kiss her, but Sandra edged in the opposite direction.

"Someone important?" she queried. Her icy tone hurt.

"Only Beverley."

The force with which Sandra pulled away from him was frightening.

"Beverley Bloody Wyatt!" she spat out as she slipped from his grasp, scooping her clothes up off the floor on her way to the bathroom.

The insult and the near hysteria in her voice as she uttered the name shocked him. He'd been an idiot ignoring the hints from Jenny, Amina and even Simeon that his deal wouldn't be popular without asking why. Now he could only guess the personal issues between the two women centred round Nick.

"She wants to discuss the property deal." He threw back the covers and went to follow Sandra, grabbing a pair of boxer shorts as he moved.

"Who are you trying to kid?" Sandra replied, the bitterness clearly detectable, as she slammed the bathroom door.

"She'll want to discuss the articles about Ol Essakut too." Martin called after her as he struggled into his clothes. Sandra didn't respond. When she emerged fumbling with the zip of the turquoise dress, he sensed reluctance to ask for help, but offered anyway.

"Let me." For a moment he thought she'd refuse, but she turned, giving him access to the zip. He resisted the temptation to pull her into his arms and carefully slid the zipper up. She flinched when he touched her shoulder. He stepped away. Tension filled the gap.

"Please don't go. Tell me what upset you," he pleaded.

Her tousled hair, her face almost devoid of make up, had never looked more beautiful. The threat of tears welling displayed her vulnerability. All he wanted was to hug her. Kiss her. Protect her.

After a moment she shrugged. "Bad timing... It's too soon."

Martin didn't know whose timing she referred to, his, hers or Beverley's, but he had enough sense to accept further discussion was out of the question. He rescued his discarded tie from the floor, slipped the looped tie over her head, and under her plaster. "Keep it, a reminder of a magical night." Then using every ounce of self-control suppressed the desire to kiss her, and moved to one side to let her pass.

As she stepped outside, he called out, "I'll be over later to drive you up to the education centre for your meeting. What time do you want to leave?"

She froze in the doorway. The few seconds she took to answer felt like an hour. Eventually she replied, "Nine, if you're sure."

“I’ll be there.” He couldn’t imagine what he’d do if she turned down his offer. He needed to be with her, to prove their night together was not a mistake.

Everything had been perfect, until Beverley called. He tried to recall every word of the conversation. Hardly surprising Sandra reacted the way she did. The wording and tone left little doubt about what sort of catching up Beverley had in mind. Persuading Sandra the only business he had with Beverley related to the sale of his land, would be difficult.

Then he started to worry. He had been so busy shying away from conversations about his selling his property and been so unapproachable no one had explained things to him. Maybe they had kept quiet because they wanted his land in the project even if it did upset the balance. Serve them right if he decided not to sell after all.

None of that changed the fact he’d have to face Beverley, if only to make it clear to her that picking up where they left off eighteen months ago was not on. Theirs was a one night stand, neither of them wanted more then, and he certainly didn’t want more now. The affair was history and staying that way.

He watched through the window as Sandra crossed the lawn from the guest cottage to the main house. He’d be a supportive friend, help her rebuild the camps and get over the crash and trauma of the armed attack, and hope Beverley’s call was quickly forgotten.

He saw Rory approach Sandra. He felt a surge of jealousy, an almost forgotten emotion. One he’d hoped never to experience again in his life.

Sandra adopted a defensive stance as Rory crowded her. Martin wanted to intervene, but was afraid of appearing possessive and interfering.

Chapter 13

Even before he confirmed the name of his early morning caller Sandra guessed.

Every nuance of the conversation gave away the nature of their friendship. Beverley had destroyed her marriage to Nick before the honeymoon ended, and was now poised to break up another relationship. Nothing would erase the intimacy conveyed in Beverley's voice.

What a fool to sleep with Martin knowing so little about him. The fact he planned to sell his land to Beverley should have served as a warning.

She'd never be able to explain the situation to Martin without confessing to the failure of her marriage to Nick. Her first meeting with Nick's ex-girlfriend Beverley, had gone well. She didn't appear to bear a grudge. In fact her friendliness made Sandra believe friendship though unlikely might be possible. Since his death all contact had been avoided as Sandra tried to forget the betrayal.

Halfway across the grass by the side door of the house Rory blocked her route. He stood so close, positioning himself between her and the entrance making her uncomfortable.

He stank of booze, and his slurred speech and scruffier than usual clothes with a slept in appearance made her wary.

"Sexy dress!" he said.

His sweeping gaze was a violation, and Amina's

gift a liability.

She forced herself to ignore his lusting gaze to concentrate on his words.

“Jacob’s been nicking stuff from Parjit.”

She took a second to work out Parjit was one of Rory’s rally driving visitors, and another second to dismiss the accusation as ridiculous. Jacob was the most trusted member of the camp staff. Why would he steal from anyone, let alone someone staying in one of the guest cottages?

“That’s crazy. Why would he?”

“Beats me,” he answered taking his hand out of his pocket to scratch his unshaven chin. “Just reporting what Parjit told me.”

“What’s missing?”

“A watch, a radio and some cash,” he said, without taking his eyes off her body.

“How much?” She realized it sounded as if the quantity mattered, when she thought Jacob would never risk his job.

Rory raised his eyebrows. “Who cares? You can’t let him get away with theft.”

As if she needed telling. Life seemed to be one drama after another.

“Don’t worry, I’ll deal with the problem,” she said, stepping backward to put space between them.

Rory inched closer, reached out and ran a finger over the tie supporting her cast, and onto her bare shoulder. “Interesting sling,” he muttered.

She flinched at his touch. He made her jumpy in a way she’d never experienced before. She wished Juma would appear, or one of the gardeners would arrive. She didn’t care who, as long as she wasn’t alone with Rory any longer. She glanced back at the guest cottage. Martin stood by the window watching. She doubted he would come. She'd been clear she wanted to be alone.

Rory had never unsettled her like this before. Today his attitude had changed. Since Nick's death she'd handled everything thrown at her but suddenly she doubted her ability to cope. She closed her eyes for a second, forcing herself to breathe deeply, and opened them find help had come. Martin stood by her side, Juma was laying breakfast on the verandah, and the gardener was filling the bird bath with a watering can.

"Problem?" Martin asked.

"Yes, Rory's friend Parjit's accused Jacob of theft," she answered.

"Go and change," he said, "Rory can fill me in, then we can go and investigate."

Rory stepped aside to let her pass. She happily obeyed Martin's instructions. Not the moment for a display of female independence. If he expected her to leap back into his bed with gratitude for his gallant rescue, he'd be disappointed.

She dressed quickly, choosing clothes that would not give Rory anything to ogle at. A pair of jeans and a baggy tee shirt seemed appropriate. Then almost in defiance she put her head and arm back through Martin's silk tie sling. Rory could read what he liked from the gesture. Confidence restored she went down to face the latest crisis. To her relief Rory had gone. Martin sat alone at the breakfast table on the verandah.

"You should eat," he said, "I sense a long day ahead. From what Rory told me, this Parjit character is determined to take the accusation all the way. He wants to search Jacob's house." Martin passed her a cup of tea.

"Jacob's not a thief. He wouldn't let me down.

He's been a godsend since Nick died."

"I agree," Martin said, "I meant to say something earlier, Jacob told me he didn't like these three characters. I asked him to keep an eye on them and report back to me."

"I wish you'd warned me."

"I'm sorry. I thought he was suffering from paranoia. Now I find it odd he's being accused of stealing." He sipped his tea. "I agree with you, I'd trust him with my life." Martin waited for her reaction. "I can't see the harm of a search to shut Parjit up."

She pushed her cup away. "I know it sounds silly. I've never spoken to Rory's friends, but I don't want them here."

"You're not alone. Juma says none of the staff like Parjit, who struts around as if he owns the place. The gardener says the other two are always rude to him." Martin buttered some toast and offered it to her. "Why don't you ask them to go?"

"How can I? They're Rory's guests. He has rights too."

"What sort of rights?"

"Not important now and far too complicated to explain."

What would he make of the fact Rory claimed she was the one with no right to live at Ol Essakut. And she wasn't ready to talk about the conversation she'd had with the lawyer in Nairobi about Rory intending to contest the will. One thing for sure she had no intention of stirring up animosity by asking his guests to leave.

"Does he often invite people to stay?"

"Never, or at least not since I've lived here." She took the toast, glad not to have to struggle with the butter knife. "I wish Simeon was back. He's good at this sort of thing."

"Don't worry. I'll stick around to back you up. You'll handle the situation as well as he would."

"Thanks for the vote of confidence."

A flock of superb starlings descended on the bird table with a flurry, giving her something to concentrate on without seeming rude for not talking while she finished her breakfast. The minute she put her empty cup down, Martin stood up, obviously ready to drive her over to Rory's house. Parjit and the other two stood outside waiting. They argued among themselves, stopping the moment she stepped out of the vehicle. Martin listening quietly as she quizzed them about the missing items.

"He stole a watch, a radio, and some cash," the shorter of the two men told her.

"It was Jacob," the spotty one said. "He's always spying on us. Last night he ran away when he saw our car lights."

Parjit, the leader of the trio added, "You must dismiss him."

Sandra had no intention of acting without irrefutable proof. Martin's assurance that Jacob was trustworthy made her extra cautious. "I need evidence," she said firmly.

"It's hidden under a blanket in his house," Lalji Singh, the spotty faced one said. His brother jabbed him so hard in the ribs with his elbow that the poor kid struggled not to lose his balance.

Sandra didn't need anyone to point out that his response was too quick and too precise. Martin's quizzical frown confirmed she was not alone in thinking it odd that these men were too sure where the missing property was located.

"How do you know?"

Parjit answered for him. "It's the obvious place."

"We'll go and check," she said. "Anything found will be checked for fingerprints." This last remark took the smile off Parjit's face.

On the way over to the village and Jacob's house Martin agreed the whole thing sounded suspect. "If the stuff is hidden under a blanket I'll be certain," he said. "Why Jacob? Did he find out something they don't want anyone to know? They'd need a reason to frame him."

"Unless Rory's responsible."

"What on earth made you suggest that?"

"He knows how much I depend on Jacob and would like to undermine my authority."

"Interesting, but I don't think so. Rory looked as puzzled as I was. I think this has more to do with the fact Jacob has been watching them."

"We'll have to hurry or I'll be late for the meeting with the funding committee."

"Don't worry. I'll get you there on time," Martin said as he opened the car door for her.

Rory, Parjit, Vejay and Lalji were heading to the village on foot giving her a few minutes head start.

"Wait here, let me talk to Jacob first, on my own," she said.

The last thing she wanted was to upset Jacob or any of the staff. He was a favourite with all the visitors, courteous, soft spoken, and caring. She knocked on his door, and waited patiently.

Jacob's surprise showed. "Is there a problem?" he asked.

"Sorry, Jacob, yes a big one. Rory's friends have accused you of stealing. I don't believe them."

"Thank you," he answered. Then he looked over at the group gathering by her car. "Lalji Singh and his brother...?"

"Yes, they say we'll find their things in your house."

"You trust them?"

"No, why are they doing this?"

"They want to get rid of me."

"I think you're right, and that the stolen items will be in your house. But I don't believe you put them there. Is that clear?"

"Thank you. What happens now?"

"Let Martin search your house. Whatever he finds will go to be checked for fingerprints. If the stuff was put here by someone else your prints won't be found."

Jacob smiled. "Thank you for trusting me. Tell Martin to look."

"Martin," she called, "Jacob is happy for you to go in." She backed away from the door, aware a growing group of off-duty staff and their families had gathered to witness the event.

Martin shook hands with Jacob, and followed him into the house. Rory and Parjit hovered in the doorway.

Simeon's father, Mr. Mugo, came over to her. "Problem?" he asked.

"Yes, and I need your help. Jacob's been accused of stealing stuff. We have to search, and will probably find the stolen property. I want you to convince everyone here Martin and I don't believe he's guilty."

He nodded, moved away from her, and spoke to a few of the people standing in the crowd. Then he came back and stood by her.

"That's the stuff," Parjit yelled, moving into the house. "Give it to me."

Martin's voice boomed out for all to hear. "Don't touch. No one touches anything until the fingerprint check is over.

Mr. Mugo said quietly, "Get them away from here."

Sandra sensed his anxiety. "Don't worry I will."

She hurried over to Jacob's doorway. "Show me what you found." Martin pointed to a bundle of blankets. Tucked into the folds of the top blanket were a watch, a transistor radio, and a plastic bank bag containing cash. "And no one here touched it?"

Everyone shook their heads. "Good." She pointed to a cardboard box on the floor. "Martin, lift the blanket and put it into the box without touching anything."

He followed her instructions and waited.

"Thank you. Lock the box in the boot of my car. Later today we will take it to the police for testing." He nodded. "Jacob, please come with us. Mr. Mugo, can you come along to make sure Jacob gets fair treatment."

A few of the onlookers nodded approval of her method of dealing with the problem.

"Rory, take your friends back to your house and keep an eye on them. I have a finance meeting at the education centre to attend. I'll tell you later what I've decided to do. The police will probably need your friends to go to the station to have their fingerprints taken."

This suggestion took the smug look off the Indians' faces. All three, decidedly put out by the prospect, huddled together arguing, assuming no one would understand what they were saying. She didn't care if they didn't like her plan.

The assembled crowd seemed satisfied, so she joined the others in the car.

Martin helped with her seat belt. "The idea of going

to the police station wasn't popular with our Indian friends."

"Did you understand what they said?"

"Not all of it, but I got the impression they were worried about their uncle's reaction."

"How odd," she answered, then turned to talk to Mr. Mugo and Jacob who were sitting quietly in the back, "I hope you don't mind being roped in to help? I ought to explain why I asked. Parjit told us precisely where to look for Lalji's things, which was very strange. I want to make sure that everyone can know Jacob is treated fairly."

"You did the right thing," Mr. Mugo answered. "Jacob says he never touched the things so having his fingerprints taken is not a problem to him. He wants his name cleared."

"So do I."

"Did you know there was a small grass fire just down there, last night?" he said pointing to a blackened area of grass beyond the goat pens. "Everyone from the village went to help. A perfect time for someone to go into Jacob's house without being seen, don't you think?"

Martin stopped, "Won't be a minute. I just want to check something."

"I have to be at this finance meeting at the Education Centre," Sandra said.

"I know. Be with you in a moment."

He circled the patch of burnt ground. Then stepped forward, right to the centre of the circle and bent to inspect something. A moment later, he picked up a broken paraffin lamp and carried it back to the car. He carefully placed his find in the boot, and without comment continued the journey.

"Perhaps while you're waiting you can all try to

work out why they accused Jacob of theft."

No one spoke for a while, as Martin took the winding route to the main gate leaving a cloud of red dust in his wake.

"They no good, you should tell them to go," Jacob said.

"I would if I could," she answered. "Tell us why you think they're no good."

"They have guns," Jacob answered.

"Guns? You saw them?" Martin asked.

"Yes, they say for shooting birds, but I tell them no one shoots on Ol Essakut. They say they practice hitting targets," Jacob added, "but they lie. I know they shoot animals."

"Are you absolutely sure?" Martin checked. Jacob nodded his eyes wide with worry.

"Why the hell didn't you tell someone?" he asked sounding rather impatient with Jacob who was looking distraught at his failing.

"I going to... but you go to Nanyuki."

Martin stopped the car in the car park outside the new building alongside several smart new vehicles.

"Looks as if I'm last to arrive," Sandra said as she got out. "I have no idea how long the meeting will take. Get a cup of coffee at the vet lab. I'll come over when I'm through."

The meeting dragged on and on. Sandra struggled to keep focussed. The quandary about Rory's friends owning guns never left her thoughts.

She repeated her needs to the committee, never compromising her demands until they understood what was at risk if they refused the funding. Her strategy paid off. The visiting representatives assured her the proposal stood an excellent chance of approval and to expect confirmation within a week.

Chapter 14

Sandra emerged into the bright sunlight to find Martin and the others sitting on the wall near the vehicle in the shade of the tall silver-barked gum trees talking to three rangers. She waved to the departing visitors and made her way to the waiting group. The rangers saluted as she approached. She greeted them by name with a handshake and inquired about their families. Learning everyone's name and their connections had been hard work, but worth the effort for their loyalty.

Aware of Martin's scrutiny, she chatted to the men. He waited to speak, and when he did, he suggested returning to the house. She willingly agreed. Her arm was throbbing because she foolishly forgot to bring any pain killers with her.

Martin waited until they moved off to give her an update on his discussions with Jacob, Mr. Mugo and the rangers.

"The Singh trio made enemies down here too. The rangers backed up reports about rude behaviour and dangerous driving and confirm Jacob's fears regarding target practice not being confined to shooting tin cans. Everyone is concerned because of the conservation rules. They wrongly assumed you had given permission."

Anger made her speechless. Without proof, she lacked the courage to order the Singhs off the ranch.

"Jacob and Mr. Mugo both agree that Jacob must go to the police station with the things we found,"

Martin offered. "They understand the accusation made and the need for you to act. I have to go back to town today, so I'll take Jacob. I'll phone and tell you what the police say. I'll make sure Parjit and the others have to go into Nanyuki to get their prints recorded. Jacob suggested taking his leave until it's sorted."

"Paid leave," Sandra said quickly. Jacob could ill afford to lose his wages.

Jacob let out an audible sigh. As for Martin, she didn't trust herself not to make a sarcastic remark about his rush to get to town to renew his friendship with Beverley.

Overhearing their call made her doubt him, but he'd been supportive, firstly saving her from Rory, and then dealing with Jacob. Maybe she should not have walked out on him so abruptly. No. She had to stay away while Beverley had a hold on him.

On their return to the house Rory and Parjit and the other two came sauntering over.

Martin nudged her, and said, "Don't say anything about the guns."

"Why's he still here?" Rory demanded, looking at Jacob. "Haven't you fired him?"

"No one gets fired without proof of guilt. If his fingerprints are on the stolen things then I will act." Sandra's faith in Jacob became even stronger. "And for your information he's waiting for Martin to take him to the police station, to get his name cleared."

The Singhs huddled together arguing amongst themselves.

"Fine. Get lover boy to take him into town. It'll be good to get him off the property too. You want to watch out for him. I wouldn't be surprised if he isn't after control of this place."

Sandra was so taken aback by the depth of

resentment in Rory's voice that she took a moment to register what he said.

The tension between the two men was so strong, it was practically visible. Martin looked ready to lose his cool, but he impressed her with his response. "I'm not leaving until Simeon gets back."

"Well," she said, "I suggest everyone gets back to work. Ol Essakut won't run itself."

Rory glared at her, but she didn't flinch. He spun on his heels and stomped off. Parjit, Vejay and Lalji scurried after him.

Simeon's father turned to Martin and said, "I'm glad you decided to wait for Simeon." He turned to Sandra, "Thank you, you've been very fair. Jacob appreciates it too."

"Good. Jacob's too valuable to lose," she said raising her voice to make certain Jacob overheard her praise. "I know you've been worried about Simeon and will want to catch up on all his news. Why not eat here this evening? That way he can fill us in together."

"You're very kind." He smiled, displaying his oddly spaced teeth.

"Make yourselves comfortable," she said, waving them towards the table and chairs on the verandah, "Juma will bring you both some tea. I have work to do inside."

The two men happily accepted her suggestion so she turned to Martin. "Martin, shall we get on with the research you asked for?"

Martin raised an eyebrow, he had no idea what she was on about, but followed her inside without questioning her in front of the others. She put her head though the kitchen door and asked Juma to give Jacob and Mr. Mugo something to eat on the verandah, and ordered lunch for Martin and herself in the dining room.

As soon as they were alone, he asked, “Research?”

“Why didn’t you want me to mention the guns to Rory?”

“Because you’ve no proof they’ve shot anything other than a few old tin cans,” he answered.

His being right didn’t make the problem go away. “So, what should I do?”

“Nothing for now,” Martin answered confidently. “I’ll find out if they have proper permits for their guns first.”

“Can you do that?”

“With Simeon’s help, anything’s possible.”

“You don’t think they’re dangerous, do you?”

“The Singhs... no... I’m more worried about Rory’s behaviour, he’s always been a bit odd but he’s definitely more strange than usual. You weren’t at all comfortable with him this morning.”

“Possibly wandering about in full evening dress at eight in the morning had something to do with that? And yes, thank you, I admit I was mighty relieved by your appearance.”

“I nearly didn’t come. I didn’t want to be accused of interfering.” He fiddled with his keys, “In the same way as I hope you don’t mind my staying here until Simeon gets back.”

“You want to talk to him, don’t you?”

“I do, but Rory’s comment just now is the real reason I’m staying.”

She stared into his deep brown eyes, happy he cared enough to want her to be safe, but the fact he had business with Beverley cancelled everything. She had to face the fact she was jealous, torn between wanting him out of her life because of his relationship with Beverley and desperate to prevent him ever seeing the woman again.

Taking the conversation on a different tangent, she said, “Rory’s never been a problem before. Do you think now is a good time to tell me the full story of why you are at each others throats? Don’t pretend there’s no problem, animosity doesn’t appear without good reason.”

His expression told her she had put him on the spot. “It’s a long story,” he answered quietly.

“I have time.”

“Well, when he first came to Ol Essakut, we had nothing in common, and at that age it’s important.”

“Come on, you know that’s not what I’m interested in. Something serious happened to bring hatred into the frame. Any fool can see it when you’re both in the same room.”

“Okay, I’ll give it to you straight. Rory had an affair with Helen.”

“Helen?” She looked across the room at the photos in pride of place on the mantle piece. “Nick’s wife?”

“Yes. I found out and I couldn’t pretend I didn’t know. Nick would have found out eventually. Nothing stays secret in this country for long. But fool that I am, I made it my duty to tell him before someone else did.”

“And?”

“He shot me.”

“Rory shot you?” This didn’t fit the gossip she’d gleaned that Nick supposedly shot Martin.

“No... not Rory... Nick shot me. I don’t blame him, he was crazy about Helen.”

“You sound rather forgiving.”

He looked at her, raising his eyebrows. “I suppose I am.” He rubbed his shoulder. “Being shot was painful, but nothing compared to what Nick went through later. About six weeks after I told him about the affair, Helen committed suicide. I've always held myself responsible. I'll never know if my interference tipped her over the edge. If I feel like that can you imagine what Nick and Rory went through?"

"No wonder Nick wouldn't tell me about her. All I got from Jenny was that she suffered severe depression after a complicated miscarriage, and hinted at an accidental overdose."

"Sadly there was nothing accidental about her death. What I can't understand is why Rory is still here. I half expected Nick to kill the bastard. Instead I find him installed in Tom Lander's house with a lifetime tenancy. It doesn't make sense."

"Don't ask me for answers. I'm the least informed person in the district."

"I'll bet the truth is in Nick's diaries. That might be a good place to start."

"Diaries? What diaries?"

"He always had black ones with a red spine, about the same size as a paperback. Believe me, he will have kept one."

"Well, in all the time we were together, I never saw one, or heard mention of one."

"How odd. We both started at prep school. Our teacher encouraged us. It was such a drag to begin with, but if we wrote an inspiring entry he would reward us by letting us read one page of his own diary. He knew the offer would encourage us. For Nick it became a personal challenge he won more often than not and got to read more of Mr. Johnson's diary than the rest of the class put together. He never divulged what Mr Johnson wrote about. By the time we left that school, diary keeping was as much a part of our daily routine as brushing our teeth. I would never have become a journalist if it hadn't been for Mr. Johnson."

"Do you still keep a diary?"

"Yes, one day I might let you read it."

"Not if it's private."

"You don't have to pretend not to be interested. One day I'll show you. I'm hoping for a happy ending." He looked her straight in the eye locking into her vision with an intensity she found unnerving. "I wish you hadn't run off this morning. I want the magic back."

Sandra found herself swallowing hard, trying to break his hypnotic gaze. Impossible. She couldn't describe the moment she found Nick and Beverley together, naked in the shower, hours before he died. She blushed at the memory, still too embarrassed and confused to tell anyone.

Nick died before she could confront him about his betrayal. With everyone so shattered by the shock of his death and the realization of what it meant for the children she had to pretend nothing happened. Rejection, anger, and confusion were swept aside. All that mattered was the welfare of Nick's twins.

To give Beverley credit, she had kept her distance at the funeral, and left the country the day afterwards, leaving Hank to deal with all matters relating to Ol Essakut, though Sandra knew Beverley continued to take an active role in promoting the ranch to her wealthy American friends, for which Sandra was truly grateful.

Martin broke eye contact and said, "I wonder how long lunch will be. I'm starving."

Sandra jumped up to go to the kitchen to check how Juma was progressing. Lunch was ready and when they moved to the table the earlier strain eased. Martin helped himself to a tiny portion. Sandra resisted the temptation to comment, eating seemed to be an issue, and she wasn't sure if he'd been ill, or just off his food. He appeared to enjoy the meal, and even helped himself to another spoonful.

After he pushed his plate to one side, Martin pointed to a pile of sketches that were lying on the table. "Can I look at those?" She nodded and he thumbed through the sheets.

His enthusiasm and knowledge surprised her, especially his ability to identify the plants, not by their common name but by their Latin names as well.

"How do you know so much?"

"My mother was a plant fanatic. I guess some of her enthusiasm rubbed off." His eyes softened as he talked about his mother. "She had two contrasting gardens. The one nearest the house was a formal English style garden which caused no end of problems with pests, diseases, heat, or lack of water, and even the lack of winter weather. The other, her African garden, was her real pride and joy. Only truly indigenous plants got in, she scoured the countryside for the best specimens available."

"What happened to the garden?"

"I'll bet the English one is a wreck, but the African one will be fine. One of her old gardeners stayed on," he answered. "What triggered your interest?"

"I had problems drawing things that moved. Plants are well behaved subjects."

"How did you and Amina team up?"

"We shared a flat when we were at college. She studied Botany, and I did art. She made me realize how much I missed Africa. We used to talk in Swahili, which annoyed the other flat mates. And we made a pact after graduation we'd work together over here. Unfortunately, my mother became ill, I had to stay and nurse her. After she died, with nothing to keep me in England, I packed my bags, let the house, and came to Kenya. Amina had just signed the contract for her first book, the rest is history."

Sandra wasn't sure whether to be pleased or sad to have her conversation with Martin disrupted by the arrival of Simeon and the twins. A glimpse of sheer joy on Simeon's face at his first sight of Martin made the moment a happy one.

Sam and Emma flung their arms around her deafening her with their screams before they insisted she went with them to search for Bambi, a tiny tame dik-dik that treated the vegetable garden as its home.

She found herself torn between pleasing the children, and wanting to be part of the reunion of friends. It wasn't hard to see the bond between these two men. Racial divisions had no place in their friendship. Simeon had shared so many experiences from childhood through to university with Nick and Martin, that at times she forgot he was the son of the village school master. The friendship had given him opportunities the other villagers never had. Sometimes she marvelled at how Simeon was able to fit into both communities with such ease. He drew respect from everyone who met him. Seeing him with Martin made her more aware of the impact Nick's death must have had on Simeon. They had been like brothers. Good that he still had Martin.

Sandra watched as the two men hugged each other. Martin towered over Simeon, but Simeon made up for it in muscular power. Simeon might have left the army, but never quit the fitness routines they instigated. He ran at least two marathons a year always aiming to beat his personal best. If he was any nationality other than Kenyan, he could have run for his country, but in Kenya the competition was too keen, even for Simeon.

Sandra let the children drag her away, but hurried back, eager to hear Simeon's news and find out his reaction to the situation regarding Jacob.

Soon Sam came back clutching a large ball and begged Martin and Simeon to play with him. His wide eyed plea won, though Sandra sat on the side because her arm still ached.

After the strain of the day it was wonderful to sit quietly on the grass and cheer the children on. Martin and Simeon were so relaxed throwing themselves wholeheartedly into the game. Their enthusiasm, laughter and sheer abandon put Nick's attempts at playing to shame.

When the game was over, Juma arrived with a tray of tea, cakes, and cold drinks for the children. Sandra sat back and enjoyed watching as they ate and drank their well earned reward. Reluctantly after tea, she sent the children off to play. It was time for the adults to talk.

The crisis with Jacob and the Singhs headed the agenda, quickly followed by an update of the situation at the camps. At one point she closed her eyes and understood why Martin appealed to her. It was almost as if Nick was talking. The voice and the enthusiasm were similar. The bond of friendship between Simeon and Martin was as strong and deep as the one linking Simeon and Nick. She envied them. Her lack of close friends was down to shyness, and a fear of losing people she loved. Amina was the exception.

Martin disturbed her reveries.

"I'm going now." He turned to Simeon and added, "Make sure she rests."

With a mixture of sadness and relief at his pending

departure, she watched quietly as he found the children, hugged them and waved good bye to them.

He called for Jacob to go, came over to her, bent down, and brushed her forehead with a friendly kiss and said very softly, “Take care.” Stepping away from her he touched Simeon on the shoulder and said, “Can we have a word in private?”

Simeon nodded and rose from his chair and followed Martin over to his Land Cruiser.

How she wished she knew what Martin said. It was probably something about Rory because he pointed towards Rory’s house. She would quiz Simeon about Martin and Rory, when he and his father came to supper.

Simeon left her to rest, saying he would catch up with the rest of the news at supper time. But when the time came, Sandra got so involved in talking about whether to relocate the camps to avoid bad feelings over the deaths she forgot to ask about Rory and Martin.

When she finally climbed into bed, her head whirled round and round, going over endless mental lists of things to do to get the camps back in pristine condition ready for the next influx of wealthy Americans.

She was just dozing off when a door creaked open. She held her breath, and listened intently. Panic flashed through her mind. The attackers were back, the children were in danger. Fear washed over her. How could she protect them from armed attackers? The door creaked again, she was about to scream, a sniffle stopped her. The intruders were Sam and Emma. Sam led Emma towards her big double bed, helped her up then he darted round to the other side and climbed in too. Sandra pretended to be asleep,

Emma wiggled over towards her, her freezing feet nearly making Sandra jump, but she forced herself to stay still. Sam inched in close on the other side. Emma's feet soon warmed up and the sniffling stopped. Soon her intruders dropped off into deep untroubled sleep.

Sandra listened to their even breathing, thinking how much these two had captured her heart. She would love them always. Being responsible for them and their inheritance reinforced that feeling no matter how badly the odds were stacked against her.

Chapter 15

Martin drove into the Mount Kenya Safari Club grounds for his meeting with Beverley. The gates closed behind him like a trap.

The impending reunion filled him with dread since the ill-timed phone call.

He'd wanted to postpone the meeting indefinitely, but only managed to delay it by a few hours. The visit to the police station with Jacob had been a long drawn-out affair. Persistence eventually got the officer-in-charge, a friend of Simeon's, involved. The saga of the misplaced property repeated yet again, resulted in Jacob's release into Martin's custody. Parjit and his relatives had to have their fingerprints taken for comparison before further enquiries could take place.

Martin dropped Jacob off at Jenny Copeland's house. Jacob would stay with his cousin, Jenny's cook.

Martin didn't expect Beverley to be forgiving. Her power and money meant few people would keep her waiting. He parked by the main building intending to walk across the lawn to her cottage rather than drive over. A few more minutes wouldn't hurt.

As he reversed into a bay, the gardener sweeping leaves nearby dropped his broom and rushed over. Martin wondered what he'd done to precipitate such a reaction. Then he recognized the man rushing to greet him, "Jambo, jambo, Bwana Martin."

Murumbi was his mother's long serving gardener, one of the few staff he'd kept on the pay roll after she died.

He stuck out his hand to greet the old man, with a respectful, "Jambo Mzee."

Murumbi gave a toothless grin, and clutched his hand, pumping it up and down. They exchanged polite enquiries about health and families, and eventually Martin asked why Murumbi no longer tended his mother's garden on Chui Farm.

The answer was not what he wanted to hear. Murumbi left because none of the staff had been paid for months. Martin promised he would sort everything out. Murumbi didn't seem bothered, being too agitated about more serious matters.

Martin shut up and let the old man talk. Even though Murumbi was miles away from the ranch he appeared better informed than the residents. He ranted on about the manager's failings, and then started on Rory's behaviour. Most of what he said didn't make sense, but Martin had enough respect for the old man not to interrupt. Finally he announced the Singh lads were only interested in finding rhino on Ol Essakut.

Rhino. There hadn't been a rhino on the estate for more than ten years. No one mentioned a sighting, which was odd as everyone would understand the importance of such an event.

He wanted to ask Murumbi for more details, but the old man got going again, this time about rumours of bribes being offered to people to take part in the attack on the camps. Martin interrupted him, and asked him to go and find Jacob and tell him everything he knew. Jacob would get far more information out of him than Martin ever would. He handed him a few hundred shillings and told him Jacob was at Mrs. Copeland's house. At the mention of Jenny, Murumbi smiled with approval.

"I go when I finish here," he said.

A tour bus pulled up beside them. Martin glanced at his watch and said, "Mrs Wyatt's waiting for me," and pointed up towards Beverley's cottage.

This launched Murumbi into a fresh illogical tirade about Beverley. "She bad woman. Bad, bad woman."

Martin was shocked. What could Murumbi know about Beverley to make him so against her? He was hardly in a position to form an opinion. Martin tried to prompt him to say more.

Murumbi shook his head. "Ask Jacob, he know. You make him tell you." The old man picked up his abandoned brush, and marched off towards the staff area.

The strange conversation with Murumbi still whirled round his head when he reached Beverley's cottage at the far end of the wide sweep of lawn.

Beverley greeted him warmly and refused to listen to an apology. She looked relaxed and had obviously been enjoying the afternoon sunshine. Her riotous coppery curls glowed in the evening sunshine, her make-up more natural looking than usual.

"Now you're here, let me get you a beer." Her behaviour contrary to his expectations threw him off balance.

She led him inside, placed a cold Tusker bottle and glass on the table beside him then disappeared through the bedroom door, saying she wanted to put something warmer on. For a second he wondered if this was a subtle invitation to follow her.

A few weeks ago, he'd have been tempted, but meeting Sandra changed everything. His lack of interest in Beverley as a woman had little to do with exhaustion. Crazy. He could name dozens of men who'd willingly swap places with him now. Hank topped the list, he adored Beverley, but she didn't seem to think of him as anything other than a friend of the family.

Martin had no idea what he would do if Beverley came out wearing some super sexy outfit and tried to rekindle the brief affair they'd had in Paris. The only thing certain, she'd be disappointed. He didn't have the inclination or the energy to act.

He must have dropped off, because he woke to find a fire crackling in the grate, the curtains pulled, his beer untouched beside him. Beverley was curled up in the chair opposite him reading a small, leather bound book. She wore an expensive looking long-sleeved silk blouse, tailored wool trousers with a mohair sweater draped over her shoulders. Very demure for Beverley, her clothes usually left little to the imagination. He found himself blinking to be sure this fresh faced natural looking woman was in fact the same person he'd last seen in Paris. She looked up from her book and smiled.

"Sorry, so rude of me to drop off." His embarrassment increased when he found he'd slept for several hours.

"Only rude if you dash off without having something to eat." She eased herself off the couch. "Stay where you are." Before he had time to protest she placed a tray filled with a dainty array of little sandwiches, cheese and biscuits and a bowl of fruit in front of him. She handed him a plate and proceeded to fill two glasses with wine.

"Hank tells me you're helping out at Ol Essakut," she said.

"Yes, he roped me in to take care of the media

coverage of the attack and I've been driving Sandra back and forth." Beverley's eyebrows rose at the mention of Sandra.

Her reaction triggered a memory of a letter from Simeon which arrived on a particularly gruesome day in Iraq. Hoping to take his mind of the nightmare situation he opened it in the lobby of the hotel. Simeon's letters were reminders of a sane world elsewhere, keeping him up to date with life in Kenya, and with Nick's latest exploits. He was not surprised to read Nick ditched Beverley in favour of an English artist. He never thought Nick and Beverley made a perfect pairing. Before he finished reading, shooting recommenced, pandemonium broke out, the building was evacuated. In the confusion he lost the unfinished letter.

Perhaps if he'd read the rest he'd have known Nick's past relationship was likely to cause tension and explain the general hostility towards his plan to sell to Beverley.

Beverley reached out and touched his arm. "Are you okay?"

He was shaking. He hated it when random flashbacks overwhelmed him. "Yes," he answered. Beverley smiled and took her hand away. She wouldn't press for details. During their time together in Paris she never encouraged him to treat her like a therapist. Deep down he was certain she didn't want details.

"Good. You've lost more weight, nothing serious I hope."

Trust her to wade in with both feet. "Bad diet," he reassured her. She didn't need to know about the depression, the nightmares, losing his nerve, and all that.

"You look different," he said, hoping to change the subject.

"Guess I grew up. Back then I was still rebelling against the old man. After he'd died, rebellion seemed pointless. Now I need people to take me seriously."

Martin understood.

Her father's magazine empire and his international properties were a massive responsibility, one he wouldn't want. Luckily she had Hank to help. Hank had been her father's right hand man for years until he became disillusioned with life in America and decided Kenya was the place to be. He'd bought land, and encouraged Beverley's father to invest as well. Conservation of wildlife was his passion. He oversaw everything up until Beverley became involved and handed responsibility to Nick. Responsibility which Sandra appeared to have taken on.

"Was I part of that rebellion?" he asked. In Paris, while taking a break from the front line she turned up to help with paperwork. Hard to remember who seduced who, theirs had been a pretty full on affair. Beverley had an open attitude toward sex. One rule only. No commitment. The brief encounter ended when she took off to the States, and he went back to the warfront. Neither had kept in touch, other than through work. News reached him she and Nick were together, he wondered where it would lead. When Nick got married, he was pleased Beverley was not the bride.

"When do you want to sign the contract?" she asked.

He wondered if she had deliberately avoided answering his question.

"Sorry Beverley, I need more time. I still haven't been back to the house."

"Have you changed your mind?"

He couldn't deny he was seriously considering staying. Until he sorted out where he stood with Sandra he'd not commit either way. "I'm wavering," he admitted.

"Fine, no pressure from me," she answered.

What an unexpected response. He had enough to think about without worrying over her motives for accepting his indecision.

He ate one of the sandwiches, and sipped the wine.

"You look exhausted. The road back into town is so bad. Why don't you stay in my spare room?"

To his relief her offer was for the spare room. A clear indication she didn't expect to renew their previous liaison, though her tone on the phone had implied otherwise. Perhaps she had a new man in her life. He hoped so. He hadn't sorted out a bed and the offer was too good to refuse.

"If you're sure," he answered. "Only problem is I need to get away early tomorrow."

"Please don't wake me. I'm still suffering from jet lag."

"Don't worry I won't, I'll go and get my overnight bag," he said.

Martin walked across the lawns again, this time lit by low level lamps between the flower beds. The air temperature had dropped to near freezing. With each stride he took he got more and more worried the seemingly uncomplicated invitation would trigger repercussions. The memory of his intimate moment with Sandra in this garden so recently was one he treasured. If he wasn't so tired, he'd drive away right now.

Martin rose early with reluctance. The glass of wine, nice as it had been at the time left a dry mouth, and a slight headache. Nightmares had haunted him but he'd managed some sleep in between.

He quietly showered and dressed, and slipped out of the cottage without seeing Beverley. The mountain stood proud and naked, glinting in the morning sun. The gardens deserted apart from a few ducks waddling from one pond to another. The early morning dew clung to the grass making it appear as if there had been a couple of inches of rain overnight. Martin chose the dry route along the roadway between the cottages and the tennis courts, making his way to the Land Cruiser to head back into town.

He hooted his horn for the watchman to come and open Jenny Copeland's gates. He was anxious to check if Murumbi had spoken to Jacob. Jenny waved through the window. He signalled he wanted a word with Jacob, before coffee.

Jacob greeted him with his customary smile. When he asked why Murumbi didn't like Mrs. Wyatt, the smile vanished.

Martin's experience as a reporter triggered an automatic change of tactic, and he concentrated on Murumbi's tales regarding Rory's behaviour. His ploy worked, Jacob happily added details of Murumbi's accusations all of which tallied with Martin's impressions.

Martin asked Jacob if he thought Sandra was a good employer, and if the staff liked and respected her. And more important, did they think she was capable of doing Nick's work. Jacob answered positively, as Martin had expected. Time to ask the tricky question.

"Do you think Mrs. Wyatt would be a good boss of Ol Essakut?"

The horror on Jacob's face was a clear response.

"I think she wants to take over from Sandra. Would that be good?" The suggestion unleashed Jacob who proceeded to tell him everything he knew about Beverley. Most damming of all was her continued relationship with Nick after his wedding to Sandra. Martin couldn't believe how hearing this triggered so much anger towards Nick. But Jacob hadn't finished.

"On day Nick die, Sandra go to room at Norfolk hotel and find Nick and Beverley together. Sandra leave hotel, she crying."

He must have thought that Martin didn't believe his story because he added. "You ask Rory. He see her. He talk to her outside hotel. Then she drive off."

"How many other people know?" Martin asked.

Jacob swore the only person he'd told was Murumbi, who told him he must protect Sandra and never tell anyone.

"You are both wise men," Martin said, noting that Jacob looked pleased at his praise, "Please don't tell anyone else. Sandra needs your silence. I shall try to make sure Mrs. Wyatt does not succeed in taking over. If you remember anything else tell me or Simeon."

As he walked back towards Jenny's house, the impact of Jacob's revelation sunk in.

No wonder Beverley's return upset Sandra. If he'd known this twelve hours ago, he'd have avoided the complications associated with Beverley's offer of a bed at the Safari Club. Sandra was bound to assume they slept together. She'd probably already worked out they'd once been lovers.

Sandra wouldn't be interested his excuses about the shock of finding himself cosseted in a luxurious hotel in Paris after months on the front line. When every noise set his nerves on edge waiting for the sound of gunfire, and unable to sleep he'd walked the streets trying to do what normal people did, except he checked for snipers on every rooftop.

He'd been stuck in Paris waiting for clearance papers to get back to the war zone. Beverley arrived to assist. She took one look and pushed her way into his suite and ordered a meal. One meal led to another and then they slept together. He'd be lying if he said he hadn't enjoyed it. The lack of emotional commitment spoilt it for him a little, but with his job any form of commitment was foolish.

Jenny lacked her normal good cheer when he joined her at the breakfast table. She poured him out a cup of steaming black coffee, added sugar without asking, and announced, "Word's out. Three more tours cancelled. Sandra will be devastated. The poor girl has enough worries. The loss of income will hit hard."

"She'll have time to do the improvements she wanted."

"The trouble is she can't afford them."

"Things can't be that bad, I thought the trust generated lots of cash?"

"Only for conservation work, the accommodation side has to pay for itself."

"Would a rhino help draw the tours back?" he asked.

"A rhino. Are you kidding? Of course it would help."

"I've heard rumours of one in the area."

"Impossible."

"That's what worries me."

"You don't think poachers are after them?" Jenny asked, her frown marks showing her concern.

"It might explain some of the fence damage."

"Oh God, I hope not," she said as she passed him

her homemade marmalade.

"I'm going to tell Sandra and Simeon. Perhaps we can locate the rhino, if it exists."

"I wish I could help."

"You can. Don't tell anyone what I've told you and keep an ear out for anything odd going on in town, especially relating to Rory, Balbinder Singh or his nephews."

"Rory?" she queried.

"Yes, he's behaving oddly, so are the Singhs. I'm wondering where they fit in," he answered.

He said farewell and left. Stopping at Ol Essakut was a prelude to the journey home. He'd put off his return long enough. But he decided he'd rather not go alone. He wanted Sandra to be with him. Her reaction would help him decide, one way or another.

Sandra stood on the verandah with Simeon when he arrived. Simeon's greeting caught him off guard.

"I tried to call you at the sports club, they said you hadn't been in."

"I stayed at the Safari Club," he answered honestly. He didn't want to lie, or more accurately he didn't want to be caught lying. Jacob's revelation had made him aware of the bitter rivalry between Beverley and Sandra. Better to be open about spending the night in Beverley's cottage as the news was sure to filter down. He didn't want Sandra to feel he hid things from her. "I discovered a few things while I was away that should interest you."

Sandra didn't comment, her smile vanished, and she rather formally offered him a seat and a cup of coffee. "Nothing bad I hope, I can't handle more drama at the moment," she said.

"Rumours of a rhino on the ranch," Martin answered.

"Rhino? What..?. Who...?" Simeon stuttered as the implications clicked. "How sure are you?"

"Sure enough to go looking for them," Martin answered.

"When?" she asked.

"Today if possible. If Simeon goes right to the top of the ranch and works back towards my place. You and I can start at the far west point and work inwards. Between us we ought to be able to find something. We can meet at my place for a late lunch. It's time I went home."

"I can't come," Sandra said looking disappointed. "Beverley's arranged to come over to inspect the damage to the camps."

"This is more important. Ask Rory to take her? I'm sure he won't object," Martin said.

Sandra looked surprised by his suggestion. "She'll be livid."

"Do you care?" he asked, challenging her to respond.

Sandra blushed, and shrugged her shoulders. "I have to work with her."

"Yes, but if we find a rhino, she won't be able to complain, will she?" Simeon pointed out.

Sandra smiled. "No, I don't suppose so."

"Come on, we can't waste time." Simeon said with enthusiasm. "I'll call Amina, she'll be happy to help with the children."

Sandra went inside, and he heard her give instructions to the staff about Sam and Emma, and to ask Juma to pack some food and drinks for themselves for lunch, and another lot for Simeon. Simeon offered to find Rory to arrange for him to take Beverley up to the camps.

"Do you believe we'll find rhino?" Sandra asked

when they finally set off.

"Yes, Murumbi our old gardener swore he'd seen it himself."

"Why didn't he tell anyone?"

"He had problems with the manager I left in charge, and didn't know who to tell. It was about the time Nick died. He didn't know you, and never trusted Rory. Anyway, he left to find work because my manager hadn't paid his wages for months."

Close to the most western point of Chui Farm, Martin aimed his vehicle up an almost vertical climb. Sandra hung onto the handle of the door as if her life depended on it. He reached the top, the track levelled out, and he turned to check how Sandra coped.

"I'd never dare drive up that," she gasped.

"Not many people would, I've only driven up here twice. It's not marked as a passable route, and would be lethal if wet." He stopped and pointed to the west." There's a perfect place further on with a clear view of the valley. I'm afraid we'll have to walk the last bit."

"Fine, lead the way."

Martin grabbed a water bottle, binoculars, and a camera, and started walking at a steady pace. The thorny bushes on the top of the bluff were thick and vicious. Sandra kept up, though occasionally she would stop. At first he thought he was going too fast, but discovered she'd stopped to inspect a plant.

"Something special?" he queried, trying to get her to talk to him.

"A grass, one I didn't think I'd seen before."

"Do you know the names?"

"No, I'm hopeless. Names are Amina's speciality."

When Martin stopped abruptly Sandra eased up beside him. He put his finger to his lip, and pointed at a tiny gap through the thorn bushes leading to an open stretch of grass. Three gerenuks on the far side stood on their hind legs, grazing the tops of the bushes. After a while he moved on to the vantage point he'd told her about. The bluff jutted out giving a spectacular view over the valley below. After a quick swig from the water bottle he carried he passed it to Sandra and then handed her a pair of binoculars, "Start looking that side, I'll look this side."

After an hour he offered her water again and indicated that they should go back. The heat was intense, the buzz of insects and the chattering of birds all that could be heard other than the pad of their own footsteps on the soft sandy soil. When he pointed his vehicle at the steep downhill slope, Sandra closed her eyes, her left hand gripped the handle on the door. He was impressed she never expressed any fear.

"Made it!" he said when he reached the floor of the valley. Sandra let out a deep sigh and opened her eyes.

"Relax. Not much further to the house. After lunch we can check the other side of the farm if that's all right with you?"

"Fine," she answered, with a little less enthusiasm than expected. He blamed the heat. After lunch in the shade her enthusiasm might return.

Martin began to worry the house would be a disappointment. In a moment of panic, he envisaged damage inflicted by white-ants on the structural timbers. Murumbi's departure was a bad omen. Nature would have overrun the garden, undoing his mother and Murumbi's painstaking work.

He drove up to the rear of the house, the least attractive side of the building, which was shabbier than anticipated. A few scrawny chickens scratched the bare earth near the back door. The only comforting sight was Njoroge, the house servant, sitting on the kitchen step eating a plate of posho.

According to Murumbi, Njoroge hadn't been paid either, so it was a relief to see him. Njoroge put down his plate, and jumped up and stood to attention. "Jambo," he said as he saluted. The old habit, a habit from years in the army, had never worn off. Njoroge's broad smile showed his four remaining teeth in their full glory. Martin's return meant he'd get paid.

Martin hoped Njoroge's presence meant the house was clean. He shook hands and said a few words of greeting, but seeing Sandra waiting by the vehicle, looking tired, decided to leave chatting until later.

He went to Sandra, and led her in. "Come on, let me show you around." He took her through the typical Kenyan kitchen, none of the fancy fitted stuff with electrical gadgets built into the units someone from England would expect. The solar electricity supply didn't allow for such luxuries. Instead there was an ancient wood stove, with a calor gas cooker and a gas fridge, the two concessions to modern times. Neither were new. He hoped the basic facilities would not put her off.

He led her into the dining room, which had a hand carved fireplace, and panelled walls. Her eyes darted from one wall to the other, taking in every detail. She reached out and stroked the top of the old carver at the head of the table with an almost reverent touch that showed how impressed she was without a word spoken. He moved on through the hall, opened the door to the main room of the house, ushered her in and waited for a reaction.

She was almost in a trance as she ran her hand over the naturally smooth surface of the granite slab that formed the mantlepiece, she traced her fingers over the silky texture of the carefully selected river-washed stones his great grandfather used in the chimney breast. Stepping backwards, her gaze travelled upwards, taking in the network of hand hewn roof timbers and downwards to soak up the beauty of the four large paintings adorning the two side walls. At last she turned towards the vast windows.

"You're mad," she said looking at him with an expression of horror. "You can't sell this."

Not quite the reaction he expected.

"Why not?" he asked. She didn't appear to be listening. She was far too intent on soaking up the view.

The vista from the window was one he had carried with him all his life. No matter where, or how low he felt, he'd close his eyes and conjure up this image. Today was more spectacular than his memory. The house perched on the rim of a ridge with the ground falling away into a wide valley. A ribbon of bright green snaked along the valley floor marking the river course, and drawing the eye away to the horizon. Not the usual flat African view, here the horizon lifted and went on, up and up, to the glistening jagged snow peak of the mountain. The shroud of cloud that habitually cloaked the mountain had evaporated. A perfect day for Sandra's visit.

He stood by her side in silence soaking up the majesty of the towering peaks.

"Years ago," she said, "I read "No Picnic on Mount Kenya". On days like this I understand why those Italian prisoners of war broke out of their camp and attempted the climb even though they didn't have proper equipment."

"The top needs proper climbing skills, but getting to the first peak isn't so hard. I'll climb with you if want."

"I don't think I've got the stamina."

"It's not so hard, and you'd find amazing plants up there."

"You know how to tempt a girl," she answered, grinning. If I ever decide to climb, I'll let you know."

"You will, those plants are calling. They want to be painted."

"Maybe, but I have more important things to do at the moment."

"Ah, yes, managing Ol Essakut. Take care not to let the place take over your life."

"And what's that supposed to mean?"

"Nick's dream. Don't suffocate your talent and creativity."

She was going to reply, but shook her head and focussed on the mountain. After a while she broke the silence.

"This is a special place. Tell me the history."

"My great grandfather camped here when he was hunting leopard, hence the name, Chui Farm. He loved the views so much he swore then that one day he'd buy the land and build a house on this spot."

"Your family have been here for three generations?"

"Yes. He bought the land, and gradually purchased more land around it. My father added more before he died."

"Don't you want to carry on? Do you really dislike the place so much?"

"No. I'm realistic. My work makes living here impossible." Seeing the sad look on her face he added, "I thought a manager was the answer. Seems I was wrong, he made a right mess of things. I can't let that happen again."

"Why didn't you get Simeon involved." she asked.

"He'd have looked after your land for nothing."

"Too complicated," he answered, not sure if the complications had increased or not.

What he did know was that his property jutted into the middle of the block of land that formed the Ol Essakut conservation scheme. It should have been included, but his fight with Nick ruined everything. When he thought about selling, his main aim had been to ensure whoever bought the land was deeply involved with the project. Beverley seemed the perfect candidate.

Now he had Sandra doing her utmost to convince him not to sell. Did she want him to stay, or were her objections a plot to prevent him from selling to Beverley? He suspected the latter.

"Have you seen what Beverley intends to do here?" Sandra asked, interrupting his wandering thoughts.

"No?"

"You should, you'll hate her plans."

"Hate is a bit strong. Why?"

"For a start, this house gets demolished.

"What?"

"Flattened to the ground, I always assumed the house was a tumble-down dump that wasn't worth restoring. Now I've seen it I can't believe that anyone, especially Nick, could have contemplated such vandalism."

"He must have been madder with me than I thought. Maybe it was his way of hurting me. He knew I loved this place."

"No I won't buy that story. I only ever got the feeling he missed having you around. He read and saved every article you ever submitted."

"Did he?"

"Yes. So rule hatred out. I think undue influence is

more to blame. The lodge they wanted to build in comparison to this is tacky, something straight out of a Hollywood fantasy."

"That bad?"

"Yes. Come back and I'll show you just how bad. I think it will be enough to make you change your mind."

"But you need the land."

"We only need the land because we can't afford to fence all the way round. You know how it juts right into the heart of the estate and cuts access between the north-west sector and the south west corner. Traffic has to go all the way back to the main ranch and out again to avoid cutting across your land. It's one hell of a detour but worth doing to save this house."

"But fixing the fencing would cut the natural animal paths," he said. "The fencing that's left ought to be removed." Her eyes were so wide and appealing he wanted to kiss her and tell her she could have the land for nothing. "Maybe we can come to some agreement."

Chapter 16

Rory resisted the temptation to tell Simeon to get stuffed when he turned up expecting a favour. Doing anything for Simeon made his resentment worse. Do this. Do that. Any job they didn't fancy came his way. He never got invited to special events but they expected him to provide cover while they had fun. They used him. But for the first time ever Simeon had given him a task he might actually enjoy.

Taking care of Beverley, spending time alone with her would be a pleasure. Nick made damn sure he never got the chance, but now he had the perfect opportunity to charm her. His mind went into overdrive. She had money, more than enough to spend on herself, worth trying to persuade her to become his sponsor.

First impressions were important. To get her hooked, he had to have a car worthy of her. With a little organization he'd fix to have one.

Rory hurried over to the garage to the Land Rover he'd rescued for his own use. An adequate motor, an improvement on the rattletrap Simeon expected him to use, but not a vehicle in which to impress a woman, especially someone like Beverley. He made sure he was alone and opened the bonnet. He took one of his largest spanners, inserted it carefully into the engine, engaged on a carefully chosen nut and applied his full body weight, first in one direction, over-tightening the nut and then in the opposite direction. Nothing happened. He levered again. Still nothing. Again. Success. His hand shot forward ripping the skin of his knuckles on the engine casing. "Shit," he muttered, and licked the salty tasting blood from the wound. Using his fingers, he gently tightened the nut, not too tightly. He smiled. He had done a good job, the threads were damaged, oil seeped out. In half an hour he could confidently claim this motor was not going anywhere.

Rory rushed back to his cottage. If he wanted to impress Beverley, he'd better clean up. He showered, shaved, and selected his least tattered shirt and trousers from his limited wardrobe and put on his newest safari boots to add the final touch. He hadn't made this much effort for a woman for a long time. Today could be his lucky day.

He ambled back to the workshop. The pool of oil forming on the ground was just what he hoped for.

Rory found a perverse sort of pleasure in fooling people. He was an expert at sabotage. He'd figured dozens of ways of putting vehicles out of action. Usually because he wanted an extra part for his own vehicle, and sometimes simply to annoy Simeon and make life harder for Sandra. No one suspected anything. He'd even managed to keep three vehicles off the road earlier in the month. All were now back in working order. But his fun was hampered by the constant presence of Parjit, Vejay and Lalji. Well, now was pay back time. He left the workshop, and strolled over to the Singh's cottage.

"Parjit, I need your help?" he called out. Parjit emerged looking as if he had just woken up. Rory wondered if Balbinder knew what a bunch of layabouts these lads were. Unless he had a specific job for them they happily spent the day sleeping.

"What's up?"

"I need a favour," Rory said. Parjit loved being needed. "My Land Rover is spewing oil all over the place, and I promised Simeon I'd take some woman up to inspect the damage to the camps, and I must have a decent motor to take her. Can I use the Subaru? I'll be back in time to take you on a trial run this evening."

Parjit scratched his chin, looked skywards then nodded. "Okay. Hang on. I'll find the keys." He emerged a few minutes later and tossed the bunch of keys in Rory's direction. "Look after her, she's running sweetly."

"I should hope so."

As he walked away he spotted a trail of dust from an approaching vehicle on the main drive. Beverley. Perfect timing. He lowered himself into the driving seat of the Subaru, revved the engine. Sounded good. He slipped into gear and eased the car down towards the main house. Beverley deserved a welcoming party. He didn't intend neglecting her even for a minute. He parked, got out and started going round the car, fiddling with bits of the trim, checking everything was in order.

Beverley swept up alongside his motor. Her hire car had seen better days, so she wouldn't need much persuasion to come in the Subaru.

He strode forward and introduced himself.

"We've never been formally introduced, I'm Rory Lyons, Simeon asked me to meet you, and take you to the camps."

"Where's Sandra?"

"I don't know. She went off with Martin Owen. No one said where they were heading.

It was hard to read her reaction.

"And I'm guessing they told you to pretend everything is running smoothly and convince me all is perfect," she said peering into his eyes.

"Far from it, I'm to show you whatever you want. With me as your guide you'll get a more realistic insight than you would if they'd stayed," he answered, determined not to break eye contact with her.

She turned away first. "Well, I suppose we'd better go."

"Do you mind if we take the Subaru? It'll be faster than that," Rory said, pointing towards her hire car.

"Not at all. This has to be the worst hire car I've ever driven in my life."

"Nervous passenger?" he queried.

Beverley shook her head. "Are you kidding? I'm a real speed freak. Only problem is I never had the time to test my limits."

"Then today's your lucky day. First I need to pick up a gun from my place. I know they've rounded up the gang, but I don't think we should take unnecessary risks."

Beverley shrugged, she didn't seem bothered if he took one or not. He stopped outside his house and ran in for the gun and back out in a flash.

"Buckle up and hold tight," Rory said as he settled back into his seat having placed the gun on the back seat. Speed freak, she'd said, an open invitation to show off his skills. He put his foot on the pedals, slipped from one gear to the next at a rate that made Beverley gasp. He knew the road well, when to twist to the left, and when to swing to the right. He braced himself for the humps and bumps. Beverley clung to her seatbelt, her knuckles getting visibly whiter with each new stomach-churning jolt. The expression on her face showed she loved every twist and turn as he took her to the limit.

He had control over her. She might not realize it but by the time he stopped she wouldn't be able to resist. Speed turned her on. He was warming her up. He took the longest route possible to Hyrax camp, but it wasn't long enough.

The moment she stepped out of the car at the camp, she became business-like, striding off to poke her nose into the tents. Rory grabbed the gun and hurried after her answering an endless string of questions.

At first he gave the standard tourist line, but gradually he started telling her what he thought should be done with the camps. He slipped in a bit about Sandra being a fool for agreeing to get a witch doctor out to remove bad spirits caused by the deaths in the camp. He had expected Beverley to be shocked, but she didn't appear to find it odd.

Beverley's cleavage was distracting. Her safari outfitters knew about style and sex appeal and nothing about survival in the bush. The material of her blouse was so flimsy, only the strategically placed pockets stopped her being indecent. He imagined her posed naked on the bonnet of his rally car, and then he registered a persistent voice.

"Rory... Hello..."

"Yes. Sorry," he muttered, feeling foolish that his imagination had taken control. This wasn't the way to impress.

"I asked how good a shot you were?" she said, pointing to the gun slung over his shoulder.

"Why? Do you shoot?"

"Not for a while. But I bet I can hit that anthill."

"Bet you can't."

"My father took me grouse shooting in Scotland every year since the age of twelve."

He pictured the scene. All his gun magazines had articles about shooting in the highlands. None of which made him want to travel. There was enough to shoot here, once you got away from the conservationists.

"Shotguns are different to rifles. This one has one hell of a kick."

"You don't think I can, do you?"

"What are the stakes?" Rory was beginning to enjoy the prospect of beating her.

"Did you have something in mind?"

"I get to choose where we eat lunch."

"Sounds fair... you go first."

Rory loaded, aimed and fired. No hesitation, no fiddling with the sights, no delay. The top six inches of the anthill exploded in a cloud of dust. Beverley gave a nod of appreciation. He reloaded and handed the weapon to her.

She took her time, but not too long. Fired. A little snick of dust on the right hand side of the anthill. She thrust the gun back in his hands and said, "You should have warned me the sights are six inches out. Can I take another shot?"

Rory laughed. "You didn't ask." He took the gun from her and reloaded it. With her second shot she hit the target spot on.

"Good shot," he said. "I still get to choose the lunch destination."

"Can I drive?"

So she was still interested. Maybe this was his chance to persuade her to provide sponsorship and get access to her funds.

"Yes, of course you can," he answered, trying to sound too enthusiastic. He hated being the passenger, but had no choice.

Rory's thoughts about women drivers rapidly changed as Beverley raced down the dusty track. Not only was she sexy, she had talent, and could hold a conversation while behind the wheel. In less than a mile she showed greater potential to be a successful driver than Parjit ever had.

"You're good," he admitted grudgingly, "I'd rather be teaching you than Parjit."

"Why are you bothering with him anyway?"

"I crashed my car, and the only way I'll get to drive in this year's rally is by helping Parjit."

"What makes this rally so special?"

Rory didn't need more prompting to enlighten her on his favourite subject. He happily described the highs and lows of the rally world. He told her about the teams that had helicopter back-up and access to spares of every description, and the individual entrants who had to battle it out, for the joy of completing the course. Beverley encouraged him to keep talking, never once taking her eyes off the road ahead.

"I'm lucky I can practise on the ranch. Not everyone has this much rough road at their disposal."

"Sandra doesn't mind?" Beverley asked over the roar of the engine.

He shrugged. "I can't see how she can stop me."

"Fair point... but why don't you replace your car?" she asked, as she changed gear.

"Cost and I'd need a navigator or co-driver."

"What qualifications do they require?"

"They have to join a motor club, get a competition licence, a medical certificate, and all the kit, helmet, and fireproof clothing."

"Have you ever thought of running a Rally Driving School?" She pressed her foot to the floor.

Rory couldn't believe he'd heard right. What a mad

idea, but he loved it. What would he have to do to get something like that up and running?

"No," he answered, "And even if I did, Sandra might object."

"She might be persuaded. The next three tours have cancelled. It'll be some time before the panic is over. Now is the perfect time to try."

"What makes you so keen?"

"I'll be your first pupil."

Bloody hell, she was serious. There had to be a catch. Did she take him for a mug?

"What do I get in return?" he asked.

"A co-driver, a new car, and an excuse to get rid of Parjit," she said without taking her eyes off the track. "What more do you want?"

He let his eyes rove up and down her body, taking in the smooth evenly tanned thighs, the swell of her breasts, the trim waist. "Do you need to ask?"

Her answering smile gave him hope.

"Getting hot in here, good thing we're heading somewhere to cool off. Turn off just after that big boulder."

The track narrowed, he was relieved she slowed without him having to say anything. She tackled the route decisively, constantly searching for the next obstacle as she negotiated the current one. He was impressed. She had the makings of a competitive driver. Eventually the track ran out, and turned into a single file path and even Beverley stopped and admitted defeat.

"Do you expect me to keep going?" she asked staring at the rocks jutting out of the scrubby grass and bush ahead.

"No, we walk from here. It's not far," he said, getting out of the car as soon as she switched off the engine. "I promise you'll approve." He grabbed his gun and the canvas rucksack Juma had handed him before they left and led the way.

The path was on an incline. When they reached the top her demeanour changed. The ground fell away steeply to a large pool fed by a narrow ribbon of cascading water that fell off the rocks on the opposite side. The rhythm of the flow of water, the sunlight on the spray forming a rainbow, all added to the splendour. Beverley seemed to like what she saw, making him confident he'd get what he wanted. He reached out and took her hand, and guided her down a rocky path to the water. When they reached a large flat sun-baked boulder, a couple of feet above the water level, he swung the rucksack off his back, and said. "Thirsty? Fancy a beer?" Her eyes lit up. He opened the bag and took out a brown Tusker bottle. "Not quite as cold as I'd like, but I think it'll taste good anyway. Sorry, no glasses," he added, as he wiped the top of the bottle with the tail of his shirt.

Beverley put the bottle to her lips and drank. "Great, thanks."

"Have a seat," he said, quickly taking off his shirt and spreading it on the rock for her. He sat down beside her, took the bottle from her and took a swig. It tasted good. But he had a more interesting challenge. He handed the bottle back to her, kicked off his safari boots and stood up. Slowly he unbuckled his belt, peeled off his shorts and pants, then balanced on the edge of the rock, lingering for a moment to check her reaction to his naked body. It was suitably admiring. He took a deep breath, tensed himself and mentally prepared himself for the shock of the cold water ahead. With a perfect dive he plunged into the heart of the pool. He held his breath and swam underwater across the pool and behind the waterfall. He surfaced behind the screen of water. After a short wait he took another deep breath and swam back to the centre of the pool, emerging to find Beverley looking panic stricken. Just the reaction he hoped for. "Coming to join me?" he shouted, "It's really refreshing."

"No, I don't think so," she answered, shaking her head.

"You chicken, or don't you want to get your hair wet?" he called back. This woman was more likely to respond to goading rather than coaxing into the water. His comment worked. He watched as she peeled off her shirt, slipped out of her shorts, and shed her tiny panties revealing a perfect figure. As she poised ready to dive in, Rory had a flash thought. She was too perfect, there had to be a catch.

Beverley surfaced beside him. "Thought I'd chicken out?" she said. "I came to check you hadn't been frozen solid." At that moment her hands grasped him.

Bloody hell. He guided her to the shallower side of the pool, where he could stand, and pulled her into his arms. "Only one bit needs warming, if you're willing to help?"

"Yes," she whispered, guiding him into her and wrapping her legs around him.

Beverley gripped him tightly, taking control. He was not used to being controlled by a woman, but this wasn't the time for a fight. Next time he would make sure he was in charge.

Desire overwhelmed him, pushing all other thoughts or emotions away. He clung to her, exploring her body intimately, then, when sated, they swam for a while before retreating to lie on the sun-baked rock to dry and warm up. Rory closed his eyes.

Suddenly Beverley sat up and announced, "It's time to go. I need to tidy up. Take me back to your place."

The unexpected switch from lying naked beside a sex loving, carefree woman to being given orders caught him off balance. His initial clumsy reaction to reach out and persuade her not to rush resulted in a brush off. Beverley slipped out of his grasp and started putting on her clothes with an efficiency that would cool any man's ardour. Her actions left Rory feeling foolish as he struggled into his own clothes and gathered up the remains of their picnic. She got to the car ahead of him and slid into the passenger seat and waited for him. Bloody women, he hated their unpredictable moods. They made life too complicated.

On the way back he wondered if her request to go to his place to clean up was a good idea. He suggested Sandra's would be a better place to freshen up, but the withering stare he got shut him up.

She didn't hide her shock. True the accommodation was basic. It had been good enough for Old Man Lander in his day, and suited Rory fine. When Helen died, Nick locked the house up, and as far as Rory could remember no one but Nick had been inside since. The old man's clothes were still in the wardrobe.

When Rory found out he'd inherited the right to live in the house he'd been puzzled and unable to figure out why Nick stipulated he must move in. Surroundings had never been important. The fact the place was rundown didn't bother him. He hardly spent any time indoors. The verandah was the most used space, except of course when he was sleeping. The rest of the time he was in the workshop, or out driving, or out drinking. As for possessions, the rows and rows of books on the shelves were of no interest at all. The only possession the old man had owned that Rory ever wanted was the gun which had once belonged to his grandfather, which had been unexpectedly handed over to him after Nick's death.

Beverley's intense interest in the place had him wondering if she was planning to renovate. He didn't mind, if it got her into his bed it was fine by him. She could make any alterations she fancied.

"Bit basic, I'm afraid. Seriously lacking a woman's delicate touch," he said, taking in the stained ceiling, the rusted wire mesh on the windows.

Beverley nodded. "Yes, I'd agree with that."

"Any suggestions for improvement?" he asked.

"How about knocking it down and starting from scratch?"

"Not sure Sandra would allow that," he answered, a little shaken that she would suggest something quite so drastic. He led her to the bathroom, noticing for the first time the green streaks on the enamel of the chipped bath, the scale encrusted shower fittings and the discolouration of the grout around the tiles. He bet she was wishing she had taken up his suggestion to go to Sandra's for her shower.

"Does the shower work?"

He checked through the window, the fire under the tank was alight. "Yes, it's not bad. I'll get you a clean towel."

Beverley reverting to her cool business tycoon mode made attempting to join her in the shower a bad idea, appealing as it might be. Beverley was too precious to make an enemy of. He needed to play a careful game to enable continued access to her body and her money.

While she was showering, he quickly cleaned the

gun and put it away. He didn't want her handling it again. Her accuracy had surprised him.

Chapter 17

Sandra wanted to scream when Martin announced he'd spent the night at the Safari Club. Instead she found herself paired with him for the morning searching for a mythical rhino. The alternative option of spending the day with Beverley forced the decision.

The awkwardness their night together might have created never occurred. Martin, a true diplomat, avoided the subject and treated her in the relaxed friendly way he had prior to the book launch.

Sandra was beginning to think she understood Martin. He resembled Nick in many ways but stepping over the threshold of his family home made her revise her thoughts.

The house at Chui Farm built using the same local materials as the Ol Essakut houses, was an inspiration, the craftsmanship breathtaking. Each stone appeared to have been hand-picked for shape, colour and texture. The beams cut and smoothed to show off their rich grain. The panoramic outlook was utterly breathtaking.

Selling this house without good reason was beyond her imagination. Money wasn't the motive, he'd said so himself. The fight with Nick no longer created an obstacle to his staying. She must convince him not to sell.

Her animosity towards Beverley had nothing to do with her objection to his selling, more about seeing this lovingly created building put in the hands of someone with no sense of history.

She had to tell him about the plans before he finalized the deal.

Simeon arrived and Martin suggested eating their packed lunch in the cool shade of the verandah facing the mountain.

Simeon joined them but was eager to get to Eland camp with some oil for the generator, wrecking Sandra's plan to ask him to drive her home. She was afraid if she stayed with Martin any longer he would bring up the subject of the aftermath of the book launch.

Martin had other ideas.

"I thought Sandra and I should check Aloe ridge. While we're up there we can inspect the wreckage."

Sandra gulped, too taken aback to protest. The idea made her dizzy. She was tempted to plead her arm hurt too much, but feared an objection would make her sound feeble.

"Do we have time? I ought to get back," she muttered.

"What for? Surely Beverley can wait," Martin answered.

His reminder about Beverley helped. Anything was preferable to spending time with her, even facing demons. If she had to visit the crash site, Martin would be a better escort than anyone else.

Once she'd agreed, there seemed little point in delay. She settled into the passenger seat and tried to memorize the route.

Martin turned off onto tracks invisible to the untrained eye. She quickly lost her bearings. He said they'd attempt to reach the site from the opposite direction to the one used when he found her. She thought she had a good image of the terrain from the air, but was amazed when he did a sharp turn, eased his way round a clump of bushes and an outcrop of rocks and stopped. In front of them lay a charred circle of bush, the centrepiece, the skeleton of her plane. Martin opened the door for her. "Come on, let's go and explore."

He reached out to take her hand. She hesitated for a second, before putting hers in his, letting him lead her forwards. She had to watch where she trod. Stubby clumps of newly sprouting grass pushed through the blackened embers of the fire scorched area.

"Good thing the vegetation up here is so sparse. The fire would have spread for miles otherwise."

She froze, unable to go on, her mouth dry rendering her speechless. The shivering started. Martin wrapped his arms round her.

"Sorry, insensitive of me, you're not ready, are you," he murmured softly in her ear. She took comfort from his closeness, breathing in the spicy scent of his aftershave. "We can leave now."

She found some strength and pushed away from him.

"Sorry, I'm being silly."

"Nothing silly about facing fears," he answered without relinquishing his hold of her.

"Yes but no one died here."

"You mean unlike the previous crash you survived?"

"Who told you?" she snapped. The only people who knew were Nick and Jim Standish. One was dead and the other swore he'd never tell anybody.

"I'm a journalist, remember?"

"I don't care what you are. You have no right to dig into my past." The pitch of her voice had risen, she had to regain control.

“Your reluctance to talk made me curious. Jenny mentioned your father died in a plane crash. You wouldn’t open up, so I made enquiries.”

“What did you find out?” she asked more calmly, as she managed to push him away.

“His plane crashed over the Aberdares. He and your brother both died. You were trapped in the wreck.”

“What else?”

“They took a day and a half to find the plane, and found you unconscious with your foot trapped in the wreckage. Your rescuers worried your foot might have to be amputated.”

“How did you find out?” she stammered, shocked by his revelations.

“I checked out old news reports of air crashes. Were they wrong?”

“I can’t remember.”

“What, the crash?”

“No, every detail of the plane coming down is clear. I still have vivid nightmares, the noise, the feeling of falling and the pain. Then I wake up.”

“When you hit the ground?”

“I remember being stuck upside down and being alone. I never get rescued in the dream.”

“Might help if you did?”

“Maybe, I’ve never allowed myself to think the accident through. I don’t recollect anyone coming. I woke up in hospital with my mother beside me crying. The doctor had to tell me about my father and brother, which made her cry even more. When I was able to travel my mother took me to England. Right up to her death, she never spoke about my father, my brother or the crash”

“Tough on you.”

"Her way of dealing with grief, which I accepted as normal until Nick wanted me to fly with him, and I refused. He kept on and on at me until I told him why. He made me face the past and my fear of small planes."

"This crash brought the whole thing back?"

"In a way, the nightmares started again, I blamed the painkillers and stopped taking them."

He put his hand on her shoulder. "Sorry, I'd never have pushed you if I'd known. Will you ever fly again?"

She shrugged, the thought made her want to cry. She blinked back a tear determined not to show how freaked out the subject made her. "Not sure."

"Come on, I'll take you back."

"No. Now I'm this close I ought to look, having you here helps."

His arms tightened around her shoulder, "My pleasure, whenever you need me." He led her towards the blackened mass of tangled metal. The smell of burnt rubber and plastic still hung in the air as they walked slowly round the wreck. She picked out the rock that shattered the wheel, tipping the plane over, starting the spin which finally halted her. Then she found the rock she'd been thrown against when the plane exploded.

"I guess I'm lucky to be alive," she said.

Martin nodded, "Yes, very lucky," he said, and bent down to kiss her on the lips. Sandra could not prevent herself from responding. She wanted him as much now as she had the night of the book launch. The memory of Beverley's intrusive phone call shattered her joy. She pulled away, and hurried towards the car.

"Please take me back," she said trying to ignore his

hurt and puzzled look at her reaction. She couldn't explain to him. Not now. Not ever. Maybe it would be good if he sold up and left the country.

Martin followed in silence and drove with care, occasionally looking over towards her to check if she was all right.

He unexpectedly slammed on the brakes, reached out with one hand and touched her shoulder. "Look," he whispered as he pointed to a narrow gap between two thick clumps of thorns.

She stared at the bushes. "What am I looking for?"

"Can you see a bird, an ox-pecker?"

"Yes."

"Watch carefully."

The ox-pecker moved sideways. Carried along on the hard wrinkled leathery hide of its host, a large dust covered black rhino. The rhino turned to face them, giving a glimpse of its horns, and a tantalizing sighting of a youngster by its side.

"No notches on their ears?" Sandra said. Notches were the accepted method of recording individual rhinos living on the nearby conservation projects. Notched ears would show where they came from.

"I can't see any either." Martin edged the motor forward a couple of yards, to get a clearer view. "No, no sign of any nicks at all. The horns are in good shape."

She guessed he referred to the practice of protecting animals by sawing their horns off to deter poachers, or of inserting a tracking device into the dead hairy spike.

All earlier tension vanished. An hour later Martin tapped her on the shoulder and indicated they should leave the browsing duo.

She didn't want to go. All she could think about

was the huge benefits a pair of healthy rhino would bring to Ol Essakut. Benefits the children would reap. But first she must deal with the added responsibility of ensuring these rhino were safe from poachers.

The children would be expecting her home soon and she longed to hug them. As for facing Beverley, delay gained nothing.

Martin eventually broke the silence. "You mentioned the proposed plans for my place, do you have a copy?"

"Yes," she answered, regretting telling him about them. If he didn't sell then he'd be around all the time and she wasn't sure she was up for that. The thought of seeing him and Beverley together as her neighbours made her feel ill. But her concerns about the plans were quickly forgotten.

Martin had been driving at a steady rate when he slowed and pointed to a group of figures in the distance. "Here," he shoved a pair of binoculars into her hand, "any idea who they are?"

"Parjit, Lalji and Vejay."

"I thought so. Who are they talking to?"

She focussed in on the Africans they were talking to. Three men, all dressed in traditional tribal dress, red shukas tied on the shoulder, their hair daubed with red mud and plaited at the back, all carried spears. "Samburu, I think?"

"Recognize them?"

"No, I'm certain they're not local, I've met most of the villagers. I don't think they come from the village on the north-west boundary either."

"So you've never seen them before?"

"I don't think so. One seems to have a limp."

"I see what you mean. We'd better go and find out more."

By the time they reached the place where Parjit's Subaru had been a billowing dust trail snaked its way into the distance. Martin followed, and found the Subaru parked by their cottage and the three Singhs ambling towards the workshop. No one else in sight.

Martin drove up, wound down his window and said, "I saw your dust trail over in the western sector, did you see anyone?"

Parjit quickly asked, "Why?"

"I thought I saw a couple of Samburu in the distance and wondered if you'd seen them?"

"No, nothing, nobody?" Parjit said, looking towards the other two who vigorously shook their heads. "Sorry."

"Don't worry," Martin said and drove on towards the main house. Before they went into the house he turned to Sandra. "That trio are up to something. Why else would they lie?"

"What can we do?"

"I'll get a message to Jacob and ask him to go to my place. If anyone can pick up the tracks he can, which might be useful to work out what's going on."

Sam and Emma thundered out of the door craving their attention, halting the discussion.

With the children clinging to her, Sandra learnt that Beverley had left. What a relief.

"Patience was never her strong point." Martin muttered.

His casual comment reinforced the belief that Martin was closer to Beverley than he'd let on.

The children begged Martin and Amina to stay for supper. Amina refused, she had to go to Nairobi, and wanted to catch Simeon before she went. Martin hesitated for a moment but sausages, mash and beans on the menu tipped the balance. He waited for a nod of approval before accepting. For the next hour they played with the children and finally read bedtime stories.

"Thanks for letting me stay," he said as soon as they reached the bottom of the stairs. "If you're not too tired, I'd love a peek at those plans."

"Help yourself to coffee, I'll get them."

Sandra brought them back and spread them out on the large low table in front of the fire. Her visit to the site made her more puzzled why Nick ever approved them.

Martin flipped through the drawings several times, making no comment at all. He hated them. The unasked question, would this stop him selling? Much as Ol Essakut needed the land, she'd never forgive herself if she allowed the destruction of his family home. Selling to Beverley made demolition a certainty.

"Do you think showing me these will stop me selling?"

"I'm not sure. I don't understand why Nick ever considered building there." It was the best response she could think of. "He talked about you so often, never gave the impression he hated you. Certainly, not enough to destroy your home."

Martin looked so serious and she wondered if she had made a mistake talking about Nick. Eventually he spoke.

"You're worried about Beverley? I know why you hate her."

Sandra's face got hotter and hotter. He had no idea. Hate was a strong word, but accurate. She had dared express her thoughts in words, and found it scary her dislike was so transparent.

"I hardly know her. Hank Bradley handles all the

trust business."

"I understand my sale could lead to a fight for control."

"Martin, my relationship with Beverley is none of your business. Back off."

"I'm not trying to interfere, but I want to be certain you understand how much power owning my plot of land will give her."

"I might be new to all this, but I'm not an idiot. Of course I understand. But what can I do? Even if you offered me the land, I can't afford to buy. It doesn't mean I won't fight to keep control. Is that what you wanted to hear?"

"Yes."

"Good, now leave me alone."

"I have another solution," he answered, "I don't sell."

"Fine, you have to live with the decision." She had to establish that she could fight her own battles. "Whatever you do, the night we spent together is not going to change anything. I made a mistake. One I don't intend to repeat."

"What happened was very special, and no matter what you say, I'm not giving up on us. The truth is I'm worried about you working alongside Beverley."

She had to end the conversation somehow. "If you want to help then find out what Parjit and company are up to."

"Fine," and with that he stood up and headed for the door. "I'll call if I find out anything worthwhile. Oh, about the rhinos, don't tell anyone we found them."

"Why not? Surely the estate needs this more than anything?"

"You don't know who you can trust. There are too

many odd things going on, and until we figure out who is responsible it would be better to keep it secret."

The excitement of finding the rhinos suddenly turned to dread. "You think they're in danger?"

"They could be."

"Surely the more people who know, the safer they'll be?"

"No. I think in this case it would put them at risk. Promise you won't say anything to anyone until I get back."

"Apart from Simeon?"

"No, not even Simeon."

"What harm will telling him do?"

"Trust me, this stays secret."

Sandra couldn't believe he was serious. It was a joke, a bad joke. But when Martin brushed her with a kiss on her forehead, his parting words left her in no doubt. "Lock up behind me."

She did as he said, but turning the key in the lock a deep sense of isolation swept over her.

Chapter 18

Martin's lack of trust in everyone she'd relied on for the last three months scared Sandra. Exhausted or not, sleep would evade her, so she might as well go in search of answers.

Martin mentioned Nick kept diaries. They must be lurking somewhere in his study. Nick often said hoarding books and paper was a family trait. His study confirmed this. She'd only scratched the surface when searching for documents for the lawyers and the accountants. The room was stuffed floor to ceiling with books, files and piles of papers, with at least twice as much stored in the gun room, a place she had only peered into twice. The first time, the week before their wedding when Nick showed her his hiding place for the key, the second when Nick's lawyer following the instructions of his will, requested access so he could get the gun out for Rory.

She checked the study first, no sign of any black books with red spines, or anything resembling a diary. Opening the gun room and dealing with her claustrophobia the next move. For the children's sake she had to find out about Rory and his relationship to the family.

She nipped upstairs to get the bureau key from the bedroom she'd briefly shared with Nick, which she'd avoided since the day he betrayed her, and she'd packed her bags intending to leave. News of his death changed everything. The children needed her and she loved them too much to abandon them. She stayed for their sake, but moved into the spare room. Everyone assumed grief made her change rooms rather than anger, and she never enlightened them.

The lingering waft of Nick's favourite aftershave still clung to the air. Leaving the room untouched was a mistake. She mustn't make a shrine of his possessions. Like an intruder, she checked each drawer in turn in case his diaries were hidden amongst his things.

Sifting through his belongings unsettled her. During her short married life she'd never rummaged in his drawers. The household staff washed, ironed and put his clothes away as they had all his life.

Nothing was hidden under his folded clothes. The wardrobe proved equally unrewarding but a timely reminder she must dispose of some of his things. As she fingered the fabrics her emotions associated to Nick changed, her pain eased, but her anger hung on.

Giving up she made for the Satsuma ginger jar on top of the tall chest of drawers where he kept the bureau key. She slipped the key into her pocket.

A noise from the children's room interrupted her. She tiptoed into their room. Emma whimpered, she knelt down beside the bed and stroked her forehead. Damp curls stuck to her hot skin.

"Don't cry, I'm here, go back to sleep," Sandra whispered, "mustn't wake Sam." Emma looked at her briefly then snuggled down with her thumb in her mouth. Her eyes closed and she drifted off to sleep again. Sandra stayed, watching the sleeping child, utterly amazed her presence had such a calming effect. Emma's skin, hot to touch, gave her cause for concern. She'd check her again as soon as she located the diaries.

Her next stop was the study. She glanced round the room. She had already checked everywhere. No excuse left to delay looking in the gun room. She sat at the elaborate roll top bureau that dominated one wall of the study, put the key into the lock and rolled the lid back, revealing an array of drawers, compartments and a little central cupboard. She pulled out the little side drawer on the bottom left hand side, slid her hand into the gap searching for the tiny catch that would open the secret compartment where the gun room key was hidden.

She fumbled, using her left hand rather than her right hand made the task harder. She had the right drawer, but wished she'd insisted on testing the catch when Nick showed her the hiding place. Her fingernail snagged on something, she quickly withdrew her hand and inspected the damage. She tried a second time. Success. With a loud click the side pillar popped forward, she eased the pillar out and tipped it over, letting the heavy key fall out.

She turned the ornate metal key over in the palm of her hand examining it before she crossed the room, slid back the wall panel that hid the door to the gun room and inserted the key in the lock. The nape of her neck tingled as the door swung towards her. Why act like a trespasser? She had every right to search Nick's private papers even the ones locked in the gun room. Nick made that clear when he made her responsible for his children and the ranch that came with them.

Her immediate problem revolved round finding a suitable wedge for the door to stop it closing behind her. This dark windowless space built into the centre of the house terrified her. She dragged a heavy chair over and pushed it against the open door, and as an extra precaution shoved the key into her pocket. The fear of being trapped inside, even for a second was unbearable.

She cautiously groped inside the doorway and found the light switch. Two naked bulbs dangled from the ceiling, flooding the interior with harsh bright light. She surveyed the space, breathing in the strong gun oil smell that permeated the air. The left hand wall contained racks, lined with guns, the small metal safe with a combination lock for ammunition at the far end. Nick had been proud of his collection of weapons, which were of no interest to her. The shelves on the other three walls were her focus. Straight ahead of her was an array of big black box files, some clearly labelled "accounts" others with no label at all. The right hand wall had an array of stud books, the remaining space filled with a mixed jumble of box files, cardboard folders, piles of loose papers, and envelopes. On the floor were more boxes with their lids askew, the contents spilling out.

She was afraid to touch anything. What if there was some logical order beneath this chaotic filing mess? She flicked through a few papers, making sure she didn't displace anything. She was quickly disheartened. It would take months to sort this. She saw nothing that looked like a diary, or a series of them.

She unearthed a box file of letters relating to the Lander property. Before she dug into it she heard Emma crying for her. She kept hold of the file, and hurried to answer the call. She turned out the light, closed the door, locked it, stuffed the key into her pocket, slid the panel closed and hurried upstairs, slightly thankful Emma gave her a reason to escape the claustrophobic space.

She got to the top of the stairs still carrying the file

which she dumped on her bed while she went into the children's room. Emma burned with fever, her hair stuck to her scalp with sweat. Sandra checked Sam's forehead, he was cooler, and undisturbed by her touch.

Scooping Emma up into her arms she took her to the bathroom. No need for a thermometer to tell her Emma's temperature was at a dangerous level. She remembered reading a cool bath was good for reducing a high temperature in a child. She put the plug in the bath, turned on the taps, and started stripping Emma's pyjamas off her. She tested the water with her fingers then gently lowered Emma into the tepid water. Hampered by her plaster, Sandra propped the child up and sponged the cool water over her neck and face, watching eagerly for the raging red to become a flushed pink. Eventually the cool water took the heat out of the fever, bringing her body temperature down.

Sandra was now terrified Emma would be in danger of catching a chill. She hauled her out of the bath, wrapped her in a towel, laid the exhausted little figure on her own bed, patted her dry and covered her with a sheet and a light cotton blanket.

Emma lay listless, thumb firmly wedged in her mouth, large eyes trustingly taking in every move Sandra made. Happily Emma was too young to understand Sandra had no idea how to tend a sick child or what caused the fever, let alone prevent it coming back. She didn't know who to call for help? She checked the medicine cupboard, found some children's asprin and gave Emma a dose. It was only four o'clock. She'd wait until six before calling Jenny for advice. She lay down beside Emma, and watched the child drop off to sleep again.

Sandra, afraid to go to sleep in case the fever flared

up again, propped herself up against the headboard, pulled over the box file she'd abandoned earlier and sifted through the contents.

The file contained the oddest collection of documents and memorabilia, relating to the Lander family. Faded sepia photos of men with their hunting trophies, one with a man proudly supporting two arching elephant tusks that towered over his head were near the top. A bundle of studio portraits of ladies in high necked blouses, along with pictures of men and women grouped round the older seated members of the family further down. A monogrammed lace handkerchief and a few foxed wedding invitations, even a small bundle of brittle envelopes tied with a dainty red ribbon lay at the bottom. Scattered in between were some formal looking papers.

The oldest document, deeds for land purchased by a member of the Lander family as far back as 1897. She found birth, marriage and death certificates most bearing the Lander name, with several old passports thrown in as well. Sandra thumbed through them, and worked out roughly the relationships of the people named. They belonged to the parents and grand parents of Helen Lander, her predecessor, who had married Nick and given birth to his children, Sam and Emma.

No matter how uncomfortable handling these rather personal family papers felt, she had to determine their importance, and preserve them for the children. One day they'd want to know their family history.

The sleeping child beside her stirred, the flushed colour creeping back. She shoved the papers to one side, and went to fetch a bowl of water and a flannel, stopping briefly to check on Sam on her way. He seemed fine, so she returned and wrung the cloth out with one hand. Her plaster cast had gone soft with her effort to bathe Emma earlier. Emma didn't seem to notice the cooling flannel going over her forehead, arms, legs and body, but Sandra kept going until the flushed colour subsided again. She put back the sheet and blanket and looked at the clock. Nearly six o'clock, she'd wait another hour before calling Jenny.

Outside the sky was changing from the blackness of night to the deep purple hue before the orange redness of dawn took over. A bath might be refreshing, and redress the balance lack of sleep had caused. She gathered the papers on the bed and attempted to squeeze them into the box.

A large, folded sheet of heavy paper wedged in the bottom stopping it from closing. She tugged the awkward document out, to find it was a beautifully drawn up family tree. Heavy black italics used for the names, fine red script for birth and death dates under the names. Blue ink for marriage dates. Five generations were recorded, ending with the birth of the twins. Helen's death date had been added in pencil. So had a new branch, leading to the name Rory Lyons along with his date of birth. Both these pencilled entries were in Nick's distinctive writing.

Sandra stared at it, thinking it a shame to spoil the symmetry by adding Rory's name. Slowly the impact of the position of his name sunk in. Rory's relationship to the Landers was not so distant after all. Nick's scribbling led to only one logical interpretation. Rory was Helen's older, illegitimate, half-brother.

Did Rory know? Was that why he thought he could make a claim for a share of the Lander property? Had anyone any proof? Or was the doubt the reason his name only appeared in pencil.

Was Nick's generous bequest to Rory of a life time tenancy at the Lander house gifted from a sense of guilt, or to prevent Rory contesting the will and demanding a chunk of land?

Then it occurred to her that Rory might not be aware of the true relationship between himself and Helen.

Sandra felt sick. A scandal could hurt the children. No wonder Nick reacted badly when Martin told him about Helen's affair with Rory. Not that shooting the messenger was quite the right thing to do. Martin probably had no idea of the complex situation he'd exposed.

Nick deserved gratitude for ensuring the Lander property was placed in a trust for the children. No one could accuse her of trying to get it for herself, and less chance of Rory being able to benefit either.

Before Sandra had time to speculate further she heard Wanjiru opening the back door. She folded up the family tree and squashed it firmly back into the box file. She was cross with herself for not leaving time to lock the file away. That would have to wait until this evening after the staff had gone when she'd bury it under a pile of papers.

Sandra nipped down to the study and slipped the gun room key into the secret compartment, listened for the hidden catch to click, slid the drawer into place and locked the bureau.

She went to the kitchen to get a cup of tea. Wanjiru was quick to ask, "Bad night?"

Sandra guessed she must have rings under her eyes from lack of sleep. "Yes, Emma's sick."

"You go up. I'll bring your tea."

Sandra didn't argue. Emma sensed her getting back into bed and snuggled up for a cuddle. Sandra hugged her, relieved to find her temperature had stayed down.

Wanjiru's reaction to the pale, listless child confirmed Sandra's concern.

"You must get her to drink," Wanjiru said, offering a cup of juice to Sandra to give to Emma. At first Emma wasn't keen, but eventually she took a sip, then another. Slow coaxing did the trick and Sandra kept going until the cup was empty, at which point Emma went back to sleep. Wanjiru swapped the juice cup for a cup of hot tea, and went off to fetch a rug for Sandra to wrap round the sleeping child.

Sandra felt trapped by the child, and trapped by the confused thoughts about Nick and the danger of his secrets having repercussions. The information had taken on the proportions of an unexploded bomb in her life. The possibility of more revelations terrified her. She tried to focus on the future and finding ways to protect the twins. She dozed for a while, waking when Sam climbed onto the bed, eager to get even closer to her than his sister. He had the same feverish symptoms though his temperature had not peaked. Sandra called for Wanjiru and asked for a second cup of juice for Sam. She adjusted her position to the middle of the bed, to enable both children to snuggle up to her, and phoned Jenny for reassurance, and discovered several of the twins' friends had come down with similar symptoms. The doctor's advice fitted with everything she'd done so far.

Chapter 19

The children had just fallen asleep peacefully when Simeon arrived. Wanjiru let him in and he came upstairs and sat in the chair opposite her.

Sandra found herself wishing he hadn't come. With all the drama of the children being ill, the excitement of the discovery of the rhinos had completely slipped her mind. Seeing him brought back Martin's insistence Simeon, a man he called his friend, one in whom she placed so much trust, should not be told. Martin's excuses about too many strange things going on at the ranch didn't make the subterfuge easier.

The minute Simeon spoke she thought Martin made a huge error in excluding him.

"We've had reports of six new holes in the fence," he announced, "all big enough to drive a lorry through, I've seen for myself."

"Why?"

"If we had more animals on the ranch I'd say poachers."

She fussed over the children to avoid eye contact, her guilt getting to her.

"Can you put extra patrols on the fence?" she managed to ask.

"If Rory gets more vehicles back on the road, at least three are still out of action. He says he can't get the right spare parts."

"Chase him. He can't complain he's short handed. He has those three Singhs available to help him. Can't he send them to fetch whatever is needed?"

"Already been suggested. I've had to put extra men out at the camps. Last night there was a fire at Eland camp. The thatched roofing on the dining room caught, and it is in a right mess."

Simeon twiddled his pen. He only did this when worried. His tension was catching. "I wish I could go with you, but I have my hands full. I can't leave the twins while they're sick."

"Don't worry, I'll manage."

How could he if she kept him in the dark. "Do you need to take on more staff?"

"With the cancelled tours I don't think we can afford it."

"Leave it with me. I'll talk to Hank. He may come up with extra funds."

"Are you sure you want to do that?"

She understood Simeon's reluctance to approach Hank. Hank would relish the chance to have her indebted to him. So far they had managed to work together but she sensed he was waiting for her to make a mistake. He wanted to take control of the consortium. Her responsibility lay with the twins, she had to keep her head and follow Nick's wishes. "Don't worry, I can handle him."

"Shall I get Amina to come and help you?"

"No, her meeting with the publisher is too important." The last thing she needed was to be hiding things from Amina. Keeping the secret about the rhinos from her closest friend would be impossible. If Amina knew, Simeon would too. "I can manage. Wanjiru is here, and they are both much better than earlier," she lied.

Simeon took her at her word and left promising to come back later and report on his progress.

The day dragged by. Sam's fever got worse, and Emma, while better, wouldn't let Sandra out of her sight and preferably not out of her reach for a moment. Sam needed cooling with a damp sponge yet again, and Sandra was trapped for most of the day on the bed, sandwiched between the two listless children.

She left them briefly to make the call to Hank. His deep southern drawl sounded comforting. She explained about the children not being well, and started to fill him in on what Simeon had reported.

"You have often said I should let you know if I needed anything. Right now, I need extra manpower. And with all the drama of the last few weeks, I don't have funding for extra patrols to keep the fences secure."

"Don't worry, I'll send some of my chaps over."

"Can you liaise with Simeon?"

"I'm not sure if I should."

"What do you mean?"

"I've found a major discrepancy in the accounts."

"What sort of discrepancy."

"Enough to pay for a new camp," Hank answered.

"I don't understand."

Hank went on to explain how he'd found the building materials ordered for work on the camps and the fence far exceeded the budget, in fact was double the agreed figures. He checked with the suppliers thinking this was a clerical error. The account had been billed twice. But he had been assured a duplicate order had been placed, the goods dispatched, and both shipments paid for in full.

Sandra remembered paying for the materials Hank was referring to. "Of course I paid them. I always settle their account on the fifth of the month. I don't remember a second bill."

"Simeon signed the second cheque."

"Well he must have assumed that I didn't do it."

"That's not the point. The point is a second load of material arrived and vanished. We need to find out who put in the duplicate order. Remember, we're talking about enough materials to construct a whole camp."

Sandra remembered Simeon saying the gaps in the fences were big enough for a lorry to drive through. She told Hank what he'd said which instigated the request for extra manpower.

Hank responded, "Leave it with me," and hung up.

Sandra hadn't told him about the fire. Sam was crying. She made a mental note to call Hank back later to tell him. Children needing attention took priority.

She sponged Sam down again, and tried to get him to take a few sips of juice. As he was settling down again she heard a car arrive.

The car door slammed, footsteps crunched on the gravel, she had a horrible suspicion she knew who it was. The voice confirmed her fears. She hoped Wanjiru would turn Beverley away. Instead Wanjiru came up and asked if she should send Beverley up.

She wanted to scream, "No." But the meeting had to happen. To give Beverley credit, she had attended Nick's funeral service, stayed at the back of the church, and left straight away to catch a flight back to the States, avoiding a potentially ugly confrontation.

Putting off the inevitable wouldn't make it any easier, so she nodded, and waited, wondering how Beverley would behave. They had almost become friends before Nick died. The memory made her angry.

Trapped by the sleeping children whose presence would hinder her desire to tell Beverley what she thought of her, also made throwing her out harder.

Beverley came upstairs quietly. She stood in the doorway hesitantly. "Can I come in?"

Sandra nodded.

"I'm sorry," Beverley said softly.

Was the apology for intruding or for sleeping with Nick? What reaction did she expect? Before Sandra had a chance to reply Beverley's eyes fixed on the children and asked, "How are they?"

"Better than earlier," Sandra answered.

"I meant, how are they coping without Nick?" The concern in her voice sounded genuine. Maybe they meant more to her than Sandra thought possible. "I'd like to help if you'll let me," she added, "but I'll understand if you'd rather I kept my distance."

Sandra didn't say anything. Forgive and forget, nice sentiment, but she still hurt too much.

"I was the one at fault. I never thought he'd marry you even though I pretended to accept the fact. I didn't realize how much I loved him until too late, and I chased after him. I didn't let up. When he thought he'd lost you, he was utterly devastated."

Sandra had no idea how to respond, and wished Beverley would shut up and leave.

"He was desperate to find you and beg for forgiveness. My feelings didn't matter."

Sandra didn't know what to say. His death ruled out the possibility of forgiveness.

"You must have forgiven him a little to have taken on these two," Beverley rambled on, "I'm not sure I'd have coped so well if I'd faced the same situation."

"Lucky for them he married me and not you." Sandra answered, realizing how catty she sounded and hating herself for allowing cattiness to creep in.

"Yes, that's true. I might not be much use with the

children but I could take the burden of getting the camps sorted out from you."

Sandra felt cornered. Beverley had worked on camps before with great results. Would agreeing to let her help make Beverley think she could slot back in as if nothing had happened. She wished no answer was required because she didn't know what to say.

"Sorry." Beverley rose as if to go. "I don't want you to think I'm pushing you, but the project is too important to let personal stuff get in the way. Can we at least try to work together?"

Sandra gave in. "Fine, carry on. Do what you can at the camps." She stroked Emma's curls almost to remind herself she was agreeing to this for their sakes. "Remember the budget is tight. I can't leave the children and I don't think you should go on your own. Maybe Rory can take you."

Taking Rory out of the workshop wasn't ideal, but if they were short of spares he probably wouldn't be doing much anyway.

Beverley looked relieved. Maybe she had expected a fight. As she left she said, "Thanks for letting me help. I won't let you down."

Sandra closed her eyes finding it hard to believe her first encounter with Beverley was over, temper intact, no tears either, which had been her dread since that fateful day. It took a while before the throaty roar of the Subaru, taking off up the road towards the camps, allowed her to relax. Rory would enjoy a chance to show off.

For the next few hours, minding the children kept her fully occupied and she had no time or energy left to dwell on the problems outside.

Wanjiru popped in every quarter of an hour bringing more juice for the children or offering to make something to eat. Everyone went downstairs at lunchtime and Sandra agreed to have a bowl of soup to keep Wanjiru happy. It must be so hard for her having so recently buried her son, Kamau.

The children ate bread and butter and drank a reasonable amount of juice, which helped fulfil the doctor's instruction of getting fluid into them.

Martin arrived mid afternoon. The children were curled up beside her on the couch reading story books. She was pleased to see him until he revealed the present he'd bought for the children.

He placed a medium sized cardboard box on the floor in front of them all. "I heard Sam and Emma needed cheering up. I thought this might do the trick."

Sam and Emma twisted themselves so they could peer at the box. Neither were prepared to get off the couch to inspect more closely.

"They really are in a bad way, aren't they?"

"I think they're over the worst."

"Well I hope you won't be mad at me for this, but I thought they would love it."

"Go on, show us."

Martin opened the box and lifted out the cutest little mongrel puppy Sandra had ever seen. "You're right. I'm mad with you." It was impossible not to be smitten by the huge round eyes and soft floppy spaniel ears. Both children reached out to touch.

"What's she called?" Emma asked.

"It's a he, and he's called Rupee. You and Sam are going to have to take extra special care of him, because he's very little."

"How big will he get?" Sandra asked, wondering what other breeds mixed with the spaniel blood.

Martin indicated below knee height. Sandra nodded her approval. "I don't suppose he's house trained?"

As if on cue, Rupee left a small puddle on the floor. Martin looked embarrassed and said, “Sorry, not yet. I’ll go and get some newspapers.”

The children shrieked with laughter for the first time all day and moved off the settee of their own accord, to sit on the floor with the puppy between them, fondling its soft silky coat. Sandra got up glad of the chance to stretch her legs. She positioned herself by the window looking out, and Martin came and stood by her. He smelt so good, she was tempted to lean against him, but the past made her step away.

“Rough day?” he asked.

Sandra nodded, and told him about the children waking in the night. She left out the saga of searching the gun room, and what she’d found, but filled him in on Simeon’s latest report of new holes in the fencing, the fire at the camp, the problems with spares and Beverley wanting to help with the camps and going off with Rory. She watched for a reaction, but his expression never changed. Finally she told him about the discrepancies Hank had found with accounts and the duplicated supplies.

“Sounds like a pretty grim day to me,” Martin said when she finished.

“It was. Last night when you said not to tell Simeon about the rhino I thought you’d gone mad, but now I begin to wonder who I can trust. I don’t suppose you found out anything useful?”

“Afraid not. But I need to know something. It will seem like a silly question, but can you remember what Rory did the day Nick died?”

“He was in Nairobi,” she answered without hesitation, “but I have no idea what for.”

“Are you certain?”

“Absolutely.” She recalled the precise moment

outside the Norfolk hotel, when Rory stopped her and he told her Nick wanted to see her urgently in their room.

She thought it odd, because less than an hour earlier Nick had helped load their bags into her car, and had been heading to reception to check out and on to meet Simeon. She'd gone shopping and returned to the hotel to collect her car. She'd hurried back to the room wondering what delayed him. The recollection made her shiver.

"Why? What makes that day so important?"

Martin checked the children were playing with the puppy, and not paying attention. When he spoke it was so quiet she had trouble hearing. "There is a rumour going round that Nick's car was tampered with."

Sandra felt her bile rise. She had to swallow hard to hide her discomfort. Her brain went into overdrive trying to remember the exact details she'd been given. "The police said it was an accident."

"I know. But rumours don't start without reason. If it was done by a good mechanic, the police could easily miss the evidence, especially in an accident where the car is badly smashed up." Martin continued, "If the rumour is true, Rory would be a suspect. He was responsible for the maintenance of Nick's motor."

Sandra answered without thinking. "But surely he'd need a motive." At which point a vision of the Lander's family tree came back to her. Then she remembered the smug expression on his face when he sent her to find Nick. It had never occurred to her before that he intended her to find Beverley and Nick together. She tried to convince herself it was silly to be sucked in by a rumour, and even madder to start suspecting Rory with no evidence. Maybe he'd intended to expose Nick's affair. In such a tight knit community she would have found out eventually. But the feeling he'd waited outside to see her reaction lingered.

It was crazy, but the memory of the moment, once triggered, refused to go away.

In her hurry out of the hotel, hurt, humiliated, and angry, she had dropped her bag on the tarmac, scattering the contents all around. Rory, who had been leaning against Nick's car, parked next to her own, bent down to help pick up the things that had rolled his way. Every detail came flooding back. The need to escape. The desperate scrabbling under the car for her things. Rory crowding her, pushing her away from Nick's car. His handing her a lipstick, a pen and an eye shadow that rolled under Nick's car. The orange stain on the hem of his shirt made when he wiped them before handing them back to her. They were still sticky to touch, but she hadn't cared. All she wanted was to get away from the Norfolk.

She shivered again with apprehension, shocked by the possible implication of that memory. It terrified her.

Martin put his arms around her, "Are you all right?"

She managed to nod, wondering if she'd paid attention that day, if Nick would still be alive.

She thought about going to the police and telling them what she had remembered. She quickly dismissed the idea. Suspicion of foul play would make them look for suspects. She would have to tell them about Rory's family connection but that was unthinkable. The complication of that information becoming public knowledge would be damaging to the twins.

And if they looked for suspects, Rory would be

quick to tell them about her discovering Nick was having an affair. She pictured him describing the jealous wife rushing out of the hotel in a rage. He would effectively give them a motive for her to get revenge on her unfaithful husband. Jealousy, a powerful and dangerous thing.

Sandra so deep in thought almost forgot Martin held her. She hadn't the energy to shy away from his comforting touch.

"Sorry, I didn't mean to upset you," he said. "I thought you should know what is being said."

"Thanks I appreciate your honesty. Don't worry I'll be all right," she said, pushing his arm away.

She still had to work out who if anyone would believe her if she told them what she suspected. The answer was simple, no one. By not confiding about Nick's infidelity at the time, and by letting everyone assume she was a grief stricken widow, she effectively betrayed their trust. Without trust, who'd stand by?

Martin's warm breath on her neck jolted her back to the present. She edged away from him and said, "Perhaps you'd better go."

Martin rescued the puppy from the children, muttered goodbye and something about telling Wanjiru what to do about feeding the little creature, and disappeared. The children, exhausted by their fun with the puppy, were curled up on the settee waiting for her to come back to cuddle them.

The last thing she wanted was for Beverley to come back. Of course she did.

Sandra couldn't help noticing the neat, well groomed Beverley who'd swept through that morning had lost her glossy magazine cover look. Her hair damp, the crisply ironed clothes, well and truly creased, and more unusual for Beverley, unaware of the state she was in.

Sandra guessed Rory had some input into the dishevelled look. Under normal circumstances she might have warned Beverly to be careful. But normal no longer existed.

She had to concentrate. Beverley sounded like a female version of Rory, extolling the virtues of rally driving and getting all excited about some sort of Rally Driving School. Sandra wished she'd go away, and then she clicked, Beverley wanted the school on the ranch. Rory would be the chief instructor.

Sandra put up her hand, "Hold on, the Ol Essakut venture is about wild life, not about motor cars."

Beverley looked ready to argue, but as if on cue Emma started a spasm of coughing. Sandra took advantage of the situation to end the conversation by saying she had to put the children to bed.

Beverley hung around long enough to ask after Martin.

"He left over an hour ago." Sandra answered, annoyed that Martin still had a part in Beverley's life.

"Never mind, he promised to have supper with me later. I'll see him then," Beverley said, with what Sandra took to be a sly smile.

"Well don't let me keep you any longer," Sandra said wondering if Beverley was trying to tell her something. She put on a brave smile to hide her anger or gnawing jealousy.

Sandra led the children upstairs to her bed. Putting them in their own would be a waste of energy as she was sure neither of them wanted to sleep alone. One story after another was necessary to get them settled, by which time she was nearly ready to join them. First she had to go downstairs and do a few things, including putting away the box file she had been reading the night before. Convincing Wanjiru she could manage by herself, and sending her off duty took ages, but she succeeded, and was able to lock and bolt the front door.

At last she could open the gun room. She wasn't sure why, she didn't feel comfortable opening it when any one else was in the house. A silly hang up, because she trusted the staff totally. One day she'd overcome it, for now returning the Lander family documents to the safety of the gun room her only goal. She couldn't risk letting anyone else get their hands on those papers.

She went into the study, and went through the ritual of taking the gun room key out of its hiding place in the desk and propping the door open as she had done the night before and reopening the gun room. Then she climbed onto a stool and placed the box on the top shelf, making sure the label was not on show and moving some out of date account files on top. As she clambered off the stool she looked around the room again, wondering what other secrets she'd find. She peeped into an unmarked box and found it contained a couple of black bound books with red spines in it. She took one out and opened it revealing Nick's spidery handwriting. The journals Martin talked about.

She scanned the page the book had fallen open at. She didn't think Martin would be particularly pleased if she told him what Nick had written. She read it twice to be sure she deciphered Nick's untidy scrawl correctly.

Nick had written, "Jealousy and greed made Martin tell me about Helen and Rory. He's so desperate to expand his empire he's even prepared to try to wreck our marriage. He wants the farm that belonged to her family for himself."

She read it for a third time, shocked by his accusation. She was afraid to read more. It was so odd having Nick influence her, months after his death.

One of the children started crying for her.

She stuffed the diary back in the box, and fled the room slamming the door shut, and hastily stuffing the key back where it belonged.

Chapter 20

Rory didn't need much persuasion to drop his tools to take Beverly to check progress at the camps.

He informed Parjit he needed the Subaru, and didn't hang about for the protest. Parjit had begun to complain about not getting enough driving practice. Rory didn't care. Parjit could wait. Getting his hands on Beverley's body again couldn't. Just sitting next to her in the motor was a turn on.

"Fancy another swim?" he asked as they set off.

"No, just drive to the camp," she answered with a distinct lack of enthusiasm. Not the reaction he hoped for or expected. He put his foot hard down on the accelerator hoping to impress. The expressionless face a sign he'd failed. Beverley was so engrossed in her own private world he hadn't a hope in hell of getting what he fancied unless he did something drastic.

He slammed his foot down on the brakes, and yanked up the handbrake. The spinning car sent up a billowing cloud of red dust. Beverley never flinched, or made a sound from start to finish. Her seat belt kept her from rocketing through the windscreen. A coughing fit started by the fine powdery dust seeping into the car the only proof she was still alive.

"What the hell did you do that for?" she demanded when the choking stopped.

"I wanted your attention. What's with the ice maiden routine?"

Her tight lips showed her anger. Her wealth

probably meant she was used to being in control of everyone around her. But needing her money, her support, and any influence on offer, didn't mean she could treat him like dirt.

She took her time answering, "Sorry Rory, I've a lot on my mind, I can't just shove everything to one side." Then with a sweet smile she stretched out her arm placed her hand on his upper thigh, "Forgive me, won't you?"

To give her credit, she knew how to win a bloke over. She was back in control. Hell, he didn't give a damn. To get her back in his arms, he'd play her game with her rules, for now. "Of course," he answered, "just checking where I stood."

"I have work to do at the camps. Afterwards a swim would be nice."

"Nice," he thought, must be losing my touch, something he'd rectify later. For now he'd do what she wanted.

"Want to drive?"

"Thought you'd never offer," she said opening her door to swap places.

He'd barely belted up before she had the car into gear and her foot hard down on the accelerator. Everything about her changed, as the thrill of speed and the danger kicked in. The Beverley he fancied had returned.

They arrived at the camp quickly, and while she wandered round making notes, he scrounged a packet of biscuits, a tin of pate, and a few beers from the supply hut. Beverley came, took his hand and led him off towards the furthest tent on the site.

"Is something wrong?" he asked.

She lifted the flap, and led him in. "Consumer testing... let's do the bed first?" She clutched his belt buckle. Rory worried about the gap in the half open flap of the tent, while Beverley undid his belt, and unfastened his trousers. Even if someone had been standing outside watching them, it wouldn't matter, he was past caring. He wanted her, as much as she wanted him, and he'd happily oblige. If she didn't mind an audience, neither did he.

Moments after he satisfied her needs, Beverley stood up, adjusted her clothes, and walked out of the tent as if nothing had happened. Rory, struggled with his trousers and belt, and followed, determined next time he'd be the one taking the initiative.

"Did you say something about a swim?" she said, as she climbed into the passenger seat.

"Are you sure you don't want to drive?

"No, you'll get there quicker."

Beverley surprised him. "Tell me about yourself."

"I drive rally cars. I like sexy women," he answered. "What more do you need to know?"

"How long you've lived here?"

"Since I was twelve." No one had ever asked about his childhood before. "My grandfather died and I came to live with Tom Lander.

"So you know Martin Owen well?"

"Why? Has he said something?"

"Oh no, but I'm supposed to be buying his land, and I think he's avoiding me. I wondered if you had any idea why?"

"Sandra has him running errands. Playing up her injured arm for all it's worth."

"Anything more than that?"

"Hard to tell. A week ago I'd have said yes, but now I'm not so sure." The moment the words were out he regretted them. He should have lied and said Martin and Sandra couldn't keep their hands off each other. He suspected Beverley fancied Martin. Time to turn the conversation to cars and driving.

"Were you serious about wanting to enter a rally?"

"Yes, Hank's trying to get hold of a car."

"Hank? What's he got to do with it?" Rory wondered about the relationship between Hank and Beverley.

"He has more connections than I do. He thinks I've gone mad, and thinks Sandra won't agree to the driving school idea. If she hates the plan, he'll have to support her decision."

"What are the odds?"

"I think they're good. You need to be organized and work out details of costs, charges, and start preparing advertising material. It takes more than a friendly chat to get a venture off the ground. Financial viability is the key. You understand that, don't you?"

"Of course," he answered, his mind turning to more personal matters. They were back at the pool site. He grabbed the bag containing the beers and food, and led her down to the rock pool. He dumped the bag, shed his clothes and dived in. Beverley peeled off each item of clothing, making sure that he watched every move. What an exhibitionist. She had the figure of a stripper and the nerve too, and he loved being her audience, but not for long. He wanted more, and wanted it now.

"Come on in," he called.

She sat on the rock. "Later."

"Now," he shouted, beginning to lose patience. Beverley gave him an odd look, but got to her feet and jumped into the water beside him. Rory grabbed her as she came up for air and locked his arms firmly round her. He let her take a breath, he had total control over her, and was enjoying every second. Judging by Beverley's physical response the pleasure was mutual.

Exhausted, they scrambled from the water and lay on the rocks to let the sun dry them. Rory offered her food from the meagre selection he'd found at the camp. He opened the tin of pate, scooped it out with the biscuits, and gave her a bottle of beer. He half expected her to moan the pate had melted or the beer was tepid, but she never uttered a word of complaint. After a short rest in the sunshine, he persuaded her to get back into the pool. Once in, he'd show her who was in control.

Rory kept her in the water until the shadow of the cliff reached the far side of the pool before he let her get out of the water to dry off.

The mood changed on the walk back to the Subaru. Beverley chose the passenger seat, and he slipped in behind the steering wheel. The aloof creature he had driven out that morning had returned, not that he cared. He'd had a fantastic day, and his head buzzed with ideas for the driving school, dreaming of the money he'd make, and the new motor he'd buy.

"Will you come over while I talk to Sandra about the rally school?" Beverley asked when he dropped her off outside Sandra's door.

"No, you get her used to the idea."

"You don't think she'll be keen."

"No, she's never been a fan, but with persuasion, she'll come round."

"Oh, I forgot." Beverley said as she undid the seat belt, and opened the door. "Hank told me there's a rumour going round that Nick's car was tampered with, his accident planned."

Rory was glad that she had her back to him otherwise she might have spotted the panic on his face. "You're joking," he said, hoping to glean more information from her, suspicious of Hank's motive for telling her.

"No, he heard it from several different sources. I wonder how Sandra will react."

"Are you going to tell her?"

"No I'm sure some other good soul will fill her in."

"When will you be back?" Rory asked.

"Don't know, I'll call you and tell you her reaction to the driving school."

Rory drove back to his house. Parjit sat on the verandah waiting for him. Rory wanted to tell him to push off, but he had to find out what made Balbinder Singh tick. The fact the rumour was out, even if Balbinder hadn't started it was bad news. The mere hint that Rory was responsible was dangerous.

"Sorry I took so long. Women. Never do what you expect. We've still got time for a run this evening." Parjit's grin was his answer. "Go and fill her up, while I grab a bite to eat."

Parjit drove off, and Rory went to the kitchen. His cook was not due back for another hour, so he raided the fridge. The only thing he fancied was cheese. He found a loaf of bread, hacked off two chunky slices, slapped on butter, chutney, and slabs of cheese. Perfect, especially when washed down with a cold beer. Sandwich in one hand, beer in the other he strolled to the door, and waited for Parjit to return.

Parjit had potential but lacked confidence. He needed to put his foot down and steer out of trouble instead of braking.

"Parjit, if you put your foot on the brake again, I'll get a stone and wedge it in under the pedal. Use the gears, steer through things."

Parjit tried. He was slower than Beverley, but for once kept his foot on the accelerator most of the time. "Better... now go faster."

Parjit did better and Rory pushed him harder. "Faster," he yelled. Parjit responded, and threw the car round bends, squeezing past boulders, scraping the sides on bushes and trees. Rory cheered. Parjit had proved he could get results. The message about not using the brakes was an undoubted success and the driving school idea, a winner.

The sun slowly slipped below the horizon. The transition from light to dark would be complete in less than ten minutes. Rory reckoned he'd done enough for one day. "Great, now turn round and go back to the house."

Parjit was just easing his foot off the accelerator when the headlights picked out what looked like a huge boulder in the middle of the road. It only took a second to realize this was no rock, but a large rhino with a calf at her side.

Parjit slammed both feet on the pedals. The car skidded to a standstill.

"Look. It's the rhino," he yelled excitedly. The rhino turned towards them, her long impressive horn curling upwards as she sniffed in their direction. She took a step forward.

Parjit frantically fumbled with the gear stick trying to find reverse. The colour drained from Parjit's face leaving him a strange pale shade of grey. The rhino peered myopically towards them, its ears pricking up at the sound of the grinding gears and with a haughty flick of its tail trotted off into the bushes, followed by its offspring.

Rory recollected Parjit's reaction.

Parjit had said, "It's the rhino," rather than "It's a rhino." Was it an indication he'd known of the rhino's existence all along?

How could he? There hadn't been any rhino sighted

in the area for years. Was this the reason for Balbinder's interest in Ol Essakut?

It made sense. It was common knowledge Balbinder was a fanatic about hunting, with the biggest collection of big game trophies in Kenya. Balbinder wanted his nephews on the ranch, to give him an excuse to come up and see them, and have access to the ranch in a way few other visitors would get

Balbinder wanted this rhino as a trophy. Its horns were big, and would be worth an obscene amount of money in an illicit deal. The monetary value being less important to Balbinder, the illegality would add an extra buzz and increase the pleasure of the hunt. Rory understood that tingle of excitement. If this rhino was about to become a target, Balbinder wouldn't be the one doing the shooting. He'd save the thrill for himself, with the added bonus of depriving Balbinder of his fun. Balbinder needed to learn not to spread rumours, or to mess with other people's lives.

"Have you seen the rhino before?" Rory asked casually.

Parjit shook his head, and answered, "No, but I hoped I would."

Parjit's answer confirmed his suspicions. He couldn't wait for Balbinder to make his move on the rhino. This would be the most thrilling hunt of his life.

Chapter 21

Rory gave up waiting for Beverley's call to tell him Sandra's reaction to the idea of a rally school. He'd fight if she refused.

Nick should never have handed the responsibility of family land to Sandra. She didn't understand its value being too busy indulging in her own personal power trip, employing a jumped up African as manager. He'd had enough of Simeon Mugo giving him orders. He needed to figure out a way of getting rid of both of them.

Meanwhile he'd get his head round setting up the driving school. Hard to believe Beverley would turn out to be such a distraction. Teaching her should be fun. But before then he needed to sort out the Singhs to his advantage.

He set off to town, dust billowing out behind him, dodging goats, cyclists and other motorists without a second glance. He had ambitious plans for the rally school in his head. Working out how to promote it, and who he could tap for sponsorship became his sole focus.

He stopped at the garage for fuel. Two familiar vehicles were at the pumps. He leapt out of the Land Rover, gave instructions to the pump attendant, and hurried to the office thinking what a great opportunity to spread the word about his new project to a couple of members of the rally driving club. As he walked in their conversation ended mid sentence. The deadly hush, embarrassed faces and the half-hearted greetings made him change his mind.

He watched them scuttle off, pretending he hadn't noticed their behaviour and paid his bill. A third acquaintance came up to the counter behind him. Rory turned to greet the man and got a swift brush off.

"Sorry, can't stop now, I'm late for a meeting."

Rory never even had time to suggest getting together for a drink.

A similar thing happened at the grocers and again at the club. Rory was grateful Beverley had mentioned the rumour going round. It explained everyone's odd behaviour. Time to take action. He positioned himself near the door and waited. The first person who hobbled in was Harry. Before he had a chance to back out, Rory greeted him warmly, put an arm round his shoulder and ordered him a drink.

"Great to see you up and about, how's the knee?" Rory said. He was in no doubt Harry wanted to run. His eyes scoured the room. "I don't suppose your wife's stopped moaning about me and the accident?"

"No chance," Harry muttered.

Rory didn't care about his discomfort. Harry was about to feel worse. He waited for the barman to pour Harry's drink before he set to work.

"Harry, we've been friends for a long time, haven't we?"

Harry took a huge gulp of Tusker from his mug and nervously nodded.

"Someone's been spreading gossip about me," Rory said. "What are they saying?"

"No. Well, not really..." Harry took another swig. "I mean... sort of."

"Go on, spit it out."

"There's talk about Nick's accident."

"What's being said?"

"Someone fixed his brakes."

Rory took a deep breath. This fitted with Beverley's report. He had to keep calm. He had to handle this properly or the situation would get out of hand.

"I suppose some bright spark figured out as I was in charge of motors on the estate, I'm responsible. No wonder everyone has been avoiding me all day. Thanks for your honesty. You don't believe I could have done anything like that? Do you?"

"No... No... Of course not," Harry answered under his breath.

Rory made the most of his discomfort. "Good, nice to know who your friends are. Another beer?" Without waiting for an answer he signalled to the barman to repeat the order and signed the chit.

Harry appeared relieved. He'd probably been surprised Rory had taken the news of the rumour so calmly. Good thing his anger wasn't visible.

The barman delivered the fresh drinks, and Rory set to work.

"Harry, I've a big favour to ask. I need help finding out who started the rumour. This has to be the work of a trouble maker otherwise the police would be involved. They checked the car thoroughly for defects, especially the brakes. If there was evidence of tampering they'd have found it."

"I guess so." Harry answered unconvincingly.

"Anyway, I had nothing to gain from Nick's death. I think someone is out to make trouble and I need to know who, if only to clear my name. Please help me. I can't prove it's a lie on my own," Rory stared into Harry's eyes. "You will help me, won't you?"

"Yes... Okay... I'll do my best," Harry stammered.

"Can you remember who told you? Find out who started the gossip." Rory had him transfixed. "We have to work back to find the source." Harry didn't look happy, but Rory, preying on his good nature added, "It'll mean a lot to me." This produced a half smile, enough for Rory to sense victory.

When the door of the bar opened again, Rory used the opportunity to turn the tables and took control. He didn't give newcomers the chance to shun him instead he marched up and boldly asked where they heard the rumour. His tactic worked well. Surprise that he'd approached them made them forget he was the chief suspect in the initial round of gossip.

To keep the topic alive he kept repeating how he was shocked at the suggestion that Nick's accident had been anything but an accident. Having got their attention he threw in the teaser.

"Why would anyone want to kill Nick?"

Once they started mulling over that one, he slipped in the suggestion, "Perhaps Nick had too many women in his life, and made someone jealous."

The conversation switched to Nick's love life. Rory listened quietly as the merits of Sandra versus Beverley got a thorough airing. Some reckoned Nick had been mad to dump Beverley and her millions in favour of Sandra. They played right into his hands. Time to give them another snippet of information to set their tongues wagging harder. "I know for a fact even after the wedding Nick was still playing around with Beverley."

There was a muttering of disbelief all round.

"Are you sure?" Harry whispered.

"Absolutely, and I'm pretty sure Sandra found out," he answered quietly to Harry, but not so quietly the others wouldn't hear.

"You...don't think Sandra...?" Harry asked, looking shocked at the prospect.

"Oh no," Rory answered, trying to sound horrified. "Even if she had found out, I can't imagine her taking such drastic steps. I doubt she would know how either."

He didn't need to say more. He made an excuse to leave the bar for a moment, to let this latest snippet of gossip ping-pong back and forth in his absence. He figured the assembled gathering would instantly take on the role of judge and jury, especially if he wasn't present.

He hovered outside the door, pretending to read the flyers on the board, listening to the excited voices in the bar.

"She has to be the main suspect. She had the most to gain."

"You mean the estate?"

"Yes, of course, must be worth millions."

"But that's all tied up in a trust for his kids?"

"Yes, but no one discovered that until after he died."

Rory was enjoying this. He couldn't let such a good opportunity go to waste. The more suspects involved with Nick's death the sooner the rumour would lose its power. He waited patiently for just the right moment, then slipped back into the bar and rejoined the conversation.

"Ask yourself, who might have wanted Nick out of the way."

"What do you mean?" Harry asked.

"Oh, I shouldn't say."

"Bloody hell, if a nut case is running loose, we need to know," someone at the bar chipped in.

"There a long list of people he's upset. Hank

Bradley for instance. He's been after Beverley Wyatt for years, and getting nowhere fast while Nick was alive. Don't forget Martin Owen? What's he come back for? They had a major disagreement a couple of years back. I'm sure there are plenty more candidates if you start delving."

Rory moved to order a round of drinks, leaving the others to continue with the discussion.

"Did anyone ever find out what the row with Martin was about?" one man said.

"No. Only that Nick shot him and he was lucky to survive. I believe he slipped over the border to Somalia to avoid getting involved with the police here," answered another.

His timely comments spun the conversation round and round, until none of them had any idea who to suspect.

Rory finished his drink and took his leave of them, boldly stating, "I'd better go, I should warn Sandra what's being said about the accident." The reaction from his audience was better than he had expected. Some even appeared sorry he'd need to break such news, others were impressed by his thoughtfulness, even though only minutes before they'd put both of them in the dock as guilty.

Once he was back in the Land Rover he remembered he hadn't told anyone about the rally driving school, but wasn't bothered. The rumour changed everything, and even though he had succeeded in turning the situation to his advantage, he couldn't alter the fact the rumour existed.

The only person who'd hinted suspicion was Balbinder Singh. What would Balbinder gain from tarnishing his reputation? Whatever it was, Rory had no intention of letting anyone manipulate him.

Chapter 22

Jealousy, the legacy Nick had left her, ruined any chance of her trusting Martin. She wanted to trust him. She needed to trust him. But her fears were compounded by one short paragraph in Nick's journal that suggested Martin was after Ol Essakut.

All night and most of the day she had been wondering why, of all the pages for the diary to fall open on, that had been the one. More puzzling was why she found his comments so hard to accept. Nick never gave any cause for her to believe any rivalry existed between Martin and himself. If anything, he gave the impression he missed Martin and would renew his friendship if the opportunity presented itself. The only logical explanation being Nick had written this in the heat of the moment, blaming Martin, rather than Helen and Rory. Her doubts meant another visit to the gun room when the house went quiet.

The children played quietly on the floor of the sitting room, giving her a chance to read the list of plants Amina needed paintings of for the next book.

The peace was disturbed by the sound of Rory's clumpy footsteps on the porch. She had nowhere to hide. Sandra opened the door, planting herself in such a way as to block the entrance. She would not let him in. He clutched a dirty cardboard box.

"I wanted to say thank you for agreeing to the

driving school. I promise you won't regret giving the go ahead."

Sandra already did, and wanted to remind him of her restrictions. "I only agreed to a trial. Any damage to the environment and the whole idea stops, and once tourist numbers pick up again you'll be restricted to off peak months."

He responded with a grudging shrug.

"I've brought something for the children," he said, and called out, "Sam, come and get your present."

Both children came hurtling out to see what he'd brought. He put the box on the floor and flipped the lid open with a flourish. The smell of rotting flesh made Sandra want to gag.

A filthy, maggot-ridden dead mongoose lay in the box giving off a vile stench. Emma began screaming hysterically, Sandra snatched her up to comfort her, letting her bury her face in her shoulder. Sam, not so squeamish, leant over the box transfixed with morbid fascination.

Rory had a satisfied grin on his face as he started to tell Sam in detail what to do with his gift.

"Bury this in the garden, after a few weeks, all the flesh will rot down, eaten by worms, ants and other bugs and you'll find a clean skeleton."

This description made Emma even more hysterical

"For God's sake Rory, get that thing out of here."

"Why?" he snapped. "My present not good enough?" His fists balled and his face flushed in a threatening way. "I suppose Martin filled your head with stories about me?"

"This has nothing to do with Martin or anybody else. A stinking animal corpse is not a suitable present for a three year old."

"Tell him, he seems interested enough," he said,

pointing to Sam. Sam held his nose with one hand, pushing back the lid of the box with the other, peering into it. “They need to learn about life and death at some point, especially if they’re going to stay on the ranch,” Rory added with the same smug expression.

Emma’s high pitched screams brought Wanjiru and Juma running to find out what the fuss was about. Rupee came with them and immediately stuck his head in the box. Sam tried to restrain him, which meant that he had to let go of his nose and the lid of the box and wrestle with the puppy on the floor.

Sandra had to admit, Rory was right, Sam’s fascination evident. But he was too young and needed protecting from the harshness of life. She had to find a compromise.

“What a stink, please leave it outside.”

“Okay,” he answered, shoving the box away with his foot. Sam had dragged Rupee away, Wanjiru caught his collar. Sam went to follow Rory. Sandra grabbed his arm to stop him.

“Wanjiru, take Rupee to the kitchen. Juma, please find the gardener.” Sandra hugged Emma even tighter. “Ask him to bury that in the vegetable garden.” Juma nodded and without further instruction picked up the stinking box, holding it at arm’s length, and vanished round the corner of the building to search for the gardener. Sam wriggled free and took off after Juma.

Juma probably thought she was mad, but at this point she didn’t care. All she wanted was the mongoose to disappear, Emma to calm down and to keep the peace. She watched from the doorway as Sam ran off determined not to miss the burial of his inappropriate gift.

Rory had a satisfied smirk on his face as he said, “It’s a tough world. A healthy dose of reality won’t hurt."

Since when had he become a child expert? The twins were far too young to face exposure to death in such a gruesome way

"Well I'm sorry, I disagree. They've had to deal with enough already, I don't want them upset again," she said with as much authority as she could muster and without showing how much his presence unsettled her.

"Don't blame me if they grow up scared of life. You're never too young to face reality. Nick would have agreed."

"I don't care, I'm in charge and I'll be the judge of what's good for them. Now if you don't mind, I'd like you to go so I can calm Emma down."

Rory shrugged and sauntered off. She wished she could pinpoint how Rory had changed. Everything seemed different, his tone of voice, his brusque remarks, his scruffy attire, his seeming lack of commitment to his work. The changes had begun the week Nick died. His reaction to the armed attack at the camp had intensified her perception of the change in him. He had become unpredictable. Maybe finding out about his connection to the Lander family made her more conscious of the threat he posed? For a moment she wished she hadn't pushed Martin away.

Emma was calmer by the time Sam came bouncing back into the room, determined to regale them with a shovel by shovel description of the internment of his dead mongoose. His detailed account set Emma off again.

This time she managed to get out the words "Mummy and Daddy."

Sandra's heart ached for her, how could she stop the tears and undo the damage Rory had done? The poor child wanted to know if what Rory described had happened to her Mummy and Daddy.

Sandra had no idea what to say, her answer mattered, it had to be truthful, because whatever words she chose would stay with Emma for the rest of her life.

She began by explaining that when someone died they went to heaven, and the body that was buried didn't feel anything, and yes after a long time it did disappear because we were made that way, not because of ants and worms. Emma didn't like her answer but didn't seem to want more detail. Sandra suspected a complete denial would have been preferable, but hadn't dared lie. A very subdued child clung to Sandra until Rupee bounded in providing a diversion.

Sandra had supper with the children, put them in their own beds, and read them several stories. Once they had settled down she told Wanjiru to lock up and sat in front of the fire to read some papers Simeon had left for her. She found herself going through them and not remembering what she had read. She pushed them to one side, and lay back on the settee watching the flames flickering in the grate. She ought to open the gun room and see what else lay hidden in there that might make sense of the animosity between Martin and Rory. Hammering on the front door shattered her peace.

Rory was back.

"Let me in," he called out. "We need to talk." His slurred speech, a warning to keep the door firmly closed.

"Sorry Rory, I'm tired, and I'm on my way to bed. Unless it's something important, come back in the morning."

"Important? Don't you think taking over all the land that belongs to me is important enough?"

"I haven't taken anything of yours. I'm only doing what Nick wanted."

"Well, he stole the land from me."

"I've no idea what you're on about. Let's talk tomorrow."

"What, when lover-boy is back? Do you think Martin cares for you? Think again... he's only interested because through you he can get my land. He's the same with Beverley... he's probably with her right now... giving her the same line he gave you earlier... he'll try to poison your mind against me. He's done it once before, he tried to get Nick to hate me. He failed. He's the one who started the rumour going that Nick's death wasn't an accident. He doesn't know your secret, does he? You didn't tell him about finding Nick and Beverley together the day he died. I'll bet you never told anyone. If they find out now, they're going to wonder why you kept quiet... they'll think you wanted him dead."

"That's not true."

"You'll be a prime suspect. You stood to gain the most from his death."

"Please go away," she pleaded. Rory wasn't listening.

"You think you can butter me up by giving me permission to drive around the property, and allowing me to live here. Well, I don't need anyone's permission. It's my land, and I'll do what I bloody well want."

"Please don't wake the children. We can talk in the morning."

Rory yelled back, "No! I want to talk now. Why should I care about those brats?" He started hammering on the door again with his fists. Emma called her name. Sandra rushed up to the bedroom to calm her. Sam was awake too, but wasn't as bothered by Rory's shouting as Emma.

"It's all right. Rory's being a bit silly. He'll go away soon," she told them, praying it was true. Rory now seemed to be shouting at someone else. She peeped out of the window. The watchman had come to investigate the noise. Rory hurled abuse at him. She lay down on the bed, the children on either side and waited for the noise to die down. Eventually, Rory shut up and stomped away across the gravel driveway. The children's breathing settled to a steady rhythm. The creak of the wooden bench on the verandah told her the watchman had chosen this as his sentry post. Peace descended on the house.

She slipped out of the bedroom and headed downstairs and she pulled back the curtain to thank the watchman for dealing with Rory.

The whole episode had unsettled her. She completed the routine tasks of putting the fire guard in place and turning out the lights. She was too emotionally exhausted to face opening the gun room. Those secrets could wait a little longer.

Sandra slept badly, unable to put Rory's comments out of her mind. Perhaps he had a legal claim on the Lander's land. Even if he found proof, Sandra was certain Nick's lawyers would insist on sticking to the terms of the trust set up in the twin's names. The last thing she needed was a battle for possession. Running Ol Essakut was challenging enough without a legal fight.

She lay wondering how Nick would deal with Rory if approached with the same demands. Perhaps he had, and Nick refused to give in, even though there was proof that Rory probably had a valid claim to ownership. She couldn't pretend Nick didn't know. Nick writing Rory's name on the family tree proved he did. Had greed, selfishness, or jealousy made him keep the secret, probably a mixture of all of those things, which made Nick less kind hearted than she believed him to be.

When she came down in the morning, Wanjiru and Juma hovered over her with more concern than usual. The watchman must have spread the word about Rory's visit. Her protection team was in action. The gardener was searching for weeds in an empty flowerbed near the front door. Juma responded to her puzzled look.

"Better, in case Mr Rory comes back."

Sandra hadn't the heart to tell him he shouldn't fuss over her. Maybe she should be grateful for his concern. Drink seemed to have made Rory so unpleasant. But she didn't want the staff to think she was scared of him, drunk or sober.

Simeon appeared half an hour later, fully aware of the previous night's events, offering to intervene. "I can talk to him if you want."

"I don't want a fuss. The man was drunk, end of story. Honestly you needn't worry," she answered, wishing she spoke the truth.

"You're mad to agree to let him run a rally driving school on the ranch. Have you thought everything through?"

"Yes and I have my reasons."

"Does Martin know?"

"He persuaded me."

"Martin? He must have gone mad too. Did he say why?"

"Yes, something to do with finding out what

Balbinder Singh is up to."

"I hope you gave yourself a let out clause. If you haven't you'll have regrets."

"I wish everyone would stop fussing. I know what I'm doing," she snapped.

"I was under the impression you and Martin had fallen out. I hope Rory's scheme has nothing to do with the row?"

"Has he been talking about me?"

"No, that's why I wondered what was going on."

"Haven't you got anything better to do, than speculate about my life?"

"I give in. Amina says you need a break. Why don't you let Jenny have the children for a few days and go down to Nairobi and see her, I know she'd love the company."

The suggestion made sense. But until she could tell Simeon about the rhino she couldn't possibly face Amina.

"I'll think about it." she answered.

Simeon looked pleased with himself at her near capitulation.

"I'm sorry. I'm coming down with something. Can you carry on running things for the moment, leave me out of decision making unless something drastic crops up," Sandra asked, not sure if her request was motivated by her physical condition or purely to ease her guilt at allowing Martin to give her doubts over Simeon's honesty. Hank had managed to trap the culprits who stole the duplicated supplies. Simeon completely vindicated was unaware he'd ever been a suspect.

She watched him leave and went into the dining room wishing she had some energy to start on one of the paintings Amina needed for the next book.

Just before lunch Rory strode over to the house. Sandra greeted him at the door, and didn't invite him in.

"Sorry about last night, had a bit too much to drink, hope I didn't make too big a fool of myself," Rory muttered. "Thought the children might like this," he said, proffering another grubby cardboard box.

Sandra didn't take it, she said, "What's in it?"

"An injured bush-baby, they can make it a pet."

"No, Rory, take it to the vet at the Education centre, they can treat it and release it back into the wild. And I'd appreciate it if you stopped offering the children unsuitable gifts. They don't need or want wild animals as pets."

"What about the dik-dik you keep in the garden?" he snapped back at her.

Sandra was stumped for an answer, The dik-dik had been tamed long before she came, but before she could make an excuse, Rory was off again.

"You want me to leave them alone, right? Not good enough for them?"

"No, just your choice of presents. You forget how young they are."

"Don't waste your breath lying to me. I know what you think about me. I don't care, I'm here to stay, like it or not." And with that he dumped the box on the step and strode off towards his house.

As she watched him go, she knew she needed to get away, even if her reasons were not the ones Simeon had in mind. Getting legal advice about Rory's claim had become top priority.

Chapter 23

Martin had to do something about the scrawny cattle still on his land. They needed fattening up prior to selling. He arranged for a delivery of feed and talked to the one remaining herdsman. Now he must reacquaint himself with the house.

He struggled to adjust to ownership and the prospect of living on the property on his own. The house being so quiet unsettled him. His mother had always been bustling about, supervising the house staff, ensuring the larder was filled and the gardens beautifully maintained.

Without her the atmosphere was different. She must have been lonely here after his father died, and he moved away. Suggestions that she live in town were brushed aside as she swore this was the only place she wanted to live. The film of dust on the furniture, the faded chaircovers and curtains, the absence of the scent of fresh flowers, filled him with regrets.

Loneliness and isolation hit him. He wished he had come back more often to see her. She refused to let anyone tell him about her illness, so he missed the chance to spend time with her before her death. Since her funeral his fight with Nick provided the perfect excuse to avoid facing up to what Chui Farm represented.

The longer he spent alone in the building the more doubtful he became that he could endure the isolation.

This place needed love and laughter to dispel the current mausoleum status. It needed to become a home, a place to love, and be loved. His disconnection from Sandra made that particular dream seem unreachable.

He forced himself to explore every room in the house, to discover exactly what he'd inherited, and the damage his neglect had done. As he went round he made a mental lists of things to attend to. He left his mother's bedroom until last, bracing himself to face the memories. He sat on her bed breathing in the faint scent of the flowery perfume he associated with her. On her bedside was a beautiful little enamel alarm clock, which he set and wound. The gentle tick filled the silence. Next, he picked up a small, badly tarnished, ornate silver photo frame, one he remembered well, a picture of himself and his sister, aged about three, taken just before his sister died. He moved towards the light to get a better view. The dust on the glass blurred the faded photo. He licked his finger and wiped the glass clean. For a minute he thought someone had replaced the photo with a different one, but decided the fading made the faces hard to pick out. He promised himself to check the family albums and replace the original with a better copy. He slipped the little picture frame into his pocket.

The empty house had little appeal, so the next day he headed off back to Nairobi to find out more about Balbinder Singh. He finally checked into the Norfolk Hotel late in the evening, but had one more task to face before he could rest.

Time to make his apologies and save a friendship. "Simeon, Sorry to call so late. Can we meet?"

"I'm in Nairobi, I'll be back in Nanyuki

tomorrow," Simeon answered.

"Tonight. I'm staying at the Norfolk."

"I thought you were on the ranch. Can't you tell me over the phone."

"I'd rather talk face-to-face."

"Okay, give me ten minutes."

Martin sat on the verandah terrace sipping a coffee while he waited, praying Simeon would forgive him. Losing a friend was not what he needed.

The terrace was populated with a typically cosmopolitan collection of khaki clad American tourists, turbaned Indians with elegant sari-wearing wives, smartly dressed African businessmen, and a few boisterous, beer filled customers who were giving the staff a hard time.

Simeon arrived, pulled up a chair and sat opposite Martin.

"Drink?" Martin asked.

"Coffee," he answered, signalling to the waiter, pointing at Martin's cup. "Okay, what's so important you had to drag me out at this hour?"

No point in skirting the issue, better to come straight out with the truth. "I owe you an apology. I insisted on you being kept in the dark about the missing supplies."

Simeon said nothing. Martin had to justify his behaviour. "Working in war zones teaches you to be cautious about trust. Mistakes cost lives. We work on a need to know basis. A habit I need to break."

"Fine, but half truths are not enough," Simeon answered.

"Sorry?"

"When the trouble with the duplicated supplies going missing got sorted, Sandra apologised. She said Hank begged her not to speak up because my name was on the order and the cheque. I accept the logic there. I'd insist on the same myself. But she's kept something else back."

"You're right. She wanted you involved but I insisted on keeping it secret."

"So what's the big mystery?"

"Rhino, a female with a calf, out on the west ridge."

"Why the secrecy?"

"We spotted three Samburu warriors in full tribal dress talking to Parjit, Lalji and Vejay in the same area. The strange part is the Singh boys denied seeing anyone."

"Why tell me now?"

"I persuaded Sandra to agree to Rory running a rally driving school."

"She told me. I think it's a bloody crazy idea."

"True, but I needed a good excuse to talk to Balbinder Singh. He's been giving me the run around. At first he sounded happy to talk about his interest in motor sports, an hour later he postponed."

"He's a busy man."

"Yes, but I made another appointment which he also cancelled. I'm used to people who feel threatened by publicity ducking out, but Balbinder is the sort who actively promotes himself. He's got no reason to suspect my interest is anything but genuine."

"So why the fascination with him?"

"Remember Jacob said something about hearing one of the gang saying they wouldn't get paid if they didn't do the job properly? Another member of the gang responded with some rude remark about a Singh. It didn't make sense at the time, but when Parjit accused Jacob of stealing, I figured there might be a connection."

"Sorry, I don't follow."

"The attack on the camps wasn't about robbing tourists, it was designed to get tours cancelled. Less people on Ol Essakut means the less chance of being seen. I asked Jacob to watch the three nephews. They considered him a threat, so framed him to get him off the ranch."

"Too far fetched for me."

"Not when you take into account the only trophy missing in Balbinder's collection is a black rhino."

"Your devious mind calculated Balbinder set everything up so he can kill a rhino?" Simeon's disbelief was clear.

"Yes."

"So explain how he discovered the rhino when we didn't?"

"The three Samburu tribesmen we spotted the other day. Jacob's been asking around and discovered they're trackers who've worked for Balbinder for years. One of them blames Rory for his limp. He says when he was a child Rory shot him, but the police never did anything about it. Anyway, that's how Balbinder found out. They told him which is why he got his nephews installed on the ranch."

Simeon raised his eyebrows. "I don't get it. They only turned up because Rory wrote off his rally car."

"That gave them a legitimate reason to be on the ranch and to go driving to parts not normally covered by tourists."

"Where does Rory fit in?"

"God knows," Martin said. "Nick did some strange things in his life but granting Rory the right to live in the Lander's house tops the list."

Simeon shrugged as if to say he didn't understand it either.

"Listen Simeon, after the way I've behaved I don't deserve any favours, but I need help."

"Try me."

"Sandra's gone cold on me, she virtually chucked me out of the house, and I've no idea what I did to upset her."

"She wouldn't like secrets between friends."

"Maybe, but the problem is more serious than that. Tell her you're up to date about the rhino, but don't tell anyone else, especially not Beverley or Hank."

"Listen to yourself! One minute you're regretting not being open with people, and then you're asking me to lie. Why shouldn't they be told?"

"Beverley's hounding me to sign the contract for the sale, and to be honest, I'm having second thoughts. If she knows about the rhino, my life won't be worth living."

"Okay, that's a fairly good reason, but if you don't sell, what will you do?"

"Still undecided."

"How are you and Hank getting on? Is he putting pressure on you to close the deal?"

Simeon's question intrigued him. "Yes, but I thought that was because Beverley was behind it. Is there something else going on?"

"Just wondered how he was handling the competition."

"Competition? Sorry you lost me."

"Hank's insanely jealous of the attention Beverley gives you."

"I've never given her any encouragement. Believe me nothing is going on there."

"Maybe not, but he won't know. The poor guy is nuts about her. He went through agony when Nick was alive, sitting and watching while she made a fool of herself. He was delighted when Nick married Sandra. He thought he was finally in with a chance. Beverley never stopped trying to win Nick back, and took off back to the States after he died. Hank hopes if she buys your place she'll come back to stay."

"Will she?"

"Good question. Hank got her interested in Ol Essakut. I don't think he expected her to hand over management control of her land to Nick. Or that Sandra would gain control of everything on his death."

"Run that past me again. Sandra controls Beverley's land?"

"Yes, and some of Hank's too."

"How does that work?"

"They had all signed an agreement with Nick. Guess they didn't read the small print. Sandra replaced Nick, and coped remarkably well. Everyone's been supportive. Hank gets to handle the petty cash."

"I got the impression he did more?"

"Only so he can protect his interests."

"So how did he take your appointment as manager?"

"Surprisingly, better than most people. We get on fine, even though he's plotting to take over."

"But Hank was the one who started negotiating to buy my land for Beverley long before Nick died."

"Yes, Nick had no spare cash. I think he hoped owning more land would shift the balance of power at Ol Essakut."

"War reporting must have deadened my senses. What else did I miss?"

"Beverley is the reason Sandra booted you out."

"But I'm not interested in Beverley."

"That's not the impression she's conveyed to Sandra."

For a brief moment Martin almost wished he was back on the front line. Working as a war correspondent was less complicated than dealing with women.

"Will you talk to Sandra?"

"Amina might do better. I'll ask what she suggests."

"Thanks."

"Where do we go from here?"

"I've got someone watching Balbinder. If he heads up to the ranch I'll know. Meanwhile we carry on as normal. And if I do anything that jeopardizes our friendship again, kick me hard."

Simeon laughed. "We've been friends too long. Nothing can damage our friendship. You had your reasons. Thanks for the apology. I'll make sure Amina gets in touch in the morning."

Amina called and didn't give him much hope for a swift resolution of the situation. Her advice was to keep in touch with regular calls offering support and practical help, and to make sure if Sandra did accept any offer of help, not to make her feel obligated to repay in any way.

"Build her trust," Amina said.

"I'll do my best, but it would be much easier if I could actually see her."

"I've persuaded her to come to the races at the weekend. Neutral territory is a good idea. Turn up and I'll steer her in your direction."

"I'll be there," he promised.

Chapter 24

The guilt at invading Nick's privacy got worse every time she unlocked the gun room door. She kept to night time visits, when the staff left and the doors were locked leaving her alone. Her discomfort grew stronger with each sortie, as did the relief of escaping the claustrophobic room and putting the key back in the secret compartment of the desk.

She had found and made sense of the haphazard filing system, and become less overwhelmed by the volume of documents. She'd unearthed several files relating to the Lander family, but nothing in them confirmed the pencilled information on the family tree.

Her most disconcerting discovery was a batch of bulging files containing extremely personal information about members of the consortium and other people living in the area. Some of the information, so personal, and embarrassing to read that she worried she might react badly if she met those concerned. The fact that the files existed left her with the sickening notion Nick had used the information to manipulate and control the parties involved. She wanted no part in anything like that, but having seen them, she wondered what to do. Burning them seemed a sensible option. She'd no desire to use the information.

She'd unearthed all Nick's journals. The majority of the black hardback books with red cloth spines, fitting Martin's description, were in three large boxes, on a high shelf, only accessible by climbing onto a chair to lift them down. The others turned up randomly mixed in with other papers. She put them all together, lining them up on the floor, in consecutive order, from prep school, until just after he met her, weeks before their marriage.

Confronted by so many she wondered how far back she needed to go to find relevant information about Rory, Helen, or Martin. She had no idea of the exact dates of events which might reveal the most important facts. The prospect of ploughing her way through all of them was daunting. Instinct instructed her to be systematic. She took a handful of the early ones sat by the fire and thumbed through them.

She found several comments in the early ones about Martin, but nothing about Helen or Rory, so she exchanged them for the next in sequence. The same applied to these. She tried again. This time enjoying the passages where Nick had written about adventures with Martin and Simeon, including his version of the forest encounter with the buffalo, which echoed the story Martin recounted to her soon after they met.

She read on, Rory barely merited a mention and what was there appeared rather hostile in nature. In the next volume, he described Helen as a scrawny nuisance. Clearly, girls and Helen in particular, did not fit in with Nick's tough adventurous world.

She persevered, and discovered the entry for the flood that she and Martin had talked about. Nick gave details of the damage, how each of the properties became isolated from the outside world and each other, by the sheer volume of water. His vivid description of the roads becoming slippery quagmires, and the dry stream beds turning into raging torrents, his graphic report of the aftermath made her picture the hundreds of bloated carcasses of cattle, goats, and wild animals swept down the rivers caught in the branches and trunks of trees torn out of the ground along the river's edge. He and Martin marked the high water line at the worst places, and salvaged several animal skins to cure to make rugs. Sandra looked round the room, realizing the skins he talked about in his diary were still in use, including the zebra rug on the floor, and a couple of others hanging on the walls. She had often wondered how someone so fanatical about conservation could adorn his walls with hunting trophies. Now she understood he hadn't killed these animals, only salvaged the hides. His action made her happier about keeping the skins on display.

She pressed on, flipped through a few more, and decided to stop. She replaced the journals she'd skimmed through, and picked up the last six journals to take with her to read in Nairobi.

Sandra had given in too easily to Simeon and Amina's suggestion she go to Nairobi. The truth was that Rory's behaviour made her eager to escape, though she'd never admit her fear to them or even to Jenny who phoned offering to have the children.

Sandra thought Jenny might have second thoughts when she found out the dog would be included in the deal. "You do realize having the children means you get Rupee as well?"

"Rupee?"

"A manic, unhouse-trained mongrel."

"Do I have to?"

"Yes, the children won't leave home without him."

"We'll manage."

The other problem she had was that Amina wanted to pin her down to go shopping, and to the publishers, and do a hundred and one other mundane tasks, which she had neither the desire nor the intention of doing.

"Sorry, I need to catch up with some pictures for you. Now they've trimmed the plaster on my hand I'm able to paint again." she told her friend firmly on the phone. "I'm not in the mood to shop or visit the publishers. They'd rather I finished the paintings and avoid missing whatever deadline they set."

"Fine, but I'd still like you to come with me to the races on Saturday. I can't let you turn into a recluse." Amina's compromise was hard to refuse.

"Okay, on one condition. I agree to go racing and you leave me in peace."

"Deal," Amina answered, seeming content with her response.

Sandra loved the little guest house in the suburbs of Nairobi where she lived before she married Nick. She maintained the lease because having a base in town enabled her to work if she wanted to between other commitments. Now it provided a haven. The tranquillity of the place removed her from the pressures of the ranch. The biggest bonus of all, Rory didn't live nearby, and neither Martin nor Beverley had cause to contact her here.

Her fear of trusting Martin had her searching for things to justify her doubts. His insistence that Simeon should not be told about the rhino had been a real concern. Rory's comment about Martin only being interested in the land had not helped. Rory's bitterness should have made her dismiss the remark, but the similarity to an entry in Nick's diary, gave it credence.

On a personal level, forgetting the night spent together was impossible. Beverley's call had tarnished the moment, and ensured the relationship could not survive. Even if she believed Martin when he said

Beverley meant nothing to him, the problem wouldn't go away.

To give him credit, Martin had been open about his relationship with Beverley. He didn't have to tell her. He was entitled to a past, but his admission added to her guilt that she hadn't told him the full story of Nick's betrayal and Beverley's role. Being the third side of a triangle was a position she never intended reliving. The fact that Beverley was currently flirting with Rory didn't fool her either. Beverley's continued interest in Martin was obvious.

Rose, the good natured house-girl, shared with the main house, greeted her effusively and brought her a pot of tea. Sandra put up with her fussing while she set up her painting easel, making her feel guilty she didn't require anything else.

No one understood her need for solitude. She sipped the tea, and read more of Nick's diaries, hoping something in them would allow her to trust Martin again.

She read for about an hour. The boyhood friendship between Martin, Simeon and Nick did seem to grow stronger as each year passed, while dismissive and derisory comments about Rory became more frequent. The more she read the more her perception of Nick altered. The way he wrote about people was contrary to his behaviour towards them in real life. This view of him made her so uncomfortable she pushed the diaries aside.

She played with her sketch pad but the mood for drawing didn't materialize. It was no good. One thing still hung over her waiting for action, talking to someone about the crash and dealing with the consequences.

The drive from Nanyuki to Nairobi had been more

stressful than ever. The flare up of tribal tension after elections more than a year ago, meant few people would drive at night. The situation had flared up again particularly in Karatina, with a spate of killings in the town. Gangs of youths crowded slow moving traffic going through the town, making her nervous. She'd had to negotiate more than ten armed police road blocks. Instead of making her more secure, their existence served as a sinister threat of trouble.

She must overcome her renewed terror of flying, if only so that she could travel as a passenger. There was no logic to the crazy notion that facing this demon might give her the power and confidence to carry on running the ranch.

One phone call got the ball rolling. Jim Standish who helped her first time round as her flying instructor invited her to his house to discuss the problem.

He lived nearby, which didn't give her time to change her mind. When she got to his house, Jim got into her car and said, "Drive to the aerodrome."

The way he gave instructions made her respond without a fight. Jim, though grey haired and weather-beaten, had never lost his air force bearing.

"But I just wanted to talk about it," she pleaded, knowing she was wasting her breath.

"I know, but I need a lift, and we can talk on the way."

Sandra didn't believe him but did what he asked.

"So what's the problem?" he said, as they pulled out of his drive.

Where should she start? Perhaps mention how important it was for her to overcome her fear. Or confess the thought of going up in a plane sent a shiver down her spine. Even the thought of driving into the carpark at the aerodrome had her breaking out in a sweat.

Why had she called him? She couldn't do this. She was about to say so, when he touched her arm, and said, "Slow down, the gateway is there on the left, just beyond the jacaranda tree."

She pulled in as instructed. Jim pointed out a parking space on the far side under another jacaranda that had deposited a thick carpet of pale blue blossoms on the ground. "Perfect. You'll get a little shade from the tree when the sun goes round," he said. "Make the drive home more comfortable."

She didn't think she'd hang about long enough to benefit from any shade the tree might offer.

"You're having second thoughts, aren't you?" he said, as he got out of the car.

Sandra nodded. He opened her door, reached in, took the key out of the ignition and took her hand. "Come, I promise I won't make you do anything you're not comfortable with." he said, leading her towards his plane. "I think you should sit in the cockpit. Spend some time watching planes take off and land. With about one flight per minute, you won't have time to get bored."

She remembered him telling her the airport had nearly as many flights per day as Heathrow, with an incredible record of safety.

"I've got to go up to the office to see someone," he said. "When I come back, if you want we can go up for a short spin... to get you used to the feel of being airborne."

She noticed a bench to one side. "I'd rather wait there," she said, pointing to it.

"Fine. But don't you dare disappear! Remember you're my transport home."

Sandra sat watching flight after flight arrive and

depart. Flying Doctor, Desert Locust patrol, private planes, the occasional charter flight and learner pilots doing frequent take off and landing practice. Dozens of planes taxied up the runway, and then flew past on take off. She talked herself through each landing as if she were bringing down the plane herself.

Jim returned with two polystyrene cups filled with coffee.

"Fancy getting on board yet?" She shook her head. He didn't give up. "No need to take the controls. If you prefer we can talk through take off, flight, and landing procedures. Then if you feel a bit more comfortable, we could go up, circle round, and come back down again."

Sandra stayed firmly glued to the bench. "What are the chances of it working?" she asked.

"A lot better than the first time when Nick brought you here. Then you didn't know what it was like to fly. You only knew how to be afraid. The fact that you have come to me at all is enough. You'll do it, but maybe not today. There's no hurry. It might be better if you wait until your plaster comes off before you attempt to take the controls again."

"Thanks. You're probably right," she answered, grateful to him for giving her an easy let out. She couldn't pinpoint what it was about Jim that had inspired confidence in her last time, and she hoped he could do it again. She smiled, he had been right to bring her here. She felt less pressured by the prospect of going up again, even if she couldn't quite face it today. Jim reminded her of someone, but she couldn't quite recall who. They sipped their coffee and then Jim asked, "Have you talked to anyone about the accident?"

Sandra shook her head, terrified he'd demand a

blow by blow description.

"It doesn't matter," he said. "If you find while we're working through this you want to talk, I'm here to listen. Let's just go for a wander and have a look at a few of the planes on the hard standing outside the hangar."

"Are you testing me to see if I'll make a run for it?" she said, with a smile.

"Oh no, you have more pluck than that," he answered, as they wandered out through the gate in the hedge. They walked on until they came to several old planes lined up, some being restored, some never likely to fly again, others in bits, broken up for spare parts. A few were kept in working order for displays, among them mono-planes, bi-planes, and even an old Catalina. She wasn't really paying much attention as Jim prattled on about the merit of one over the other. It was only when he stopped talking, cupped his hand under her elbow and tried to turn her away that she focussed on the mangled remains of one particular plane. She shivered and wanted to throw up. The wreck matched the plane in the nightmare which had haunted her most of her life.

Jim put his arm around her shoulder supporting her. He stayed quite still, then after a while he said quietly, "Sorry."

She saw concern in his eyes. "Why sorry?" she managed to ask as she glanced back at the wreck.

"I forgot... I shouldn't have brought you down here... "

"I don't understand,"

"That's the plane your father died in." His voice so quiet, so full of pain, she regretted putting him in this awkward position.

His words sank in.

"This... this one?" Then a flood of questions tumbled out. "Who told you? How can you be certain?"

"Your father was a friend of mine," Jim said.

His revelation silenced her for a second. She had to ask, "How did you know he was my father?"

"When I first met you and heard your name I guessed your fear was caused by the crash."

"Why didn't you say something?"

"You didn't seem keen to explain your fear," he answered. "I didn't want to upset you further. How much do you remember?"

"Nothing. No recollection at all."

"And you weren't curious enough to find out?"

"No. I was far too busy blocking the whole thing from my mind. I never thought of seeing what records existed."

"That figures. Shall I fill you in?" She nodded and he continued. "These were reliable planes, and according to the accident report, there was nothing mechanically wrong. A bird strike was the most likely cause of the accident."

"I remember birds, a big flock, but I never connected them with the crash."

"Well, it is a miracle more strikes don't occur. Locating the crash site took a long time. The plane came down in the forest, in the late afternoon, and by the time the alarm went out darkness prevented a search team from going out. Overhanging trees hid the plane. They found it at noon the following day, and spent another six hours getting a rescue team through the forest to reach the plane to rescue you. Do you remember any of that?"

"No. In my dream I'm alone. No one answers me, and my foot hurts."

"You've never talked to anyone about this, have you?"

"No. Is it obvious?"

"Only to someone who's been in the same position."

"You?"

"Yes."

"What should I do?"

"Write down every detail, getting the whole thing clear in your mind helps. Everyone who's done this has thanked me afterwards, especially the people who blamed themselves for doing something to contribute to the accident."

"I'll try. Thank you."

"Do the same for both accidents." he said, "not just the one you dream about."

"But I know why the second one happened."

"Doesn't matter, write every detail down. The insurance company will want the information anyway. I assume you'll put in a claim."

Sandra was too embarrassed to admit an insurance claim had never entered her head. Maybe she had a subconscious avoidance of having to admit she'd been shot down.

"They'll want every detail from take off until you knew you had a problem. I'm surprised the accident boys haven't been clamouring for details."

He must have sensed her reluctance to talk, and left her for a while on her own. When he came back, he told her about his conversation with Bill Huxter, the American beaten up during the attack on the ranch. Jim told Sandra he thought Bill had been genuine when he offered to fund a replacement plane, because he understood how vital a plane was for the work they did on the ranch.

Chapter 25

Martin trawled bars talking to anyone and everyone trying to find out more about Balbinder Singh and his business dealings. Balbinder was involved in so many different enterprises including a business trading with the Far East, which would provide perfect cover for smuggling goods out of the country. Afraid Balbinder might discover his interest, he stopped digging.

He called Sandra and offered to take her out for dinner. She politely refused, keeping the conversation short, leaving him more frustrated than he had been before speaking to her. Only the thought of seeing her at the races kept him from calling her again.

He had always enjoyed going to the Ngong race course, even though he had little interest in horses or gambling. This was one of the few places in Kenya where alterations had been minimal since his childhood. The same didn't apply to the once empty tract of land on the other side of the road. The flat black cotton plain had vanished beneath a crazy mix of houses, ranging from palatial looking mansions surrounded by high walls with razor wire round the top, to mud and wattle huts with corrugated iron roofs with cardboard and plastic shanty dwellings propped up against them. The main road leading to the race track was lined with open air displays of wrought iron wares, chunky upholstered furniture, huge garden pots painted in bright colours, old lawn mowers, and row upon row of young plants grown in plastic bags, interspersed with charcoal vendors, stone masons, and water-tank drivers all vying for trade. In the dry weather it was a dust bowl, and in the wet a mud bath.

Within the racecourse compound a different world existed. Here one found order. White painted railings surrounded well tended, well watered, perfectly mown lawns and neat flowerbeds overflowing with colourful bedding plants. The members' enclosure reminded Martin of race courses in England in the summer. Even now some people still took the trouble to dress up for the occasion, though he suspected hats were for sun-protection, rather than fashion.

He had arranged to meet Amina at two thirty by the winners' enclosure. While he waited, he filled in time by buying a sweepstake ticket. He hated hanging around, his fault for arriving early. He hadn't been this nervous about anything let alone meeting a woman for years. This alien reaction was a fair indication of the strength of his feelings. Reciprocation would make him a happy man.

Amina's height made her easy to spot in a crowd even without a hat. Sandra stood beside her, dressed in a crisp white dress, looking more relaxed than he'd ever seen her. Martin was pleased. In the short space of time he'd known her she'd had more than her fair share of worries to contend with. Perhaps the break away from the ranch would help her get over her ordeal and make his task easier.

He didn't wait for Amina to reach him, but headed towards them giving Amina a brief kiss on the cheek, an unspoken thanks for honouring her promise. He turned his full attention to Sandra. He put one hand on her shoulder and moved to give her a more meaningful kiss. As he leaned closer he sensed a slight flicker of tension and she pulled away. Not the reaction he hoped for. He pecked her on the cheek and gently released his grip, pretending he hadn't noticed her reaction.

"Lovely to see you both," he said, trying to sound cheerful. "You're looking well. How's the arm?"

"Getting better," Sandra answered, adding, "What about your research?"

"Not so good. Lots of conflicting information, but so far nothing I can act on. I've still got a few leads to follow."

Amina tapped Sandra on the shoulder and said, "I'll meet you on the stand later."

Then she put her hands to her mouth. "Oh Martin, I'm sorry I nearly forgot to say. Simeon has something important to tell you." She waved as she walked away leaving them together.

"You asked her to fix this?" Sandra asked, raising her eyebrows.

He couldn't lie. "Do you mind?" Thinking she would rush off, he blurted out, "I need to explain about Beverley." He didn't have to finish the sentence to know he'd blown his chances. The tension in her jaw gave her away.

"I'm not interested," she said firmly, starting to turn away from him.

He grabbed hold of her arm, "But you have to understand there is absolutely nothing going on between us."

"And what difference does that make to me?"

"The night of the book launch, didn't that mean anything?" She blushed and seemed to be looking for an escape route. This was too public a place for such an intimate discussion, but he didn't have a choice. "It meant a lot to me," he said, desperate to keep the conversation going.

"I'm sorry Martin, we had a wonderful evening. I've no regrets. But trying to recreate the event would be a big mistake."

"But worth a try."

"Martin, stop pressuring me." Her voice sounded so firm, her decision final.

"I would if I thought you meant it." He looked into her eyes and added quietly, "I know why you're holding out on me. I'm prepared to wait." He pulled her forward, she turned her head away. He kissed her cheek regardless, then released his grip of her arm and spun round to walk away.

With each step he took he cursed himself for his stupidity. He stopped when he reached the racetrack railings, leaning against them looking out across the grass towards the wooded area and cemetery bend, his whole body aching with longing. He'd been a fool. He should have listened to Amina, instead of alienating Sandra even more. He'd missed his chance to say he knew about Beverley and Nick's affair and understood her fears. He doubted he'd get a second chance for a while.

A tap on his shoulder brought him back to the present. "I've been looking everywhere for you," Simeon said. "Did you find Sandra?"

"Yes, and I blew it."

Simeon shrugged. He had such a calm attitude to life, Martin could almost hear him mentally working out he'd waded in too soon, and given time the situation would change.

"Amina said you had something urgent to tell me," Martin said, sensing Simeon's reluctance to get involved with his love life.

Simeon nodded. "Problems with Rory."

"Rory... ... What the bloody hell is he up to now?"

"He's been making a nuisance of himself, knocking on Sandra's door late at night, shouting his head off demanding to be let in."

"What happened?"

"She had enough sense not to open up. Eventually he went home."

"God I wish I'd known half an hour ago, though I don't suppose it would have made a difference."

"Between you and Sandra?"

"Yes. A disaster, I couldn't have handled it worse if I'd tried."

Simeon looked around. "You're right, she doesn't look too happy. Should I go and talk to her?"

"Where is she?"

"Over there behind you, further along the railings."

Martin turned to see for himself. "No, I'll go. There's something I forgot to say."

Sandra gazed out at the vista across the race track, probably to avoid contact with him, the crowd and the world. He stood at the rail next to her. She turned to face him, her eyes brimming with tears. She said nothing. He reached into his pocket for a handkerchief. His fingers touched the little photo he had taken off his mother's bedside table, reminding him how much he wanted to show it to her. This wasn't the right moment. He took out his handkerchief and handed it to her. He was full of regret. His behaviour had made her unhappy. She mopped her eyes, and blew her nose. Then he plucked up courage to say what he had intended to say earlier. "Sorry, you don't want to listen to me, but I forgot something."

"What?" She said in a whisper.

He leaned in closer, "That I love you." He eased her gently toward him. There was no resistance, so he covered her lips with his. This time she relaxed, the contour of her body pressed against his, reviving memories of that night, locked in intimate proximity until a booming voice over the Tannoy system shattered the peace. Martin relaxed his grip on her, drew back. She looked shocked. "I mean it, I love you. Tell me when you're ready to talk."

What should he do next? His instincts screamed, give her time to make up her own mind. Simeon had gone so he walked back to the grandstand, pushing his way through the crowd gathering for the start of the next race. He stopped once and turned to check if she was still where he'd left her. Sandra had disappeared too, but standing a few feet away was Beverley.

Her shocking pink dress with a vast wide brimmed orange hat, made her impossible to ignore. For a brief second he thought the colour combination with her coppery hair was outrageous. Her dress clung to her generous curves leaving little to the imagination which changed his impression from mad to brave. But whatever effect she hoped for, made him want to run.

Unfortunately he wasn't quick enough.

Beverley flung her arms around his neck and kissed him firmly on the lips. He gripped her shoulders to push her away. As he did so he caught a glimpse of Sandra over her shoulder. It was obvious she had seen the kiss.

He wanted to yell it wasn't his fault, and that Beverley had made all the moves. He watched helplessly as Sandra spun round and ran headlong into the crowd, leaving him stuck with Beverley who blocked his way, preventing him from chasing after her.

"You're hurting me," Beverley snapped. Martin released her shoulders immediately.

"Sorry," he muttered, still trying to pick Sandra out

in the throng of people in the distance.

"What happened to you last night? I was expecting you for dinner?"

"I'm busy working on something. I couldn't get away."

"Well you might have phoned. Anyway if you're so busy, how come you can take time out for the races?"

"Oh I was hoping to meet up with someone here." As if on cue his mobile phone rang. "Excuse me," he said, stepping away from her while pressing the necessary keys to answer the call. Another blast on the Tannoy gave him a reason to put more distance between himself and Beverley. He made gestures to indicate he couldn't hear the caller, and backed away, slipped through the passageway that went under the grandstand, and kept walking until he reached the exit.

The caller knew someone who might have information about Balbinder. He agreed to a meeting. Martin thought the contact was looking for a free meal in a posh restaurant. He didn't mind, he needed a perfect excuse to avoid an evening alone or one with Beverley. He was tempted to leave, but wanted to explain to Amina what had happened and hope for help with damage limitation.

The informant was as expected, a complete waste of time, and when he decided he was unlikely to get any useful information from his dinner companion, he ordered a round of drinks, and pleading a sick stomach, left them. He went back to the room he had booked at the Aero Club.

He slept badly, and woke later than planned. The first thing he did was ring Simeon. Neither he nor Amina had managed to speak to Sandra, but they promised they would talk to her later. Then he phoned his contact from the previous night only to be told to call back in an hour.

He showered, dressed, and drank another cup of coffee, impatiently waiting as the minutes ticked by. He was about to pick up the receiver and dial again when the phone rang.

Word was out. Balbinder had left town. Destination unknown.

Unknown to most people, but not to Martin. His gut instinct told him Balbinder would be heading to the ranch. Now the challenge was to stop him.

Two people needed to know. He called Hank first, then, he phoned Simeon. He didn't give details. He didn't want Amina to find out in case she told Sandra. He said he'd pick Simeon up in ten minutes. If Sandra had any inkling Balbinder was heading to the ranch she would insist on returning. He preferred things as they were, the children safe in Nanyuki with Jenny, and Sandra out of danger in Nairobi.

He hurried to the office and settled his bill. Jim Standish happened to be there waiting for a pupil, and insisted on chatting for a minute. Eventually Martin said, "Sorry Jim, can't stop I have to get back to Ol Essakut, I was supposed to pick Simeon up ten minutes ago."

Jim waved him away, apologizing for delaying him.

Martin drove off hoping his instincts that Balbinder was heading for the ranch were wrong. Knowing Sandra and the children were safely off the ranch was a boon. He had a horrible feeling that an encounter with Balbinder could turn nasty.

Chapter 26

Sunlight dazzled Rory out of deep sleep. He attempted to move out of the range of the blinding rays. The front seat of the Land Rover didn't offer room to move, or much in the way of padding for comfort. All he got for his efforts was a dig in the ribs from the gear lever and a bruised elbow from hitting the steering wheel. He had numb legs and one arm tingled with pins and needles. Added to which, his head throbbed and his tongue felt as though someone had coated it with lard. He closed his eyes trying to recollect the cause.

Gradually odd memories of the previous day came back to him.

He'd been so pissed off because everyone had gone to Nairobi leaving him in charge. They'd all gone to the races. Not that he'd have joined them even if asked. He'd had enough of Rory do this and Rory do that.

Damn it, even Beverley went to join them. He hadn't figured her out yet. Her switching moods made her damn hard work. She'd go from steamy passion one minute to icy cool the next with not much in the middle. Hell, that woman could freeze the balls off a guy in ten seconds flat, but when she was hot... bloody hell... she was on fire.

He'd worried about her interest in Martin, but decided she was buttering him up to make sure he sold her Chui Farm. She didn't believe in taking chances and he didn't blame her. He'd willingly bet that as soon as Beverley had ownership of the land Martin would be out of the picture, which suited him fine.

The sitar playing finished him off. God, the noise was dire enough to send any man crazy, but add three nasal singing voices to the sitar noise and life became unbearable. He needed to hit town before he did something drastic at home. The Subaru was out of commission having a puncture repaired, so he took the Land Rover. The decision to escape had been a good one, as he found drinking companions at the club and a good session followed. More details eluded him. His feet tingled as the blood circulated again. Next he'd get out of the motor and walk around for a while to get rid of the cramps in his muscles. What he really needed was coffee.

The club house was locked. He wandered round the back to the kitchen and found someone to fulfil his demand for coffee. Cup in hand he walked round to the front of the building, pulled a chair into the sun and sat facing the mountain while waiting for the caffeine to kick in and his headache to subside.

As soon as the doors unlocked he moved to the dining room for breakfast. Even though he was the only person eating the service was infuriatingly slow. He ordered toast, but hadn't the patience to wait, he'd get better service at home where the staff responded to his orders. A few hours sleep on a comfortable bed might help his mood.

He got back into the Land Rover intending to go straight home. The throbbing headache made him change his plan and stop to get something to deaden the pain.

What a mistake. Having purchased and swallowed the most powerful painkillers available, he went to reverse out of his parking space. Jenny Copeland driving Sandra's Peugeot blocked him in.

He watched her in his mirror, expecting her to reverse to let him out. Instead, she got out of the car and hurried towards him. "Rory, thank God I caught up with you," she said breathlessly. "I rang the house and was told you were still in town, and when I called the club they said you'd just left."

He gave her a moment to catch her breath, and with a forced smile asked, "What's the problem?"

"I need you to take the children home with you. My brother's wife is ill and I have to go and care for her. Sandra isn't due back until late this afternoon. I can't get hold of her. Please take them back with you. Wanjiru will cope until Sandra gets home. I'll leave a message to tell her where they are."

Rory racked his brains for an excuse to get out of taking them. "It's a bit difficult. The Land Rover isn't fitted out for kids."

"That doesn't matter, you can drive Sandra's car home and I'll take the Land Rover, I'll get it back as soon as I can." Rory accepted defeat, he was stuck with them, like it or not. Jenny had spoken, and as usual she would get her way. He wordlessly got out of the Land Rover, handed over the keys, and followed her over to the car.

"Let me get my things out first," she grovelled round to pick up her handbag contents which had spilled onto the floor. He waited patiently. Then she said something which didn't make sense. "You must be so pleased they sorted out the mystery of the stolen materials."

"Did they?" he asked, hoping she might elaborate.

"Surely Simeon told you. Hank's men caught them red handed driving the lorry through a gap in the fence."

Rory had no idea what was going on. No one bothered to tell him anything. That could only mean they'd suspected him. Jenny said building materials, not motor spares, still he must be careful. He helped her transfer her stuff, checked there was nothing in the Land Rover he needed and got on his way.

Two screaming brats and a yapping puppy were no cure for a hangover. He put up with the noise for about five minutes before he yelled, "Shut up," which made them even noisier than before. He put his foot down hoping speed would shut them up.

God, what a piercing scream, he thought. I'll not be responsible for my actions if she doesn't stop soon. He slammed his foot harder on the accelerator and turned the stereo up to full volume to drown her out.

As he roared down the road he realized the two brats were at his mercy. Did he have the guts to use this opportunity to get rid of them? With so little time staging an accident would be hard.

His mind went into overdrive. If he let them wander off, at this age, and in this heat survival chances were limited. No, too careless. Better to take them swimming in the water hole. Everyone said they were strong swimmers, but if one got sucked under the waterfall, he could say that while he tried to rescue one the other got into trouble. The intense heat made taking them swimming plausible and worth serious consideration. A few minor details needed working out.

Rory reached the gates of Ol Essakut and slowed down. One of his mechanics was sitting on a log chatting to one of the education centre staff. "What are you doing down here?" he asked, annoyed the staff would take advantage of his absence to slack off.

"Parjit told me to take day off," the man answered. Rory was about to shout at him, but had second thoughts and asked, "Why?"

"He said, no spares, so nothing to do. He go off with man from Nairobi."

"What man?"

"Big Singh," he said, demonstrating a big stomach.

Rory had little doubt he was describing Balbinder Singh. "Where did they go?"

"Eland camp road."

Rory had heard enough. He put his foot down and roared away. When he reached his house, he saw that the Subaru wasn't outside the guest house nor the workshop, making the bad feeling worse. He hurried inside to fetch a gun from the safe. He decided to take his grandfather's rifle and stuffed two boxes of ammunition into his shorts pockets.

Back at the car, the children had finally quit screaming and gone to sleep, they started to cry again when the door slammed.

Rory paid no attention. All that mattered was finding Balbinder Singh. His arrival meant one thing. The trophy hunt was on. Balbinder would be aware everyone was away, giving him the perfect opportunity to have a go and assume he could get away without being caught. Balbinder had made one serious mistake. One he would regret.

Rory stopped briefly at the workshop to double check which direction their cars had headed in, and to get a second description of the visitors.

It confirmed his fears that Balbinder had come. He had been alone. He and Parjit and the other two had gone off in convoy heading north-west. Before he set off in Sandra's Peugeot, with the children still strapped in, Beverley swept up in a new rich-sounding rally Subaru, blocking his way.

"Do you like it? Fancy taking me for a spin?" she asked in an enthusiastic voice.

"I'm busy," he snapped back at her, annoyed that she should pick this moment to crowd him.

"What's on?"

"Nothing."

"I thought you'd be pleased, I'll take it back if you're going to be so ungrateful."

Rory, gritted his teeth and leaned over, kissing her through the open window, "Sorry, I'm in a hurry. Can you move your car out of the way? You can wait but I don't know how long I'll be."

Beverley reversed a couple of feet, as if she was going to get out of his way, then she came back, "Let me tag along."

Emma began to cry again. "Shut up," he yelled. She screamed louder.

"I'll take the children, or come and mind them," she pleaded, reaching into the car's open window to hold Emma's hand. The ear piercing noise stopped. "See, you need a woman's touch."

"Never saw you as the maternal type," he answered, wishing she would push off.

"You'd be surprised what I can be," she said, her tone holding the threat of intimacy out of kilter with his present mood.

Rory hesitated for a minute to consider her offer. If he didn't hurry, Balbinder might beat him to the rhino. And he'd never get an opportunity like this to deal with the children again. He didn't need Beverley on board, but couldn't leave her here either.

"Okay, shift that," he said, pointing to her new Subaru, "and jump in."

As he gave the instruction he regretted his decision.

Now it was too late to withdraw the invite. She wasted no time in getting into the seat beside him. He drove off without waiting for her to buckle up.

Beverley kept quiet for the first fifteen minutes, and then she started to look worried. "What's the hurry?" she asked. When he didn't answer she repeated her question, her voice more demanding. Still he ignored her. Finally she shouted to him to stop. Enough. First the children, now this woman, he couldn't take any more. He slammed his foot on the brakes. Her seat belt didn't lock in time to stop her banging her head on the dashboard. She bounced backwards with a neck cracking jolt against the headrest. He reached down, released her seatbelt catch, leaned across her lap, yanked the door handle, then, using both hands shoved her out of the car. He didn't bother about the door. He put the car in gear and drove on, not even bothering to look in the mirror to check how she'd landed. The children miraculously went quiet. Best they stayed that way.

Chapter 27

The betrayal hurt. After the initial shock of his declaration of love, and his passionate kiss at the races, Sandra had for a brief moment considered taking the risk. She turned to face the crowd only to witness Martin and Beverley locked in an embrace.

He saw her watching, his guilty expression enough to make her run. Any sort of conversation with him would be impossible, an ordeal too hard to contemplate. As for facing Beverley, she shuddered at the prospect. The most sensible course of action must be to put distance between them. She'd never manage to pretend she didn't care because she did.

She hurried away in search of Amina.

"I've a blinding headache coming on, so I'm going home. I'm going to take the phone off the hook and go to bed."

"I'll call tomorrow," Amina said.

"I'll probably sleep till lunchtime."

Amina didn't look happy with her response, but shrugged as if she accepted her decision

Back at her little studio cottage she took the phone off the hook. Amina calling was not the problem. The possibility Martin might try to make excuses for his behaviour was too unbearable to contemplate.

Jim Standish's suggestion she write down every detail of the crash to get perspective had more appeal than thinking about Martin. She dug in her desk drawer and pulled out a pad of paper and a pen and started writing.

Cowardly or not, she decided to deal with the more recent crash first. Every detail from checking her fuel, filing her flight plan, to taking off got jotted down. She included the colour of the sky and described the thin wisp of smoke, spotted in the distance which reminded her of Nick's warnings about poachers. The call from Simeon, even thinking he might be fussing about nothing. On and on she wrote. She stopped writing at the point when Martin appeared and helped straighten her arm.

By two in the morning she had only done the easy one. The recent accident, when she had been behind the controls, much easier to face than the earlier one when she had been a child passenger. Best to sleep first. She'd figure out where to begin in the morning.

When a shaft of sunlight fell across her face, Sandra opened her eyes, peered at the clock and turned over and snuggled down again. The silence that engulfed the house was oddly unnatural, and she lay straining to pick the everyday sounds she had become accustomed to since her return to Kenya. Birds chirped in the background, but something was missing. The splashing water from the gardener's hose as he washed the car, giggles from Rose as she flirted with the cook from the main house, the absence of barking dogs, and reduced traffic all contributed to the strangeness. Of course it was quiet because of the holiday. The owners of the main house were away. The servants had time off, apart from the watchman, who spent most of his working hours perched on the concrete culvert by the gate chatting to passers by.

Rare moments of solitude, seldom experienced in this country must be treasured. She tried to think how many times had she been this alone since her arrival, and could only remember two occasions since meeting Nick. The first had been on the day he betrayed her, the day he died, when she had taken herself off to the most remote spot on the ranch to hide her tears. Simeon tracked her down to break the news of the accident. The next was the time after her plane crash landed on Aloe ridge. Even then her isolation seemed longer because of the dark and the pain. The only other times alone were when driving or flying. The constant company of either friends, or Nick before he died, and now the children and the network of staff working in the background, meant she'd almost forgotten the delight of an undisturbed daydream.

What a treat to wake up unaided, no alarm clock, no patient knocking on her bedroom door to herald Rose or Wanjiru bearing the customary early morning tea tray. No child clambering onto the bed, no manic puppy trying to chew her ears or her toes if they stuck out of the bedclothes. The luxury of tea in bed happily skipped in exchange for this peace.

The magnetic pull of the shaft of sunlight that snuck through the chink in the curtain overpowered the desire to turn over and go back to sleep. Sandra longed to bask in the full glory of its brilliance. She threw back the covers, had a shower and pulled on shorts and a tee-shirt, and went on a barefoot skirmish to the kitchen. Even in her absence Rose's enthusiasm for serving greeted her. On the table lay a breakfast tray complete with a posy of flowers from the garden. The layout suggested the menu. In the fridge she found sliced fruit, a little jug of milk for her tea, a neatly prepared dish of butter, and a small bowl of marmalade. Rose had decreed fruit and toast for breakfast, good thing she didn't fancy a feast of porridge, followed by a full English breakfast. If she made one, Rose might forever worry she had forsaken her employer on her only day off. She wouldn't risk offending Rose, especially not on a public holiday. Fruit and toast suited her fine.

Sandra unlocked the verandah door and carried her tray outside. Normally she ate on the verandah, but today, because of the unexpected privacy, she decided to eat in the middle of the lawn. She put the tray down on the grass, near the Bombax tree, and went back indoors to collect a cushion to sit on, her sketch pad and paint box. Sitting cross legged she tucked into the juicy mango Rose had prepared. She studied her immediate surroundings, soaking up the vibrant colours. The fallen bluey-purple jacaranda flowers had completely covered an area of lawn below the tree. Scarlet bouganvillea tumbled out of a tree, and the fence was a tangle of jasmine, morning glory, and so many other plants whose names remained a mystery. The combination of the intermingled scents triggered by the warmth of the morning sun was intoxicating, lulling her into a dream-like state. Her gaze moved to the unobstructed view of the knuckle-like Ngong hills. All this beauty topped by the startling colours of the birds, yellow weaver birds, iridescent green sun birds, sapphire blue superb starlings and brilliant carmine bee eaters, who flitted between the bird table, the trees and bushes to splash in the birdbath.

Having finished her breakfast, she reached out for her sketch pad intending to draw the hills, but instead found herself holding the pad of paper on which she had written her description of the plane crash as instructed by Jim. She shoved it aside. She didn't want to stir up memories, but perhaps she needed to face the challenge.

For sixteen years she'd avoided this moment. At

first avoidance had not been intentional, she genuinely didn't remember a thing, Gradually odd snippets had tried to return and been blanked out to avoid the pain. Foolish, but the only way she knew to deal with her fear. Now that she had decided to try, would she be able to conjure up the pictures again? The aftermath was vividly clear. The weeks in the hospital, when her mother sat next to her bed crying and crying. The doctor and nurses prodded and poked her and asked questions that didn't make sense. She hadn't a clue what they were talking about. They even showed her pictures of a man and a boy and tried to convince her that they were her father and her brother. It made no difference, she couldn't remember them. Later with her mother sitting beside her with tears in her eyes, they showed her the pictures again. This time telling her both people had died. They probably expected a reaction, but she felt nothing. No, not nothing... Anger... Anger at the two people in the photo who made her mother cry so much. Anger that still lingered today.

The prospect of leaning against the rhinoceros horn shaped spikes that adorned the Bombax tree was unappealing, so she lay on the grass with her head on the cushion and closed her eyes. Soon a tickling sensation on her wrist forced her to open them. Sugar ants. The tiny little creatures were scurrying over her wrist towards her abandoned tray. Sandra found their frenetic progress fascinating. So hard to imagine these minute, harmless creatures were related to the larger, savage safari ant, whose name had been coined from their habit of making wide route marches after heavy rain, attacking any unfortunate creature that strayed in their path.

She gently brushed the ants from her wrist, and

rolled over onto her stomach to monitor their activity more closely. The speed of their progress, the hurried examination of the tray by the initial invaders, then as if by magic the troops arrived. Which one was the leader, who gave the orders, impossible to decide? The relentless march would continue as long as a supply of sugar was available. One by one the porters scurried in procession onto the tray, picked up a granule of sugar and rushed back along their incoming route triumphantly waving their load over their heads as they passed unladen late-comers. Any dropped load would be snatched by another ant, leaving the original owner no choice but to return to fetch another one. The continuous stream of ants flowed into and out of a tiny hole in the ground, reminding her of a speeded up aerial film of people going into and out of a tube train station. She'd never know how deep the hole was. Their entrance was next to a large earthenware pot containing an anthurium lily in full bloom with its stiff red waxy single petal flowers with rigid stamens jutting out of their centres. A few ants climbed the flower stems. They either had not learned about the convenient haul of sugar sitting on the tray, or were fussy eaters who considered refined sugar too tasteless.

A tiny movement caught her eye. About three inches away from the entrance to the ant nest was the first trap. Five more ran right round the base of the pot plant. They resembled miniature volcanic craters, each one about half an inch high, and an inch and a half wide. Sandra watched in a trance. Was the ant-lion going to have a bad day because she had provided sugar in such abundance, or would the sugar ants tire of fetching and carrying from the tray and explore the area round the base of the pot?

With intense concentration she watched. Then she pictured a hand hovering right over the sand trap holding a blade of grass. On the grass was an ant. The hand shook the grass, the ant fell and struggled to climb out of the crater, but the walls were made of such fine soil that the ant never had a chance.

Sandra often felt like that ant in the trap. As fast as she thought she was in control, of life, Ol Essakut, the twins, everything else, something happened to push her back down and into danger.

She pictured the floor of the volcano crater erupting, the ant-lion grabbing its prey and vanishing back below the surface, the sand settling, leaving no sign of activity. Then she heard a voice in her head clearly saying, "Do you want to know their full Latin name?"

Sandra shook her head and closed her eyes. Sixteen years she had waited for a glimpse of her past, and now not only had she heard her brother's voice, she could picture him clearly, magnifying glass in hand, showing her one of his secret finds. Bugs were his passion. He knew them all, he collected them, he studied them, and made notes about them the way their father did. Notes that filled dozens of exercise books, notes she had never been able to bring herself to read. They were all still in boxes in storage in London waiting for her to decide what should be done with them. Then a second voice, her father's voice came to her. He sounded just like Jim Standish, and she realized that Jim actually looked like her father too.

Sandra plucked a blade of grass, scooped up an ant, and shook it over the trap. The ant fell, struggled to climb the sheer sides, but within seconds it vanished without a trace. The soil in the trap was so fine it worked just like quicksand, sucking the victim below the surface so the predator hardly had to reveal himself. Sandra touched the surface of the sand with the blade of grass. A little pair of pincer like claws grabbed the grass, she pulled, the ant-lion hung for a moment then let go and vanished, refusing to be tricked into exposing himself.

The ant-lion was, like her brother and her father, elusive. For so long she hadn't been able to picture them, and today it had been as if they were in the garden. She had always hoped coming back to Kenya would help to bring back those buried memories. Tears filled her eyes. The lack of memories left an empty space, especially after her mother died. Finding them might bring sorrow, but also give her something to treasure.

She sniffed, and went inside for a tissue and to put the phone back on the hook. She shouldn't have cut herself off. What if the children needed her? This thought jolted her back to the present. Becoming a recluse and wallowing in long forgotten memories or indulging in self pity over an affair that should never have started wasn't going to solve a thing.

Regaining memories of her father and brother was in some ways a joy, but there would be pain too. She had to accept there was no need to rush into trying to remember everything at once. It was more important to look to the future, which curiously meant delving into Nick's past rather than hers. And the sooner the better.

With renewed positive energy, she scooped up Nick's diaries and returned to the garden to read them.

Chapter 28

Sandra plonked herself down on the grass beside the breakfast tray, poured herself another cup of tea and started reading Nick's diaries again, this time with a purpose.

She skipped through his last years at school and college, his relationship with Martin stayed constant, though the mention of Martin's name started to become more sparse, replaced by a succession of girls names.

The first vibes of rivalry between them appeared. They both fancied the same girl. She dented their egos, dumped them and went off with another of their friends. The friendship suffered, until Martin came round and bulldozed Nick into shaking hands, and making a pact, never to let any woman muck up their life long friendship.

Sandra easily imagined Martin at his most persuasive. Nick had been lucky to have such a friend. She envied their bond, having never experienced anything as strong herself. This daydreaming wouldn't get her anywhere. She sipped her tea. It had gone cold, but she hadn't the energy to make more. She read on.

The following summer they both came back home. The majority of the entries filled with adoration for Helen. He was smitten. The scrawny nuisance of a child had become a heart-stopping beauty. He filled pages and pages praising her, describing her efforts to help her father run the property while managing to break every heart in the district. Her presence next door obviously influenced Nick's decision to stay at Ol Essakut.

Getting Helen to fall into his arms became his challenge. He wasted no time making his interest known, but she strung him along, one minute seeming keen the next ignoring him. She kept a string of boyfriends on the go and claimed to be too young to settle for one man. Fun first, commitment later.

Nick wanted to join the fun, but his father became ill and all the responsibility piled on his shoulders. Helen didn't have the same burden and frequently took off to stay with friends. In her absence Nick got on favourable terms with her father Tom, commonly referred to as Old Man Lander, who came across as a formidable old man, with a long white beard and a notoriously sharp temper. Not a man to meddle with, but a source of sound advice about running the ranch.

Martin got an occasional mention when he came home between trips to Somalia, Ethiopia, Sudan, Uganda, Tanzania. The local stories frequently enabled him to come home for a few days. Nick wrote how he envied Martin's nomadic life especially his ability to dash off to the coast or head to Nairobi at will.

It took nearly two years before Helen accepted an invitation to go out with him. The evening ended with a chaste good night kiss. Her kisses got more passionate as the weeks went by, but never as passionate as Nick wanted, leaving him frustrated beyond reason.

Sandra chuckled at the thought and read on.

One day Helen suggested a weekend at the coast, Nick assumed the invitation meant she was ready to sleep with him. Her timing couldn't have been worse.

His father suffered a massive stroke, and he couldn't leave the farm. Helen came to comfort him, and they slept together, but still she went away without him.

She popped back for his father's funeral. He tried to persuade her to stay. She wouldn't. A month later she returned, her attitude different. She suddenly had unlimited time for him, frequently coming across the vlei to seek him out, in a way she'd never done before.

Within a month they married.

Sandra wondered at Nick's need to rush into marriage. Her own experience was so swift she hardly had time to get used to the idea before she had to deal with the name change. Maybe the difference with Helen stemmed from having childhood connections.

Fatherhood swiftly followed. Nick recorded mixed feelings. One part thrilled, and the other part resentful. He wanted Helen to himself. He'd waited so long to possess her, and didn't want to share her so soon, but at the same time thrilled at the prospect of parenthood.

Helen hated pregnancy. Morning sickness, getting fat, and mood swings made her hard to live with. The premature birth of healthy twins, a boy and a girl took everyone by surprise. Helen didn't share his joy, and sank into a deep depression. She ignored the twins, often locking herself in her room, leaving Nick and the ayah to cope.

Nick adored the children and when Helen insisted she needed to go alone to the coast to recover from the ordeal of childbirth, he let her go. She completely lost track of the problems he faced. Drought, her own father's declining health, went unnoticed leaving Nick to shoulder all responsibility. She flitted back and forth, occasionally with friends in tow. On those occasions she'd act out the doting mother role, because her friends expected it.

Sandra wiped a tear from her eyes. What torture for Nick to live with someone capable of ignoring the twins.

Nick even wrote that given a chance he'd do anything to find a good mother for his children. The comment made Sandra sit up with shock. Choosing her over Beverley now made sense. She'd adored the children from the first moment she met them, and had been happy to spend hours playing with them. Beverley on the other hand, always backed off when the children demanded attention. The likelihood of this having influenced him hurt and explained the ease with which he broke their marriage vows. She had to accept he never loved her. To him she represented the perfect mother substitute for his children.

At least she had the satisfaction of knowing she'd do the job well and willingly. She'd do everything possible for those children to protect their stake in the ranch. She'd fight off bids to take control away from her, deal with the staff, and anything else required. She understood the meaning of responsibility.

She read on.

Helen came home for longer periods, still paying little attention to the children.

She used the excuse of Old Man Lander's health going down hill to move back across the vlei to care for him. Nick tried to get her to bring the old man over to their house so she'd be near the children, but she wouldn't listen. When the old man finally died, she moved back home with Nick, but her moody behaviour nearly drove him mad. She frequently spent hours at her father's house, supposedly sorting out his things. With no evidence of this happening Nick wondered what made the empty house so attractive. There wasn't anything of interest there. Before his death, Old Man Lander, had insisted Nick take a huge stack of family papers from the house, with the instruction they must be kept in his gun room, away from prying eyes. Natural curiosity made Nick read the papers and discover the Old Man's secrets.

Sandra wondered if the positioning of Rory's name on the Lander family tree was one of those secrets.

Old Man Lander left his whole estate to his grandchildren Sam and Emma, with Nick named as trustee. Nick was honoured, Helen furious. Rory received a small bequest, enough to buy the rally car he had hankered after. Nick sensed Rory's disappointment that he didn't get more.

About this time Nick wrote he suspected Helen was having an affair. He intended staying silent to avoid confrontation for the children's sake. Things must have been bad, because for several weeks he made no entries in the diary.

The next thing recorded was Martin's return for his mother's funeral. The sad circumstances took some of the joy out of the reunion. As did the idea Martin was hiding something. The following entry described how on the night after the funeral, they had dinner and retreated to his study for a drink. Nick wanted to clean two guns before putting them away. The two weapons lay on his desk awaiting attention. Simeon had promised to join them. He expected Martin to offer to clean one, but he was too preoccupied to get involved. Nick put pressure on to discover what he had on his mind, even though he suspected it had something to do with Helen and her affairs.

He concentrated on the gun, wondering how to react when Martin made his revelation. He was far too proud to admit to anyone let alone his closest friend that he had a miserable sham of a marriage.

He continued polishing his gun, bracing himself for the disclosure, wishing Martin would hurry up.

"It's Rory," Martin announced.

The name of Helen's lover triggered so much anger he lost all sense of reasoning.

Rory. The shock of hearing that name uttered in the context of Helen's lover, triggered an unstoppable reflex action. He loaded and pointed the gun he held at Martin. He wanted to shoot. He wanted to kill him. He wanted those words taken back. But he knew they would never go away. His anger made him irrational. Martin knowing made it worse, not better. The situation was unthinkable. Impossible. Helen and Rory. How had he been so blind?

Martin never flinched, beads of sweat formed on his forehead. Nick kept the gun steady. He played with the trigger. He wanted to see Martin squirm. He wanted to punish him for bringing this travesty into the open.

A noise behind him distracted him for a second. His trigger grip so tight it only needed the tiniest extra pressure to complete the process. He couldn't stop the action. The bullet left the chamber before he could release the tension. Fortunately the distraction made him pull to one side, and the heart shot he'd aimed for turned into a shoulder shot.

Simeon rushed forward, grabbed the gun out of his hands, snatched the remaining ammunition off the desk and went to check Martin's condition.

Nick went over and over the manic moment. What madness made him point the gun at Martin? Would he have pulled the trigger? How much worse if Simeon hadn't turned up? Could he blame the distraction of Simeon's appearance for his squeezing the trigger? The distraction had thankfully altered his aim.

Without it Martin might have died.

Nick recalled how the deafening blast inside the confines of the room compounded his shock. He couldn't move. He watched helplessly as Simeon locked the guns in the safe and pocketed the key before he hustled Martin out of the room. Nick never attempted to explain his actions.

Three hours he sat waiting for Simeon to return, knowing he would demand a logical reason for the shooting. He didn't have one to give. But Simeon didn't come back that night, or for the next week.

Simeon reported Martin would survive, and that he would drive him up to Uganda, to get him out of the country to avoid unnecessary police hassle. Martin swore the shooting was an accident, and as long as Nick promised he wouldn't do anything crazy, he'd not go public.

Nick made the promise which Simeon relayed. The pact made.

Simeon returned the key. Nick put the guns back in the cabinet and swore he'd never take them out again.

A rumour got out about the shooting incident. Endless debates followed. An accident or a deliberate shot was the most asked question. The police never got involved and soon the story died down. But Nick couldn't forget.

Nick was living a nightmare. He had isolated himself from the one person who he might have been able to confide in. Martin had no idea why his revelation merited such a bizarre reaction.

Nick's curiosity was his undoing. If he had resisted the temptation to read Old Man Lander's papers he would not be in this situation. Neither Helen nor Rory knew the truth and he had the dilemma of whether to tell them or not. One thing for certain, was that their affair had to end.

It took him a week to decide on a course of action. He'd tell Helen he knew about the affair and insist it must stop. If she agreed he'd say no more.

Helen's reaction didn't fit his plan. She seemed relieved he'd found out and demanded a divorce, as she was pregnant with Rory's child.

Nick's anguish was made worse by the fact Helen seemed happy for the first time in months.

Shocked, he pleaded with her to reconsider. She seemed set on leaving and setting up home with Rory. He told her that she couldn't marry Rory. She responded as he expected. If he wouldn't give her a divorce she'd go and live with Rory anyway.

Nick had no option. He had to tell her. Rory was her brother.

Cutting her veins might have been kinder.

Her anger kicked in and she accused him of lying to hurt her. Nick had to physically restrain her and promised to stand by her, treat the child as his own, as long as she ended the relationship.

She retaliated by screaming that the twins weren't his.

Nick tried to ignore this, thinking she was seeking revenge. Nothing she said would make a difference to how he felt about the twins. But the doubt, once sown, refused to go away. If he wasn't their father, who was? She wouldn't say.

Helen demanded proof about Rory. He showed her the letter her father wrote a few weeks before he died.

Unable to cope she spiralled into depression, which led to her taking an overdose. She survived but the baby didn't. Nick never discovered if she'd told Rory he was her brother. Rory became more aggressive than ever, but kept more distant. Six weeks later Helen took a second overdose. This time she killed herself.

Nick and Rory's relationship though full of tension, was bound together in a peculiar way because of their mutual adoration of Helen. Nick made a pact not to go public about the affair, or the miscarriage, and they agreed Helen's overdoses were caused by her depression. He still wasn't sure if Rory knew the full story.

Nick never found the courage to ask Rory if Sam and Emma were his children.

The telephone interrupted her reading.

Sandra ran inside to answer it, relieved to hear Amina's voice rather than Martin's.

"Hope I'm not disturbing you. Do you fancy lunch?" Amina said, "I've been abandoned and could do with some company."

"I haven't really thought about food." Sandra answered honestly. "Abandoned? That doesn't sound like Simeon."

"Oh, he's gone charging off to do something with Martin and Hank." Amina sounded sorry for herself which was unusual. "Wouldn't even hint what they were up to or when he'd be back. So why don't you come over?"

Sandra shivered. Simeon, Martin and Hank going off together filled her with dread. Amina would have to find someone else to spend the day with. Sandra had to get home. She cried off, pleading her headache had not quite gone. She got off the phone to avoid Amina detecting her panic.

Those three going off together in a hurry meant one thing. Trouble. And the one place where they were likely to head was Ol Essakut. They should have called, but she remembered, she'd taken the phone off the hook which gave them a let out.

A quick change of clothes followed by a mad dash round the house locking up, something she rarely did, made her wish Rose was on duty. All this would normally be Rose's responsibility, but today the onus fell on Sandra. She went to lock the door to the garden and remembered Nick's diaries. She shot out, picked them all up, put them on the tray and hurried back in. She didn't bother to wash up, there was no time. Rose would deal with it when she returned.

She tried to ring Jenny to say she would collect the children earlier than planned. She didn't answer. Unusual, but perhaps Jenny had gone into town.

Happy everything was secure, she got into Jenny's car intending to head straight back to Nanyuki, where she would swap cars and pick up the children on her way home.

A few miles down the road she decided her mad rush was foolish. But the ominous dread wouldn't go away. And then she hit traffic. The queue stretched back for miles right out to the game park entrance. She had forgotten that public holidays usually involved a major political rally in the centre of town. She needed to work out an alternative route across town. On reaching the turnoff to the Aero Club she decided to take a break, to get out of the heat of the car for half an hour and get something to quench her thirst.

It was as if fate had a grip on her life. She'd seen Jim's car and enquired after Jim, and while she waited for an answer she overheard someone say Hank had rushed off to deal with poachers.

Sandra didn't need to hear more. She guessed the target. The rhino they'd found. That's why Simeon and Martin departed in such a hurry.

Flying would be quicker than driving. She had to shed her fears and hang-ups fast. Jim Standish was out with a pupil, and due back in a few minutes. She hurried out onto the tarmac to wait, to catch him the moment he landed.

His plane landed bumpily and taxied towards her. Jim climbed out and gave her a bear hug of a greeting, before waving farewell to his departing pupil.

"What brings you here?" he asked.

"I'm ready. Can I go now?"

Jim put his hand on her shoulder. He wanted to refuse, but she willed him to say yes.

"It'll have to be a short flight," he said looking upwards. "The weather is closing in fast. I've already cancelled my next lesson, but it will probably hold on long enough for you to get the feel of things again."

"What about fuel?"

"That's okay. The tanks are about three quarters full. Give me a minute to fill in a flight plan."

"Can I wait in the plane?" she asked.

"Sure, I'll be back in a minute."

Sandra climbed up and got in, did up the seat straps and put her hands on the controls. Yes, she was ready. She checked the fuel gauge. Jim was right, three quarters full, enough for her to get home. Come on, Jim. Damn. She couldn't wait any longer. She thought he'd understand. She taxied down the runway, got in line, and called the control tower for instructions. Said she'd decided to fly solo. Explained she was aware of the deteriorating weather conditions, and convinced them she only planned to make a short circuit. She nearly lost her nerve as she waited for her allocated slot. At last her clearance for take off.

Up, up and away.

God it felt good to be up in the sky again. She knew she'd be in trouble if she didn't inform the control tower soon of her change of plan. She waited until the last minute to make the call. When she did, there was so much static interference she found it difficult to make out what they said.

"Sorry, change of plans," she shouted over the crackle. "Tell Jim I'm heading to Ol Essakut to deal with an emergency."

They came back with repeated warnings of the storms ahead, strongly recommending she turn back. She pretended not to hear their objections, ending the call with a promise to report back after landing.

The storm clouds threatening to break the drought were building up in density and certainly looked ready to burst. Ahead of her was a particularly black volatile looking cluster she decided to skirt round. She reported her altered course to the control tower.

She had little time to dwell on the contents of Nick's diaries as she battled with turbulence which made the flight one of the toughest she'd ever faced. All she thought about was what to do when she arrived. Should she stop off and collect the children? No, no time and better and safer for them to stay with Jenny for a bit longer. She could fly over the area and try to spot the rhino from the air. It would save time later. She deeply regretted not sorting things out with Martin at the races. She needed his friendship more than ever. She had to talk to him about Rory and Helen. Tell him what she had discovered. Then he might be able to help her make a decision as to what action to take, which led to her wondering if Rory was involved with the poachers.

Flashes of lightning and rumbles of thunder kept her alert. She'd have to land on a road rather than fly through one of these storms. But as long as she could find a gap in the clouds she'd keep going.

Chapter 29

Rory climbed to high ground. He lay on rocks at the top of the ridge trying to locate Balbinder. The heat sucked every ounce of moisture out of existence. He wished he'd remembered to bring some water with him and hadn't abandoned his vehicle so far away. He glanced back to where he'd parked. A rising trail of dust headed that way. The speed of the moving vehicle worried him. The only fast driver around was Beverley, who had her new car to test. Damn the bitch. He scrambled down from his rocky perch and jogged back to where he'd left the children. He didn't need her interfering with his plans.

He got back as her dust settled, to find her reaching into the car to give the children a drink.

He yanked her away from the car window.

"What the hell do you think you are doing?" he asked.

She stared back defiantly and said, "Giving the kids a drink."

He pointed his gun at her stomach, and said, "Move."

Fear replaced her defiance. Much better. He'd had enough of her telling him what to do. She turned around, as if she expected to find someone to help her. "Move, and bring that bag," he said, this time poking her in the ribs.

"Where to?" she whispered. He nodded in the direction he'd chosen.

Rory enjoyed the unmistakeable fear in her voice. He'd never had complete control of her before. Their brief relationship had always been rather one-sided, one in which he'd only experienced a few brief moments of being in control, but nothing compared with the pleasure this gave him.

"Over to the top of that hump. I need a better overall view."

"Too far," she pleaded.

"You should have thought of that before you invited yourself along."

"Let me go back. The children need me."

"Do you think I care what happens to them? How come you're suddenly so fond of them? When Nick was alive you'd have done anything to get rid of them. I know because I overheard you saying his kids were the only thing wrong with him."

That shut her up, but soon her silence began to annoy him.

"Who knows you're out here?" he asked. He got a sneer in response so he prodded her with the gun. "Who knows?"

"Juma... and... Wanjiru," she stammered.

What kind of idiot did she take him for thinking he'd believe she hadn't phoned Martin or Hank. Wouldn't do her much good though, the deed would be done by the time they got back from Nairobi.

He noticed her dragging her feet. Poor cow, trying to leave a trail to show which way they'd gone, she must think he was stupid.

"So aren't you going to ask what we're doing here?" he said to break the monotony of the hike. She didn't reply.

"We're after poachers. They're after a rhino."

Still no response.

"I should mention I know the poacher?"

At last, a reaction. "Who?"

"Balbinder Singh."

"I thought his interest was rally driving, not animals," she answered as she tripped over a stone, scraping the skin off her ankle. She stopped to inspect the damage. He nudged her on.

"Me too."

"What are you going to do?"

"Stop him."

"How?"

"Proper little journalist, aren't you? Probing away, waiting for me to let loose some telltale snippet, so you can dig deeper. Well I'll tell you how. I'm going to kill him. The thing I haven't decided is whether to put a bullet through his heart, or simply blow his brains out."

Her mouth fell open.

"Which do you think would be best?"

She stared at him, no doubt regretting being so inquisitive.

"You think I'm joking. Well I'm not." She still didn't say anything. "I'm veering towards the head shot. Blow his bloody turban off. Think you'll enjoy watching?"

The colour drained from her face. Good, she was scared, but still capable of a nervous whisper. "How can you be certain he's after the rhino?"

"I have my sources. The rhino gives me the perfect excuse to shoot Balbinder."

"But I thought you liked him."

"Nobody likes that blackmailing bastard." He laughed, this was fun. He'd give her enough to keep her enquiring mind at work, try to get her on his side.

"Blackmail? You're kidding. What could he

possibly know about you?"

He didn't answer, but pushed her on towards the high ground. Beverley stumbled along, exhaustion and fear starting to slow her down. At least she had the sense not to complain. They reached the base of the rocky outcrop which poked up in the seemingly flat terrain. He made her scramble up onto a ledge. From the top, the criss-cross of bone dry dips and gullies became clear. The area was not as flat from here. Huge black clouds on the distant hills threatened to change the terrain. A cloudburst was the last thing Rory wanted. He made Beverley sit down, she didn't need much encouragement. The oppressive sticky atmosphere of the pending storm was debilitating. He grabbed the bag he'd made her carry, hoping to find something to drink inside. He pulled out a Tusker, rummaged a bit deeper and found a bottle opener to remove the cap. Beer fizzed out in a rush, he put the bottle to his lips and let the froth fill his mouth, then when he'd had enough he raised the bottle in the air and said, "Cheers."

Beverley didn't respond. She was too busy catching her breath. He surveyed the ground below. At first he saw nothing, but he kept looking, waiting for some telltale sign of human activity. The heavily laden clouds cast black shadows on the ground, interspersed with beams of sunlight. A momentary flash of sun bounced off a shiny surface to pinpoint a vehicle. Once in his sights, he soon made out the second car, Parjit's Subaru. Now he searched for movement. Then he could pick his route.

He checked Beverley. She had removed her shoes exposing huge blisters on her feet. Tough, he thought, her fault for wearing such ridiculous shoes, but impressed because she hadn't demanded a drink or whinged about her feet.

"Don't get too comfortable," he said, as he pushed the bag back towards her. "We'll be heading off in a minute."

He squatted down beside her, shielded his eyes from the sun and continued to scan the terrain below. He concentrated so hard he almost forgot she existed until she spoke.

"Did Balbinder start the rumour that you had tampered with Nick's car?"

He had to admire her. She didn't give up.

"Well am I right?" she continued, "because the idea of you tampering with Nick's car doesn't make sense to me. I can't figure out a motive? I even asked around and no one else came up with a single reason for you to kill him."

Rory felt his neck jar as he turned to face her. Those bloody rumours kept haunting him. Too many people believed them. His attempts at the club to point the finger elsewhere had been moderately successful. Should he tell her he'd put her in the frame? "Oh, lots of people had reasons for wanting him dead. Maybe I had some. I certainly wasn't alone. Sandra had a motive, insane jealousy. I know she found you together at the Norfolk the day he died.

Beverley turned away from him. She didn't seem to like the way the conversation had turned. Well he did. "I know you hated being second best," he went on, "and you've been chasing after Martin just to rub her up the wrong way, haven't you?"

Beverley threw him a sour look and didn't answer.

"Martin wanted him dead too. Martin has always wanted to own all the land round here. He'd never get possession with Nick around. And he had a score to settle after that shoot out two years ago."

"What was that about?" Beverley asked.

"That's not important. You wanted him dead as well, because you want control of Ol Essakut. And don't try to deny it. You hated him for going off with Sandra."

"Maybe, but Balbinder Singh wasn't pointing a finger at any of us. Nor did we have the expertise or opportunity to tamper with his vehicle. And none of us are threatening to kill anyone for starting a rumour."

"Perhaps you're too clever for your own good," he snapped back, wondering if she realized he'd have to get rid of her. First she'd provide a perfect distraction for Balbinder.

Half an hour later he spotted the movement he had been searching for. He concentrated on the sighting for a while making certain he'd found Balbinder before making his move.

The hunt was on. He told Beverley what to do. "We're going down there now. Don't make a sound or the rhino might kill you or worse still you'll get caught in the cross fire. Is that clear?"

The terror in her eyes confirmed she understood. "One foot wrong," he whispered as he gestured with a throat cutting action. She nodded. She appeared to have difficulty swallowing and her hands were trembling as she fumbled with her shoes waiting for his signal to move.

It took longer than expected to reach the place where he'd seen Balbinder, during which time Beverley never put a foot wrong.

Balbinder's tracks were easy to find. So were the rhino tracks that Balbinder followed. Extra caution was required. The rhino and calf could easily circle round. The parched scrub provided ample cover for both the rhino and Balbinder and his three nephews.

A branch snapped. He signalled to Beverley to take cover behind a bush. Slowly he edged his way forward looking for a flicker of life. He waved to Beverley to stay down. He raised his rifle and eased off the safety catch, then lined his sights onto the spot where he thought he'd detected movement. He waited. Yes, there was something there. Who was it? The minutes ticked by. A spooked bird took flight. Had to be Balbinder. He turned to check on Beverley. Damn, the bitch was sneaking backwards away from him. He couldn't call her without giving himself away. He wasn't bothered, she wouldn't get far. He turned back to focus on his quarry. He located Parjit. Balbinder must be close by. He scanned to the left and then to the right.

Parjit spotted Beverley, and whistled softly to attract Balbinder's attention. Balbinder, who had been kneeling, obscured by a bush, twisted his head to check the direction Parjit pointed. This slight movement gave Rory his chance. Beverley had unintentionally created the perfect diversion. He couldn't have orchestrated it better. In those few seconds of distraction Balbinder let his guard slip and made himself a perfect target. Rory's dilemma of whether to aim at the head or the heart, still remained. His finger tensed on the trigger. He waited for Balbinder to move.

The static laden air almost crackled with tension. Beads of sweat ran down Rory's forehead. He let them run. The slightest movement would give Balbinder an advantage. Balbinder seemed to sense his presence. He turned and stared, too late for action, but enough time for Rory to glimpse his fear.

Rory squeezed the trigger. A surge of satisfaction washed over him, as Balbinder toppled backwards with the force of the bullet as it ripped through his chest. Rory's second shot was ready in the chamber in seconds. He watched for a flicker of movement from his victim. Nothing. Now Parjit. He had him in his sights. He cowered under a bush, his head buried in the ground. Did he think he'd become invisible? Rory's finger nursed the trigger as he waited for Parjit lift his head. He wanted to witness his fear.

He was aware of Beverley behind him on his left. He hoped she wouldn't do anything stupid. The sun vanished behind a thick, dark cloud. The tension levels rose. Thunder rumbled around them. Beverley was on the move, coming his way. She was rushing towards him. He had no idea what she intended, so braced himself. Seconds before impact, he spun round with his rifle butt held high catching her smack in the face, knocking her off balance.

She crumpled at his feet without making a sound. He lashed out at her with his foot, rolling her over on her back. She lay still, her eyes shut, her mouth open, blood splattered all over her face.

Those few seconds gave Parjit the chance to escape. Rory didn't think he'd get far. The hunt was on. Rory headed after him. He had to be careful. Parjit had a gun. He couldn't afford to let Parjit and the others get away. He stopped when he saw something khaki coloured on the ground, took aim and fired thinking it was Parjit lying low, but when he got closer he found his bullet had hit an abandoned rucksack. He heard the Subaru engine revving and a car door slam. Then he saw the tell tale billowing trail of dust as it roared away. What would they do? They wouldn't dare report what happened. If they did, they would have to admit to being out here with Balbinder to hunt a rhino.

He didn't care. He'd deal with them later. What Balbinder started, he would finish. This rhino was his. Stopping Balbinder from the pleasure of getting his trophy didn't mean he couldn't.

He hurried back to pick up the rhino trail. He grabbed Balbinder's rifle off the ground and slung it over his shoulder. The tracks showed the direction the rhino took, but not far away the tracks reverted to a normal browsing, feeding pace. This rhino didn't seem to be in any hurry to go far, in fact appeared to be moving round in a circle, heading towards where Balbinder lay. Rory was pleased. All he had to do was shoot the rhino with Balbinder's rifle, and claim the glory for killing a poacher. Nice one. He doubted the three stooges would dare to dispute his version of events.

At last he caught up with the beast. The wind was in the right direction, blowing his scent away from the great grey tough skinned creature. Rory was not in a hurry. He sat watching the mother and calf chomping away. His greatest regret was that the rhino had the biggest horns he had seen for years, which would be worth a fortune in the Far East, and he wouldn't be able to reap the rewards. Freedom was more valuable, and depended on his being able to blame Balbinder for the killing.

He spotted an old scar on the rhino's front shoulder which accounted for her uneven prints. The injury had left her with a limp. The calf looked healthy enough, though still too young to stray more than three feet away from its mother. He wouldn't kill the calf. Let someone rescue it. One of the orphanages, either in Nairobi or on one of the other ranches would be happy.

A fly buzzed round his face. He swatted it away,

but his movement seemed to act as a signal for another fly to home in on him. Aware of the danger of unnecessary movement, he tried to ignore them in the same way he ignored the trickle of sweat running off his forehead. Another rumble of thunder made the rhino twitchy. Rory knew he should act soon. He lifted the rifle and took aim. All he needed was for her to shift another foot to the side then he would have the perfect shot. She raised her head, and snorted. She started to lift her foot to move. He waited, keyed up, ready to pull the trigger.

A branch cracked behind him. The rhino's ears pricked up. Rory glanced back. Beverley stood about five yards away with a gun pointed at his head. Her swollen, blood covered face made it impossible to read her intention. He could only guess at what she was thinking. He didn't think she had the guts to pull the trigger, and even if she did the chances were she'd miss. Any gambler would say the odds were bad, but he'd never get another chance to shoot a rhino. After that, he'd sort out Beverley. He turned back and calmly took aim. As his finger tightened on the trigger he heard a shot. The impact of the bullet hitting his leg jolted him. His rifle lifted. His shot went wide, the mother and calf blundered off into the bush.

Rory dropped his gun and rolled onto his back. He couldn't believe Beverley had shot him.

He wanted to scream in agony or rage, he wasn't sure which, but he didn't want to give her the satisfaction of knowing how much he hurt. Warm sticky blood seeped out of the wound, soaking through his trousers. He raised his hand, hardly daring to inspect the damage her shot had inflicted. He faced her. She raised the rifle to her shoulder again. Shit, he thought, she's going to finish me off. A disturbance in the bush behind him made him look round. The rhino headed straight towards them. Beverley stood her ground, and fired her shot. Even from where he lay he knew she never intended to hit the rhino. She'd aimed well over its head.

With her gun discharged, she turned and fled. Selfish bitch, he thought, leaving me here alone, bleeding to death and at the mercy of a rhino. He checked behind him, her shot seemed to have put the rhino off for a moment. He had two choices, reload, or try to do something to stop the flow of blood. Thunder cracked overhead. Lightening split the sky. The storm was about to break.

Chapter 30

Martin got word Balbinder had left and hurried over to collect Simeon. He made a feeble excuse to Amina that he needed Simeon's help without giving details. Together they went to the flat on the edge of town where Hank stayed when he came to Nairobi.

Hank had his phone pressed to his ear when they arrived. He waved Martin and Simeon inside and carried on his conversation.

"No Beverley, stay where you are. Martin and Simeon have just come. We'll set off straight away." He raised his eyebrows to show his frustration.

"I know you're worried," he continued, "but it's too risky and you might make the situation worse."

He pointed towards the sofa. Martin moved forward wishing he was able to pick up the other side of the conversation

"Damn it, Beverley, I love you, which is one more reason why you shouldn't go rushing off into the bush." After a long silence he added in a softer tone. "I know you want to save the children, but I don't want you taking unnecessary chances. You said it yourself, he's nuts."

Martin noticed the sweat breaking out on Hank's forehead. The conversation got more worrying by the second. The children being involved changed everything.

"This isn't the best time to be telling you I love you, but I've waited too long already."

Martin caught Simeon looking uncomfortable with Hank's unexpected declaration of love. God knows what Beverley's reaction would be, maybe she'd guessed long ago.

Hank stuffed his phone into his pocket, grabbed his keys, and said, "We've got to get to Ol Essakut fast. Rory's gone nuts. He's got Sam and Emma with him."

"I don't understand," Martin said. "What would he want with the children?"

"Beverley isn't sure. She muttered something about poachers,"

"Possibly something to do with Balbinder Singh, I got word he's headed out on a hunt," Martin said. "But that doesn't explain the children being with Rory?"

"Sam and Emma were in the car he's driving. No idea why he has them. She says it's stinking hot out and they've no food or water with them."

"We must contact Sandra. She needs to be kept in the picture," Martin said,. "Simeon, please call her, she's not taking my calls."

Simeon nodded, and tapped in Sandra's number. "Phone's switched off. Shall I leave a message?" he queried.

Martin signalled no. "Try later."

"We need guns." Hank said, as he ushered them out the door. "You go straight to the ranch, I'll swing by my place and pick up some guns and catch up with you."

Martin drove off first, wondering if they'd arrive in time. Strange, but the fear of facing Rory armed with a gun didn't bother him as much as the prospect of facing Sandra if anything happened to the kids.

Simeon distracted him with the suggestion that he call Amina and ask her to tell Sandra.

"No, better she doesn't know," Martin answered.

"Are you sure, I reckon she'll be mad when she finds out," Simeon said.

"Better mad than in the way," Martin muttered. He'd been relieved when Simeon failed to get through. He didn't want Sandra in the line of fire. He couldn't bear the thought of her being in danger again. "Blame me. Technically the rhino is on my land, which lets you off the hook. Anyway, it's not your fault. She's the one who switched off her phone."

The roads were jammed with cars and matatu's flooding into town for the holiday celebrations. Eventually they got clear of the worst of the traffic and Martin put his foot down, regardless of the risk of speed traps. Martin didn't give a damn. He was determined to stop Balbinder from destroying the one thing that might make Ol Essakut a success.

He slowed down for the numerous police road blocks, each time being waved through without problems. Several of the local matatu drivers did not appear to be so lucky. Police checks were referred to as ATM's, automatic transfer machines, because the police demanded money to supplement their income. It was a case of pay up or be inspected. Knowing they would fail for having too many passengers or for some mechanical fault, they found it more cost effective to pay. More often than not the passengers had to share the cost.

He hadn't gone very far up the road when they had to slow down for the first of many blinding downpours. Martin had forgotten the ferocity of an African thunderstorm. The deluge was so heavy the windscreen wipers were almost battered off the windscreen, unable to cope with the volume of water lashing down at them. Steering became difficult as the vehicle aquaplaned on the sheets of water covering the tarmac. Twice conditions got so bad Martin had to stop and wait for the rain to ease and the road to become visible again. They pressed on and after a few miles came into a bone dry area.

"Won't take long for the rivers to flood," Simeon commented. "By the look of the last one we crossed they've had a lot of rain up on the Aberdares."

"Do you remember the terrible flood we had about fifteen years ago?"

"How could I forget? Especially, after you and Nick went round painting trees and rocks to show the high water mark. Some of those marks are still visible today and I'm forever explaining to visitors what they are."

"I'm glad they're still visible. I pointed them out to Sandra the other day. She didn't believe the water rose so high. I hope we aren't in for another like that now. It might put her off the place for life."

"I doubt Sandra will ever be put off." Simeon answered with respect in his voice.

The rain pelted down as they reached the Harriman house. There was lots of activity on the verandah. As he stopped Wanjiru rushed over to greet them. Martin ushered her out of the drenching rain, and tried to calm her down to make sense of her version of events, and to discover the significance of the stuff piled up on the porch.

It didn't take long to realize Wanjiru's only concern was the children. Beverley had run back to the house asking for food and water and gone off again to find them and Rory. Wanjiru begged her to wait and take someone with her. But Beverley hadn't listened. Eventually, Wanjiru remembered that Beverley had left a note.

The note, addressed to Hank, wasn't sealed. Martin read it.

She apologized for not waiting, she didn't dare to leave the children with Rory any longer than necessary. She said she had loaded up with supplies for the children, and told the staff to get more supplies ready for them too, in case the storm heading this way caught them.

Judging from the stuff piled on the porch Wanjiru and Juma had done more than follow her instructions. They'd alerted all the available staff still on the ranch, and even sent a couple of trackers ahead on foot to try to follow Beverley's trail. Everyone was concerned that rain might wash away her tracks if they left it too long. The trackers were to leave clear signs to show which route to take.

Martin, impressed with their organization, started loading up the back of the land cruiser with blankets, tents, food, and lamps while they waited for Hank.

The first thing Hank did when he arrived was hand Martin a rifle, and ammunition. Martin, reluctant to explain his lack of desire to handle a weapon, took the gun and prayed he'd not need to fire it. As he was already loaded up with supplies he left straight away, up the slippery road in search of the trackers' promised markers.

The rain had obliterated every tyre track that ever existed. He spotted the first marker, and not long after, found another. Without them the search would have been based on guess work as to which way she had driven. The light was fading when he came across a ranger standing by the side of the road waving his arms. The poor man was soaked through. They got him into the vehicle and he guided them into the bush, straight to one of the vehicles they were looking for,

Jenny's Peugeot.

Simeon grabbed his gun. Martin didn't bother, he only cared about the children and keeping them safe. If something had happened to them, Sandra would struggle to cope. She'd blame herself for leaving them and putting them in danger. Jenny would too. He peered through the steamed up windows but couldn't see anything. He opened the door, and stuck his head in. Emma lay slumped in her seat on the far side of the car, her childseat preventing her from falling sideways. Sam sat wide-eyed, one hand up to his face, his thumb firmly stuck in his mouth, the other hand stretched out to stroke Emma's arm. He looked suspiciously at Martin, his fear evident. Martin made a gentle approach to avoid alarming him further.

"Are you okay?" he asked quietly. Sam nodded his head. "What about Emma?"

Sam shrugged.

"Has she been asleep for long?" Again Sam shrugged. "Simeon's here with me. Would you like him to give you a drink?"

This time the little boy took his thumb out of his mouth and reached out towards him. Martin quickly unclipped the seat belt and passed him out to Simeon. "Give him a drink, while I check Emma." He went round to the other side of the car and opened that door. Emma still hadn't moved. Martin put his hand on her forehead. She was warm, limp and obviously dehydrated. He spotted a bottle of water lying on the seat beside her. He wondered why they hadn't drunk it, until he tried to open the bottle. No wonder. He struggled with the stiff cap, eventually it gave. He tipped her head up, her mouth opened. He put his finger in her mouth and dribbled a few drops of water down his hand letting the liquid run into her mouth.

She swallowed, and tried to push his hand away, he dribbled a few more drops and then a few more. When he took his hand away, she slowly opened her eyes, and reached out for the bottle. He helped her, making sure she drank a little at a time. Then he heard a whimper from behind her seat.

"Rupee," Emma whispered.

"Don't worry, Juma's here. He'll take care of him." He held the bottle up for her to take another swig, and shouted to Juma to open the back and do something about Rupee. Martin undid her seat belt strap and lifted her out of the seat and hugged her tightly while he kissed her forehead. His eyes brimmed with tears, no one noticed because of the lashing rain.

They all sat huddled in the back of the Land Cruiser trying to find out from the children which way Rory and Beverley had gone. Sam pointed in one direction, Emma in another.

Hank arrived, and wasn't happy no one knew for sure which way Beverley had gone. He scoured round looking for tracks, and decided there were several possible paths they might have taken.

"Follow Sam's directions," Martin said. "He's quite clued up about such things."

"You think so?"

"Yes, but I won't come with you, I'm taking these two back to safety and Sandra. I'll take Juma and enough supplies to last us if we get stuck in this storm. The rest you can keep for yourselves and the men. Set up camp here." He wasn't sure if the others would realize his enthusiasm to take the children back wasn't just for their benefit. He was terrified that under pressure, he might become a liability. He didn't think he could handle the gun Hank had so thoughtfully supplied, and in this sort of situation hesitancy to fire would put both Hank and Simeon in danger if they were relying on him. Hank paid little heed to the children. He was far too worried about Beverley, and desperate to find clues as to the direction Rory had taken her.

"Well, if you're going, you'd better hurry," Simeon said.

More deafening thunder, followed only seconds later by a bolt of brilliant white lightning which made Emma scream and cling on to Martin even tighter than before.

"You're right," he answered, "I'll take Jenny's car because of the children's seats." Simeon and Juma helped him pick out a few things from the mass of stuff the staff at the house had piled into the back of his Land Cruiser. Then Martin hugged the children and said, "Sam and Emma, we have to get back into your seats, so we can take Rupee home. Are you ready?" Sam nodded nervously. Emma was crying again. "Come on. Let's make a dash for it."

Simeon carried Sam back to the car and strapped him in. Martin managed to get Emma back in her seat, and buckled up. Juma sat in the front, clutching Rupee. Martin ran round to the driver's seat. The key was in the ignition. The engine fired at the first turn. He let the motor run long enough to check he had enough fuel to get back. The needle took ages to rise to a level he was satisfied with, one third of the way up the gauge, more than enough, he slipped the car into reverse and started to turn to get back on the road. Hank and the others waved as he pulled away. There was just enough light to make out the graded surface of the track. He prayed that the rain would not get much worse before he had the children safely home.

The road was more slippery than earlier, the

beating rain turned the loose soil into slime. Martin couldn't remember the last time he'd driven in such bad conditions. He must continue he had precious cargo aboard. The children were so quiet he adjusted the mirror so he could watch them. Juma tried to make them laugh by teasing Rupee, who had made a complete recovery. His efforts failed they were not in the mood for laughing. Tears trickled down Emma's face. Martin longed to stop to reassure her, but any delay might mean they didn't get home at all.

Martin sighed with relief when the car finally slid to a halt outside the house. How would Sandra react when she heard?

He lifted Emma out of the car. She clung to him with a stranglehold that nearly choked him. Sam was happier now and started playing with Rupee. Wanjiru eventually managed to persuade Emma to release him and sit on her knee.

The first thing he needed to do was contact Sandra and let her know the children were safe.

Wanjiru told him there was a message from Jim Standish. It seemed he was desperate for news of Sandra and wanted to be contacted the minute Sandra landed.

The message didn't make sense so Martin called Jim, and got his answer machine. He tried Sandra's house phone, no answer. He tried her mobile, no signal. He tried Amina's number. No luck there either.

The children clamoured for attention. He must settle them before he made any more calls. Wanjiru magically produced their favourite supper, spaghetti, and he found himself sitting with the children encouraging a speed eating contest. Who could suck up a single strand of spaghetti fastest? He was sure no one in the medical profession had ever suggested this as therapy for traumatised kids, but it made them laugh, the best medicine of the day. Wanjiru pretended to be cross when she saw their tomato covered faces. She produced a cloth to clean them up and made them finish their glasses of milk. Getting back to their normal routine, hopefully would cancel any after effects of their extended stay in the hot car. Only time would tell if Rory's behaviour had left mental scars. He tried to treat them as normally as possible. He read them a story, and played with their building blocks with them before Wanjiru whisked them off for a bubble bath. Reassuring squeals of delight came from the bathroom, and Wanjiru emerged covered with foam, a towel wrapped child tucked under each arm.

Once they were in bed he went to read them a final bed time story. One story led to another and another. They took advantage of his good nature. Fear the events of the day might flood back at any moment made him an easy target. Sandra could handle awkward questions with ease, with luck she'd be back before they started asking any. Emma's eyes kept closing, but she fought to stay awake. Eventually she lost the battle. He carried on reading, his voice getting softer and softer, and Sam nodded off too. At last he could ease his cramped limbs, and sneak back downstairs.

It was strange being alone in the house. He didn't think he had ever been here without either Nick, or more recently Sandra for company. Wanjiru made it clear leaving wasn't an option, she expected him to stay until Sandra got home, announcing the spare bedroom was ready for him. He wondered how Sandra would react to his presence.

Being stuck in the house for the children's sake didn't stop him thinking about Simeon and Hank and their search for Beverley. Funny how his earlier concern for the rhino had now been totally overshadowed by fear for others.

Hank's public declaration of love had come as a surprise. The look on Simeon's face had nearly made Martin laugh. He would have if the situation hadn't been so serious. Rory was obviously unstable and dangerous and Balbinder unpredictable.

Martin tried to call Sandra again. There was still no response, nor from Amina. Then he tried Jim Standish again wondering what the pilot wanted. He couldn't believe Sandra had found the courage to fly again.

Jim answered his phone, and wasted no time with pleasantries. "She said she wanted to try a take off and landing," he fumed. "Next I hear she's landed on some dirt track on your land."

"What the hell did she think she was doing? No one would want to fly in this weather. Not unless they had a death wish."

"Exactly," Jim shouted back down the line. "Still, I suppose we ought to be grateful she landed in one piece. At least that's what she told the control tower before she got cut off."

"I never heard a plane. The storm's been raging since I arrived. The rivers are flooded, so I can't get anyone out to search for her until daylight."

"You tell her I'm not happy."

Martin didn't blame him. Without the plane, his livelihood was at stake. Lessons provided his only income.

What made Sandra so determined to get back? Maybe someone told her about Balbinder, unlikely and not something she'd want to deal with alone. Or did Beverley alert her to a problem with the children? Fear for them would explain her reckless behaviour.

When Jim hung up, Martin suspected he'd be relieved to have raised the alert that Sandra was at Chui ranch. Jim might feel better, but Martin had never experienced such unease in his whole life. The only glimmer of hope he clung to was that she'd landed close enough to his home to find shelter.

He abandoned his half formed plans to head off in search of Sandra. Sam crept down the stairs with a tearful Emma in tow. The two children clambered up onto the settee on either side of him. He hadn't the heart to shoo them back up to their beds. Instead he wrapped his arms around them and promised them another story. For now he would let them snuggle up to him down here by the fire. Sam shoved a Thomas the Tank engine book into his hand. Emma pushed it away firmly. Sam passed him another about a pink striped cat. This time Emma, still a little tearful and edgy, accepted his selection. He knew the importance of calming them down, and keeping up the pretence nothing odd was happening. Best they didn't learn Sandra was stranded by the storm, or anything about the tricky situation with Rory and Beverley.

He read one story after another, once more forcing himself to read very slowly, hoping to bore them to sleep. This trick worked again.

Martin waited for a while before he untangled their arms and legs from around him, and lay them down flat on the settee and put a rug over them. He stoked the fire and flopped into the nearest chair. The picture of Helen staring down at him from the mantle shelf, made him uncomfortable. He rummaged in his pocket, and pulled out the little photo frame he had taken off his mother's bedside cabinet. His sister would have been about the same age as the twins, he looked across at them. The resemblance was startling, making him think about the past.

The soporific effect of the fire put him to sleep. A loud clap of thunder shook the building and woke them all. The terrified children clambered onto his lap and snuggled up. Emma calmed down quickly, Sam more awake tugged at his sleeve, demanding to look at the photo he still held.

Sam peered at the picture for a moment and said, “Emma.”

Chapter 31

What crazy instinct made her fly home in such atrocious conditions? Too late to turn back now. She hoped Jim would be pleased his advice worked and got her past the fear and forgive her for taking his plane. He'd be furious with her for taking off without telling him, and in weather like this.

Dodging storms became her focus. The plane buffeted in all directions by the gusting wind, made the controls hard to handle especially with her hand in a cast, but she hung on, ever watchful of the cloud formations as well as constantly checking the landmarks below. She couldn't afford to go off course.

As she got nearer, a huge cloud bubbled up between her and the ranch leaving her no choice but to circle north, and tack backwards. This plan had one advantage, she'd be flying over the area where they'd found the rhino. She'd check for activity. On reaching the point she wanted she became aware of a shift in the wind. The storm had surrounded her, thunderous clouds advanced every direction. She must land before they engulfed her, but she desperately wanted to make one low pass over the rhino territory.

She dropped right down, well below the heaving cloud, into the dark purple grey haze preceding the storm. Her eyes adjusted to the gloom. In the distance she caught a glimpse of a fast moving vehicle. She watched the dust trail thinking how much the ranch needed rain. A more subtle coloured green Range

Rover, parked off road, attracted her attention. She shivered, suspicion rising fast. Poachers meant guns. She yanked the controls to gain height. She'd no desire to become a target for a mad gunman. She circled the area, keeping as high as possible without entering the base of the cloud, this time searching for the occupants of the car. The light made the task hard. A movement distracted her. She braced herself to risk swooping in for a closer look. The rhino and calf were there, so was a man lying on the ground about twenty yards away, he didn't appear to be moving, the angle of his body awkward, not a natural hunting position. She circled the rhino and calf. The rhino made to move, nose down in a charging position straight at a second figure she'd missed earlier. Without a second thought, she dived down towards the rhino to head it away from its intended victim. After she had passed over, she registered the second person on the ground was Rory. She spun the plane round and once more tried to drive the rhino away from its quarry. This time she focussed on Rory. His injuries looked serious.

A flash of lightning and a low growling rumble of thunder along with the deteriorating visibility, made the need to land a priority. No hope of getting back to Ol Essakut. At least if she put down here, she'd be able to check on Rory's condition. She picked out a few land marks so she'd be able to locate him from the ground, wishing she knew the terrain on Martin's property better. His house by the river gorge was too far away from Rory. She needed to be closer.

A graded track near where the green Range Rover had parked looked fairly smooth without many dense bushy patches along its edges. She lined herself up for her descent, bracing herself for a bumpy landing. The wheels touched the ground, bounced up, then touched again, this time staying on the ground. What luck. This had to be the smoothest bit of road on the estate. The plane came to a halt, and the first huge drops of rain fell. Within seconds they beat down on the roof of the plane with deafening intensity. Before doing anything else Sandra called control to report her status. She fiddled with the controls. The radio hissed and crackled, the storm static creating severe interference. She reported her position, stating she'd set down on a roadway unharmed. She didn't get a reply, so repeated her status again and eventually over the crackle heard a staccato voice say "message received." She wanted to say more, but the radio crackle made further conversation impossible. She flicked the switch to off and scrambled to the rear of the plane to gather emergency equipment.

First aid kit, some form of shelter from the rain. She ferreted in the little lockers in the back of the plane, found a small folded tarpaulin and a blanket in one of them. She hauled them out and put them with the first aid kit, then found a torch and a bottle of water, and compass, an essential as long as she concentrated.

Once she'd collected everything she could carry, she fixed a point on the compass, opened the door of the plane and climbed down. The rain soaked through her clothes in seconds and streamed down her face. Undeterred she walked on in her chosen direction, quickly reaching the tree selected as a marker. From there she headed east into the bush to the Range Rover she'd spotted from the air. Its doors were locked. She moved on, to the first figure seen from the plane. His turban made her wonder if this was Balbinder Singh, the man Martin had been so concerned about. No need to check his pulse. A huge dark circle of blood in the centre of his chest drew her eye to a gaping bullet hole. The rain spread the blood across his chest staining his shirt pink. She checked around him expecting to find a gun nearby. Nothing.

The missing gun worried her. Not knowing who'd shot him or why, did too. She couldn't dwell on that, Rory needed her help. Maybe the driver of the vehicle creating the dust cloud had gone to fetch someone, more likely they had been responsible for the bloodshed.

She double checked her compass and headed towards the place where Rory lay, not far away. Perhaps she should call out to warn him of her presence. A precaution, she'd rather not get shot by mistake. "Rory. Rory. Can you hear me?"

She picked up a faint reply. "Over here."

Sandra followed a trail of blood leading towards the voice, and found Rory lying on his side, tucked in against a small rock. At first she wasn't sure where the blood had come from, because the rain had spread the blood from the top of his leg right down to his ankles. Soon the growing pool beneath his thigh highlighted the spot. She knelt down beside him, to make a closer examination.

"Can't stop the bleeding," he said faintly, pointing to the hole in his leg.

"I'll do what I can." She unfolded the tarpaulin, spreading it over him, making him stand his gun on its butt to make a sort of tent. She peered in under the newly created shelter and opened the first aid kit she had brought with her. She tore open the biggest dressing pack and pressed the wadding against the bleeding wound. Rory flinched, but she didn't stop. She took another wad of dressing and attempted to dry the surrounding area, a losing battle. Her only hope was to pack the wound and bind something tight round the leg to stem the flow.

Rory groaned, but she ignored his pain and carried on, and managed to get a bandage round his leg, winding as tight as possible.

"I can't do more in these conditions. What else is injured?"

"My foot got crushed, and I think my shoulder is dislocated," he gasped. "Been a hell of a lot worse if you hadn't flown over when you did."

"Who does the Range Rover belong to?" she asked.

"Balbinder."

"It's locked, but is the only shelter around. Is he the dead guy over there?"

"Yes."

"I'll try to find the keys. Be back as quick as I can."

Sandra hated the thought of rummaging through a dead man's pockets, but what choice did she have? She wanted to say a prayer when she stood over him, but wondered if a prayer would be appropriate. His safari jacket had numerous pockets. Which one held the keys? She tentatively touched the right hand pocket, no keys there, tested the left one, ammunition. His trouser pockets felt empty, which left only the blood stained breast pocket of his jacket. The blood made it stiff and sticky to touch, inside lay something hard and lumpy. The congealed blood made the button hard to open. Squeamish or not, she had to continue. These keys might save Rory's life. She slipped her hand into the pocket and dragged the contents out. Three keys on a fancy key-ring.

Sandra ran back to Rory. "I've found them. I'll move the vehicle closer so you can climb in. Here, take a sip of water while I'm gone."

She made her way back to the Range Rover,

unlocked it and struggled to adjust the seat so she could reach the pedals. She had never driven one before. A quick check of the switches and controls, find the headlights, the windscreen wipers, try the clutch and test the gear change. All done, time to switch the engine on, get into gear, ease the foot off the clutch and edge forward. She struggled to see through the sheet of water on the windscreen. She left the clearing where Balbinder lay, wishing she could pick up his body but she couldn't afford to delay getting back to Rory. The headlights helped as the storm clouds reduced the light to night time levels. She inched up as close as she dared and jumped out to open the rear door and went to help him get into the back.

Rory was slipping into unconsciousness. She knew the importance of keeping him conscious even if it meant he was aware of the pain. She tapped him on the shoulder. "Rory, can you move?"

He shifted his position and groaned. "No."

"Try," she pleaded.

"I can't," he whispered.

She tried to put an arm round him to help him sit up, but he didn't seem able or willing to move. She sank onto the ground next to him, tears of frustration mixing with the rain streaming down her face.

Because of the darkness she left the headlights on and the engine running while she worked.

"I can't lift you on my own. I'll try to make some sort of shelter here. Hang on I'll check what they have in the back."

She was struggling to rig up a more substantial tent to cover him when she heard voices.

Two drenched figures appeared out the darkness. Jacob, and an old man called Murumbi. Jacob seemed as shocked to find her as she was to see him.

Her lights had guided them her way. She explained what she could. Rory's condition didn't need words, but news of Balbinder Singh's death had them worried.

"It's too late to help him, Rory needs help now. We must get him into the vehicle to save him."

Jacob nodded to Murumbi, muttered a few words to each other, they clambered up onto the roof of the Range Rover, ripped the canvas canopy off the top to slide the tough fabric up under Rory's feet and up towards his bottom. At one point they indicated she should lift Rory's legs.

Jacob's plan seemed as good as any, so she bent down beside Rory, trying to get one hand in between the rock he was leaning against and his spine. "You understand what we're going to try to do?" she asked softly. "Go with us, don't fight. We won't drop you."

Jacob caught hold of her hand behind Rory's back, and said, "Ready. One, two, three." And together they lifted him away from the rock.

Somehow between the three of them they raised Rory on the canvas and placed him onto the tailboard.

"Now we splint his leg," Jacob said, as he reached over and picked up Rory's discarded rifle, checked it wasn't loaded. "Good for splint."

Sandra handed him a roll of bandage, found in the back of the Range Rover and watched as Murumbi lifted Rory's legs slightly so Jacob could bind them to the rifle.

Rory grabbed Sandra's hand, squeezing so tight she thought he'd break her bones. His teeth so firmly clenched together the veins in his forehead stood out in some mad effort not to show any sign of weakness. Jacob worked quickly considering the conditions preparing Rory for the next stage. Jacob scrambled in and slid Rory round so the door would close.

"Can you drive to Ol Essakut Jacob? I'll stay in the back with Rory," Sandra said, as she inspected her earlier dressing. The bleeding had slowed but not stopped.

"River too high to go home tonight," Jacob said. "Best we go to Mr. Martin's house."

Sandra, so focussed on Rory hadn't paid attention to the fact the rain was coming down as hard as it had been when she landed. Jacob was probably right, better to get to proper shelter than stuck in the mud.

"Fine," she answered, "the quicker the better. He's getting cold."

The drive to Martin's was shorter than she expected, but not the welcoming haven she'd hoped for. The place was deserted so Jacob had to break in. There was no fuel for the generator, and the telephone line was dead.

Rory slipped in and out of consciousness. They had to get him inside fast. She waited while Jacob lit a hurricane lamp and Murumbi put a match to the kitchen range. Jacob found a camp bed to use as a stretcher and brought it out to the vehicle. With a lot of pushing and pulling, they lowered Rory onto it, and carried him inside, putting him down near the stove.

In the lamp light his injuries looked more serious. He had turned a sickly shade of grey and was shivering violently. Jacob helped remove his wet clothing and together they cocooned him in towels and blankets.

The dressing she put on earlier stayed in place. She was afraid to touch it in case she triggered further blood loss. He could ill afford to lose more now. She looked at Jacob to gauge his opinion. He shook his head when she pointed to the dressing, waving his hands to indicate to leave it alone. Jacob's expression didn't inspire hope of Rory recovering. The deterioration was fast, and without qualified medical help comfort was the only thing she had to offer.

She kept talking to him to keep him conscious.

"What happened?" she asked.

Rory let out a sort of laugh. The sound so unexpected, so callous, it made her shudder. "I shot Balbinder," he said.

"Why?"

"Got what he deserved." He grabbed her hand. "Blackmailing bastard."

Sandra didn't know how to respond, but Rory didn't wait to elaborate. "He wanted to tell everyone about Nick's accident."

"What has Nick's accident got to do with Balbinder?"

Rory shook his head. "You heard the rumours..."

Sandra decided the pain had made Rory delirious and paranoid. Perhaps encouraging him to talk wasn't a good idea. He coughed finding it harder to draw breath, possibly his ribs had been broken. His chest was badly bruised.

"He used me... He started them..." he gasped. "He wanted the rhino..."

"I don't understand..."

"His rumours... they're true, I fixed the car."

She couldn't believe Rory would confess so readily. Pain must be causing his confusion. "That's ridiculous. Why would you want to kill Nick?" As she said it, she knew he had many reasons for wanting Nick to die.

"Secret," he muttered.

"To do with Helen?" she asked quietly.

Rory tried to sit up. “How do you know?” He choked and fell back into a lying position.

Sandra dripped water onto his lips.

“Know what?”

“She died... because of my baby.” Tears trickled down his cheek. “Nick made her... He hated her because she told him the twins weren’t his kids.” He gripped her arm so tight it hurt. “Bet he didn’t tell you that.”

She couldn’t pull away, and she hated having to press him to talk, but she needed to know. “Were they yours?”

“No... Do you think I’d have wanted to get rid of them if they had been?

“What do you mean, get rid of them?”

Rory stared at her, but he seemed far away.

“He poisoned her mind against me. That’s why she killed herself. He didn’t have to tell her... to hurt her.”

Sandra had to defend Nick. “No, you’re wrong,” she said. “He never wanted either of you to find out. He asked her to end the affair with you and she refused. That’s why he told her. He had no idea she was pregnant.”

“He swore he’d never tell anyone.”

“He kept his word. I discovered his diaries.”

Rory closed his eyes. Beads of sweat formed on his brow. She wiped them away and wondered what else to do.

“Diaries... Bloody diaries.” he mumbled. “Full of secrets... he liked secrets... Balbinder liked secrets too.” He tried to lick his lips, so she dribbled a few more drops on them, which seemed to help.

“Why did Balbinder shoot you?” she asked, to keep him talking, afraid of letting him lose consciousness.

“He didn’t shoot me... I got him first... perfect

shot... smack in the heart," he gasped, his breathing more laboured with each outburst, "right where I wanted. Then Beverley shot me."

"Beverley? I don't understand..."

"Stupid interfering bitch... thought she could save the twins."

"Save the twins? What the hell do you mean?" She panicked. "How do they fit into this story?"

"Told you... I wanted to get rid of them... but Balbinder came after the rhino... before I had time... then Beverley pitched up. Silly cow tried to charm me with a few cold beers. Nearly had her fooled, but I figured she'd distract Balbinder... it worked... but then the crazy bitch came at me with Balbinder's gun."

"Where is she?"

"God knows, she took off into the bush... went to find the twins, maybe."

"What do you mean? Where were they?"

"We left them in the car."

"Where?" She demanded, aware of the higher tone of her voice. She felt numb inside. None of what he was saying made sense.

"Don't know... somewhere off the track..." His voice weakened. "Beverley's never going to find them."

Sandra didn't know what to say next. She now knew the details of his part in Nick's accident, but more important was getting clearer information about the children. Had he really abandoned them in the bush? If he had, how and who could she alert to go and find them? The pool of blood on the floor underneath Rory became too obvious to ignore. His chances diminished by the minute. No one could lose that much blood and survive. His eyes were becoming less focussed, and his skin drained and clammy.

She felt cruel for attempting to keep him talking, but there were things she had to ask.

"Who is their father?"

He shook his head weakly.

"Did you kill Nick?"

"You'll get it all..." he mumbled.

"What?"

"Ol... ..Ess... kut." He was barely coherent.

"Don't give up," she pleaded, "Please Rory, hang on."

He squeezed her arm and whispered, "Watch... out... for... Martin. He wants it.

Before she had really registered what he had said, his grip on her arm relaxed and he lost consciousness.

What did he mean? Why the warning? She didn't know what to do other than to sit and hold his hand. His breathing was shallow, getting weaker and weaker with each gasp.

Jacob put a blanket over her shoulders. His simple kind gesture was nearly her undoing. She shivered. The chill from her soaked clothing and the cold hard floor she knelt on had seeped into her bones. Her legs were stiff with cramp but she wouldn't abandon him. Not now. Not yet.

Jacob came back with a little stool for her to sit on. Gratefully she moved onto it, but the resulting pins and needles nearly made her cry out.

Jacob and Murumbi had been busy. The stove was delivering heat to the room. The kettle boiled and Jacob offered her a cup of hot tea. She looked at Rory, as she guiltily took the cup, wishing he were fit enough to have some too.

The tea was hot and she clung to the cup, savouring the warmth from it. The heat raised her awareness of her wet and cold state. What about the others?

Murumbi huddled near the stove, steam rising from his soggy garments while Jacob bustled round the kitchen in a rather lost way.

"Go upstairs and find dry clothes for yourself and Murumbi," she said.

Jacob nodded and left the room, returning shortly with a couple of shirts and pullovers and tracksuit trousers. She guessed relics from Martin's college days. He checked with her they were suitable, and they disappeared into the passage to change. Murumbi, swamped by the clothes, looked happy to be dry.

Jacob suggested she should change her clothes, but the tempo of Rory's breathing changed, and so did the atmosphere in the room. Time was running out. The rasping breath the only sound she focussed on. When he finally stopped breathing, she became aware of all the other noises she'd filtered out. The drumming of the rain on the corrugated roof, the splash as it overflowed from the guttering, cascading onto the path outside the window, rumbles of thunder, the crack of lightening, the sound of Murumbi and Jacob drinking their tea, even the sound of her own breathing.

Jacob coughed. "You go change, not good to get cold."

Sandra did as he said, unwilling to accept Rory had gone. Gently she released her grip on his hand, and stood up.

To encounter death was difficult enough. Two dead bodies in one day more than she could bear.

Jacob spread a sheet over Rory, and led her through the hall into the big sitting room. He pointed to a selection of clothes piled up on the table in front of a roaring fire. He had laid out a couple of towels as well.

"You stay here. I bring hot water to wash."

She wanted to protest it wasn't necessary, but a quick glance in the mirror made her accept the offer. Her jeans were red, caked with a mixture of blood and mud, one a deeper stain than the other. Her shirt was much the same. And as for her plaster cast, the rain turned the plaster to a limp lump, and Rory's blood created a stain that went right up to the elbow.

Sandra perched on the seat by the fire while she waited for him to bring in the bowl of water. She thanked him, and as soon as he had gone stripped off her clothes, and attempted to wash off the mud and blood, a harder task than expected. The water soon turned so red she wondered if the process added more dirt than she removed. She'd have loved another bowl of clean water, but was too cold and tired to ask. She briskly towelled herself dry and pulled on a rather baggy pair of trousers with a stretchy waistband, topped with the smallest and warmest looking of the jumpers Jacob had lined up.

Once dressed, she tried to lift the bowl of dirty water but it was too heavy for her without the support of the plaster cast.

She went into the kitchen, Rory's body had disappeared.

"Too hot here," Jacob said without prompting. "Other room better."

Sandra thanked him, pleased he'd acted without asking for permission. Now she needed his support.

"Will you help me to find the children, and Beverley?"

Jacob's eyes widened, and he shook his head. "Not safe to go out now."

She peered out the door. The rain was heavier than

before. Rivers of water swirled round the wheels of the Range Rover obscuring the shape of the driveway. Jacob's common sense didn't make the decision any easier to accept.

"Someone will look for them," Jacob said. "No one will get here. River too high."

"What do you mean?"

"We cross the river before rain start. Very deep then, but we want to save rhino," he explained.

"Where have all Martin's staff gone?"

"Some take cattle to Rumuruti, and stay away for holiday."

"What about Balbinder Singh's body?" she asked.

"Rain too bad, we get stuck. Better tomorrow," Jacob answered. Sandra trusted his judgement. Of all the staff on the ranch, Jacob was the best person to have around.

"Perhaps if the storm dies down the radio in the plane will work." She knew she was just trying to give herself some hope.

Jacob smiled. "We check in morning."

"Did you find anything to eat?" she asked.

"Store's locked." he answered shaking his head.

"Break it open."

Jacob didn't need more encouragement. Within minutes he had forced the larder door open, and disappeared. When he didn't immediately come out, Sandra followed him in. He held a tin of lobster bisque trying to work out what it was. Sandra couldn't imagine Murumbi tucking in, so shook her head, and pointed to tinned peaches, tinned tomatoes, and a couple of cans of corned beef. Jacob accepted her suggestions and found a bag of maize meal and a small bag of rice, in amongst some weevil infested packets of cereals.

Armed with the ingredients of his choice Jacob took his offerings back to the kitchen. Murumbi cheered up at the thought of food. Sandra wasn't hungry but knew she ought to eat something. The lobster bisque would suit her fine. How many days would they have to survive on the meagre contents of the store? Martin had described the great flood, but she couldn't remember any mention of the duration of the isolation. Still she had two people on hand who'd proved themselves capable of improvisation in difficult circumstances.

"I'll try this," she said pointing to the lobster bisque. In response to the puzzled look, added, "Fish soup." Jacob didn't look keen. "You and Murumbi should open the tin of corned beef, and cook some rice. And I want you both to stay here in the house, find blankets and camp beds and set yourselves up."

"Thank you," Jacob said, rather formally. "You go by fire in the other room, I heat this up." He took the tin out of her hand. Sandra was tempted to say she could do it herself, but decided it was better to do as he suggested. Murumbi would not be used to eating with his employers and might be uncomfortable if she stayed to eat in the kitchen with them. Jacob mixed with tourists often enough to cope without a problem.

She went in and plonked herself down on the big old fashioned settee to wait for her soup. The paraffin lamp Jacob lit hissed gently in the background. A big pile of old photo albums lay on the table in front of her. She leaned forward and started turning the pages, trying to find pictures of Martin. She found some of him and Nick, and there were a few fitting descriptions of events in Nick's diaries. She shivered. Those diaries were supposed to clear up mysteries. Instead they triggered more questions than answers.

And most of them concerned Martin. Every time she had tried to get him to talk about Nick, or Helen, or Rory he had avoided the subject. Her conclusion being he didn't want her to know the truth about his interest in Ol Essakut. Nick had expressed doubts about his desire. Now Rory had added his warning. Beverley shared their concerns too. Only Simeon stood up for him, but Martin hadn't been loyal to Simeon in return.

Jacob appeared with her soup, which brought her back to the present. She asked if he had everything he needed, and while he stoked the fire he assured her he had. She ate the soup and a little later he returned, to take the dishes away, and to bring her a rug to put over herself. She wondered if he sensed she wouldn't feel happy sleeping upstairs in a bed, with a dead body in the house. She thanked him, and wrapped the rug round her legs. She was exhausted, physically and emotionally, because she spent the night before reading Nick's diaries, and then she had experienced the return of memories of her father and brother, overcome her fear of flying, had a hair-raising flight, and then listened to a death bed confession. More than enough for one day, she thought as she absentmindedly flicked through the last of the photo albums.

One particular photo caught her attention, making her wish the identity of the people in it had been indicated.

Chapter 32

Martin had done his fair share of hanging around waiting for news to break, and something to happen. He didn't mind being stuck with the children, he loved their company, but the frustration of not being able to go and find Sandra made him edgy. She said she'd landed safely but she might have lied and pretended everything was fine to protect the children from worry. He'd experienced her expertise at playing down events with her dodging telling him about being shot down previously.

The hurt on her face at the races when she caught Beverley kissing him still haunted him. He couldn't bear that he'd caused her pain. She needed to understand only one woman interested him, and she was the one. Now he couldn't get near her let alone speak to her.

Martin woke as dawn broke. The rain still fell and the vlei had become a vast shallow lake. He prayed the description of the terrible flood had stuck in Sandra's mind, with enough impact, to prevent her from attempting to cross any of the streams or rivers between his property and hers.

He desperately wanted to head off to find her, but she'd never forgive him if he left the children alone. By mid morning he wondered if Hank and Simeon would ever find Beverley, never mind Rory and Balbinder Singh. The radio crackled into life. Simeon announced they'd found Beverley and would be bringing her back immediately. As far as they knew, Balbinder was dead, and Rory injured. Both were on the other side of the river and unreachable.

Martin had to sit and wait for their return, using the time trying to work out a way of crossing the river. The weather made flying impossible even if he'd had a plane available. Simeon's comment about the river turning into a raging torrent made him sure all the normal bridges, and fords would be underwater and too dangerous to contemplate. Trying to approach his property from the opposite direction was out. He couldn't even get to the main road from here never mind back in to his home.

The only other possibility was the old rope bridge.

He doubted anyone had risked the route in years. He hurried to the kitchen and asked Juma if he remembered the bridge. Juma, shook his head and sent a message down to the gardener, who asked around the residents in the village. Not one person could remember seeing a rope bridge anywhere.

A vehicle approached and Martin rushed out to meet them. Hank carried Beverley in and gently lowered her onto the settee in the lounge. Her face was a mess, black eyes, swollen nose and lips made her almost unrecognisable. Hank propped her foot up on a couple of cushions, and checked if she was comfortable. She mumbled she was fine, the injuries affecting her ability to talk.

"What chance of getting Beverley out, or of getting a Doctor in?" Hank asked.

"None," Martin answered. "The road is impassable, both the bridge this end, and the one near the Education Centre are underwater. You can raid the medicine cupboard, I'll show you."

Hank went upstairs with him, and while they were

out of range of the children, relayed what Beverley had told him about Balbinder dying and about Rory hitting Beverley with his rifle butt.

"She also said Rory had been about to shoot the rhino, and using Parjit's abandoned gun she fired at him to stop him. She intended to shoot the ground near him to put him off, but the gun pulled to one side and she hit him in the leg," Hank said. "She was too scared to stick around to find out how badly hurt he was."

"I don't blame her. I don't think I'd have bothered after being smacked in the face like that."

"Luckily she crossed the stream and found an overhanging rock to give her shelter before darkness descended. She heard a plane flying round, but couldn't work out where it landed. With all that thunder and lightning and her face hurting so much she wasn't too bothered about other people at that stage. This morning she hung her shirt up on a branch hoping someone would be looking for her as she had no idea which direction to head."

"What about her foot?"

"Twisted ankle and raw with blisters, nothing rest won't cure. But I'm not so sure about her face."

"Nose is probably broken, but I doubt the doctor can do anything until the swelling goes down."

"Exactly what I told her. Seems we get to stay here for a while. I hope Sandra won't mind."

"She's got problems of her own."

"What?"

"She borrowed Jim Standish's training plane, and flew up here yesterday afternoon without his permission. I spoke to Jim. According to the flight recorder she made radio contact to say she had put down on a stretch of road on my property as the storm broke which ties in with Beverley's account. Bad static made radio contact almost impossible."

"What will she do?"

"I don't know. If Rory's gone mad enough to shoot Balbinder, and injure Beverley, I want to be with her, even if Rory is injured. He's more dangerous than we ever imagined."

"Maybe she'll have taken shelter at your place," Hank said.

A comforting thought, but Martin needed certainty. "I hope so. Would you mind taking charge of the children? Or will caring for Beverley be too much?"

"I can handle both. What's your plan?"

"I want to check out an old rope bridge we used years ago. If it still exists, I'll cross the river and give her some support."

"What does Simeon think?"

"I haven't asked."

"Asked me what?" Simeon said, having overhead the tail end of the conversation.

"You remember the old rope walkway we rigged up over the gully above Kingfisher Gorge?"

"How could I forget? That rope must have rotted by now."

"Will you come with me to check?"

"Are you mad?"

"Probably, but I have to try."

"Okay. I'll bring some ropes, harnesses and other tackle. No one goes over unless I think it's safe."

"Fine. I'll ask Juma to pack some food."

Hank said nothing. His normally brash behaviour seemed tempered by his concern for Beverley. Martin wondered if the change in him had anything to do with his declaration of love the day before. Would Beverley take it seriously? She certainly seemed keen for Hank to stay by her. Martin hoped it wasn't just because he'd always stood by her at bad moments in her life. Hank deserved more.

"Hank I'll leave you to contact the police, they can decide whether to inform the Singhs. Maybe they can locate Parjit and his brothers. Someone said their car went through the main gate at about nine last night, no one is sure who the occupants were. And you might be wise to get legal advice for Beverley. Fighting her case shouldn't be too much of a problem. And can you witness my signature on this document and get it to your solicitor to deal with at the same time." He handed Hank a pen and a few pages of paper, and large white envelope. "Simeon, can you sign this too?"

Simeon did as requested, and then showed him the assortment of ropes and other equipment including spare radio batteries he'd gathered.

"If you get over, I'll bet the ones at the house are dead, otherwise I'm sure Sandra would have called in."

The preparations reminded Martin of the days when Nick, Simeon and himself had gone off on their adventures together. This was different. This had an urgency those adventures lacked. Simeon said nothing but Martin guessed he remembered those days too. They stopped a couple of times to check the river levels as they went. And then they got to the old rope bridge. The roar of water pushing through the chasm and down into the pool about fifty yards from the rope bridge made talking almost impossible.

Even when Simeon shouted Martin had trouble hearing what he was saying. Simeon signalled for him to move away from the edge to a fractionally quieter position.

"I can't let you take such a risk."

“Sorry, you can’t stop me,” Martin answered.

“Damn, I thought you’d say that. You do realize if you get over, you might not be able to get back,” Simeon said.

“Don’t worry. I can take care of myself.”

“I hope so, but at least wear a helmet and a harness with a safety rope. So, if you fall, we might manage to haul you up before you drown.”

“I’ll do whatever you want, but quickly, please.”

Simeon pulled out the ropes he’d loaded up, sorted them and handed him a harness. He checked Martin had fastened his correctly, and offered him a helmet and finally snapped on the safety rope. Martin didn’t comment that the precautions wouldn’t be much use if he did fall.

All he wanted to do was inch his way over the three strand rope bridge.

“Remember, when you get to the other side attach the safety rope to the tree over there, so we can winch supplies over to you,” Simeon instructed in the commanding tone he had learned in the forces.

Martin gave the thumbs up signal and turned to face the rope walk.

The old construction consisted of three heavy coir ropes, two to hold on to, and the third thicker one to balance on. Finer inter-connected ties, set about three feet apart, supposedly kept the main trio of ropes from separating too far. Most of these looked rather frayed and fragile.

He gripped the hand ropes, and put one foot tentatively on the lower one. He felt slight tension on the safety rope, which Martin would feed out as he went. He put his full weight down on his front foot. The structure swayed as the rope tightened under his weight. Slowly, he lifted his back foot and stepped forward, and he slid one hand along the top rope, followed by the other. The timber supports creaked as did the rain soaked rope, as it tensioned. He moved on, slowly, steadily, being extra careful not to set up a rocking movement. He didn't trust the frayed rope to stand violent pressure. He got more comfortable the further he progressed. About three quarters of the way across the rope beneath him sagged. He tightened his grip on the hand ropes. He took six more steps when it sagged again, the strands separating. The temptation to rush the last few feet was powerful, but he forced himself not to. One more step, then one more. He was almost at the end, he lifted his foot, and as he went to put his weight on it, the rope snapped. His arms nearly jolted out of their sockets as his full weight transferred from his legs to his arms. He hung a couple of feet from safety. He had to decide, which of the two remaining ropes to trust to support him. He made his choice. Letting go of one he swung one hand over the other, ape fashion until his feet hit the ground.

He didn't dare look back until he had both his feet firmly planted on the ground a few feet away from the edge. He waved to Simeon and got a signal of congratulations back. He secured the safety rope as instructed, and a few minutes later his pack made it across. The rope would stay in place in case they were stranded for any length of time, but Martin wasn't bothered. All he wanted was to find Sandra.

As he approached the house he saw smoke coming out of the main chimney. A possible indication she had reached safety. He hurried on and found signs of a forced entry. The staff should have been there to let her in. Then he remembered about the holiday, and the cattle drive.

He entered and found a heap of blood stained

clothes lying on the floor. He flew into a panic. He couldn't bear the thought of her being injured. He called out. No answer. He hurried in through the kitchen, through the dining room, into the lounge, an empty cup and a discarded blanket showed someone had stayed. He opened the door to the downstairs office, and discovered Rory's body.

A dead body and a pile of blood stained clothes and an empty house were not enough. He tore round the house looking for Sandra, finding evidence that more than one person had sheltered in it. He went back outside looking for clues. Several sets of foot prints and fresh tyre tracks in the mud added to his confusion. Whose were they? The sound of a vehicle made him duck behind the doorway for cover. His relief when Sandra climbed out was so intense he couldn't stop himself from rushing over and flinging his arms around her.

"God, when I found all those bloodstained clothes I thought I'd lost you," he said kissing her forehead.

Sandra pushed him away. "What happened to the children? Where are they?"

"They're fine. At the ranch..."

"Are you sure?"

"Yes, I got them home yesterday evening, tired, a bit thirsty, but otherwise fine." He could tell she didn't believe him. "Hank and Beverley are with them and Simeon is around as well."

Sandra stared at him, her eyes filled with tears. He gently pulled her back into his arms to comfort her. This time she let him.

"I've been so worried." Her fears poured out in a rush. "Rory said he'd left them in a car out there somewhere. I didn't know whether to believe him or not. He said so many things that didn't make sense.

He even said Beverley shot him."

"It's true. Beverley told me herself. You can speak to her on the radio if you want."

Sandra shook her head and wiped her eyes with the back of her hand, and eased away from him. "How did you get here? Jacob said there was no way in or out with the river flooded."

"I came over an old rope bridge, up river. A bit dodgy, but I made it. Sadly it wasn't safe enough for anyone else to cross with me. I'm glad you had Jacob and Murumbi to help."

"They've been great."

"Where have you been?"

"To the plane to try to radio, but I didn't have much luck. And we collected Balbinder Singh's body. We didn't want some animal to get hold of it. You know Rory is dead?"

"Yes, I found his body."

Martin peered over her shoulder at the covered figure in the back of the Range Rover, and Jacob and Murumbi standing by patiently waiting for Sandra to give them instructions. "You go in. I'll give them a hand to move him."

While he helped them, they told him how they had heard that Balbinder was around so came to keep an eye on his activities, and had been lucky to find Sandra. He thanked them, and told them he'd left food in the kitchen for everyone and he went back to give Sandra his full attention.

Sandra seemed reluctant to talk so he had to coax the story out of her. "What made you feel you had to dash up here so fast? Jim Standish wasn't too happy with your sudden departure, especially in such dicey weather conditions."

"I came because I heard that you and Hank and

Simeon had charged off to deal with some poachers. I felt I should be around."

"I thought somehow you had got wind that the children were in danger, but couldn't figure out who'd have told you. Tell me what happened. Beverley said you circled the area."

"I spotted the Range Rover, and someone lying on the ground, so I risked flying low to check. Then, I saw Rory. The rhino was in full charge. I came in as low as I could to scare it off, but not before it tossed him in the air. I landed as close as I could and went to help. I couldn't do much. Then Jacob and Murumbi appeared out of nowhere."

He sensed she didn't want to say more, so he prodded her with, "Jacob said you and Rory talked a lot. Did he tell you why he killed Balbinder?"

She nodded. "He was blackmailing him."

"Did he say what Balbinder had on him?"

"He knew Rory had sabotaged Nick's car and caused his accident."

"I don't suppose he told you why he did it?"

"Jealousy. He blamed Nick for Helen's death."

"I should never have told Nick about their affair."

"You can't blame yourself. He would have found out soon enough."

"I suppose so. By the way, Jim, when he wasn't ranting and raving about you taking his plane, wondered what got you over your fear of flying?"

"He told me to write down every detail I could remember of the accident. I did the one up on Aloe ridge first. It took quite a long time, but doing that stirred up memories of the one when I was a child. I put down what kept recurring in my dream. Then I went out into the garden to have breakfast and I saw an antlion crater and that triggered a memory of my brother, and I recalled my father's voice telling us about antlions. He was a bug expert. This was my first clear memory of either of them since the accident."

"I don't understand... first memory?"

"I lost my memory, or at least lost all the bits that they had a part in." she explained. "I learnt to recognize photos of them, but only because my mother got upset when I said I couldn't remember them at all."

"And now?"

"I keep getting flashes of things that remind me of my brother. Silly things, like running round in the rain... splashing in puddles. I suppose my father is harder to remember because I didn't spend quite so much time with him. It's mainly his voice that keeps kicking in."

"Does it make you sad?"

"No, I'm glad. I just wish all this stuff with Rory hadn't happened. I want to concentrate on the memories. But now they've started they'll keep coming. I hope so anyway."

"I had the opposite experience. My twin sister died when we were very young. I missed her so much they put all her pictures away because they upset me. I suppose because of that I almost forgot what she looked like."

"Is there a photo of her in those albums?" Sandra asked, "I hope you don't mind. I had a look through them yesterday."

"I don't mind at all, must be one in here." He reached out and picked up one of the albums, flicked through the pages then passed the open album across to her.

He guessed from her expression she'd seen the picture and made the connection.

He didn't want to talk yet, so he suggested they call Simeon and update him on the situation.

Chapter 33

Sandra was so relieved to find Martin at the house she nearly forgot her earlier concerns. His news of the children made his arrival even better, to the point where she wanted to kiss him, but old hurts stopped her from getting close. Not helped by Rory's dying comment that resurfaced as well, adding to her confusion.

Martin probably thought she still hadn't forgiven him for kissing Beverley. Let him believe whatever he wanted, much easier than trying to explain the doubts caused by entries in Nick's diaries and the comments Rory made before dying.

Jacob overheard Rory's confession. She hoped he'd be discreet. Maybe he hadn't made sense of what they had talked about, and she didn't want to make matters worse by begging for his silence.

Did it matter if Martin knew? Their relationship had been on a downward spiral since Beverley's early morning call after they slept together. He'd done nothing since to convince her he'd ever be completely open with her. Until he did, she felt justified in holding back herself.

The strong physical attraction made her decision hard. She liked being with him, found him easy to talk to about anything except the one topic foremost in her thoughts. She blamed exhaustion for relaxing her guard, allowing her to open up to him about her family, which led to him showing her the photo of his twin sister.

She had gasped so loudly he must have noticed. He said nothing. Never asked what shocked her. Instead he'd stared at the photo for a moment in silence, closed the album and pushed it aside. His silence added a fresh layer of tension between them.

Jacob came in with a tray of food and the chance passed. She was too tired to reopen the topic, and took herself off to an upstairs bedroom to sleep. The presence of the two bodies in the downstairs room the least of her worries.

Daylight came with brilliant sunshine and clear skies. Martin spoke to Simeon on the radio, and told her Hank had organized a helicopter to fetch them, it would return later to pick up the two bodies, and probably take Beverley to Nairobi to the hospital.

Sandra longed to get back to the twins. She dreaded to think how upset Jenny would be over her part in asking Rory to care for them.

Flying over the flooded landscape, Sandra realized how lucky she'd been, first to have had help from Jacob, and to reach shelter when she did. Water from the Aberdare mountains, had turned the normally dry gullies into raging torrents making the landscape a no go area for vehicles.

When they touched down and got clear of the whirling blades, the children charged across the wet grass to greet her. They jumped up and gave her smothering hugs and kisses. She'd removed the soggy plaster cast and found holding them painful, so gently lowered them to the ground, letting them free to hurl themselves at Martin, who lifted them with ease. Sandra found herself almost envious of the attention they lavished on him.

Beverley intervened. She limped up and hugged

Sandra in an uncharacteristic display of friendship.

"I'm sorry I've been a bitch," Beverley said quietly, "I don't know what got into me. Nothing happened between us. I wished it had, but Martin's so besotted with you I hadn't a hope. I made a fool of myself. Please forgive me."

Sandra found herself speechless, not sure why Beverley needed to apologise, she was obviously in pain. The battered nose, swollen lips and black rings round her eyes were the most visible injuries. Sandra suspected her clothing hid more.

Sandra muttered, "Forget about it," and tried to pull away. Beverley clung on.

"I thought I was going to die. A sobering experience," she explained, "which made me wonder who'd care, and I decided apart from Hank, no one would give a damn. I asked myself why, and didn't like the answers."

"What didn't you like?" Hank asked.

Beverley seemed surprised to see him standing beside her. She took a deep breath, and said clearly, "That I've been a spoilt and selfish bitch most of my life."

Sandra felt embarrassed. "Beverley, don't." She wanted to put an end to the conversation.

"Bear with me," Beverley continued. "Everyone needs to know Nick loved you more than he did me. His rejection hurt. Jealousy made me chase after Martin the way I did. I knew he wasn't interested in me, although we did once have a very short fling a while back. I wanted to hurt you. I even fooled around with Rory, because he fancied you too."

Sandra couldn't understand why Beverley would want to broadcast her jealous behaviour. "So why tell me this now?"

"Hank asked me to marry him."

The information only added to the confusion. Hank and Martin looked equally mystified. "What's his proposal got to do with me?"

"Everything," she answered, "I can't give him an answer unless I make peace with you."

"I don't follow?" Sandra said, wondering what she would divulge next. Would her revelations make Hank regret his proposal?

'"Hank is passionate about the Ol Essakut project. I didn't understand how much until now. I've always solved problems by buying my way out, which is why I wanted to buy Martin's land. I hoped to gain control and squeeze you out. That was a huge mistake. Ol Essakut needs you. It needs Martin, and Simeon, and all the people currently on board. I am the one who should bow out."

"Rubbish," Sandra said.

"You only say that because the project needs my financial backing."

"That's ridiculous. Ol Essakut needs you too," Sandra managed to say. "Not just for your money. And how does our friendship affect you and Hank?"

"I'm worried if I back out, he might be tempted to quit too."

"Listen, I hope you and Hank can be happy together. The only issue I have over you buying Martin's property is your plan to demolish his house. Perhaps we can talk about it later."

"No need. He's not selling."

"What?"

"I thought you'd be happy." She turned to Martin. "High time you started talking honestly to each other. Honesty works wonders."

Martin looked rather embarrassed and muttered,

"Thanks."

Beverley smiled as best she could with her battered face and said, "I'll leave you to sort yourselves out. I won't interfere or be a bitch again, and if I ever look as if I'm dropping back into my old habits, I'll expect you to speak up. Deal?"

"Deal," Sandra replied.

Beverley nodded and hobbled towards the house. To Sandra's surprise the children followed her, chattering as they went, odder still Beverley responded warmly.

Martin broke the silence. "Bet you didn't expect an apology."

"No, but what have you got to tell me?" Sandra said, looking intently into his eyes. "I'm tired of you skirting round the truth."

"Okay, as long as you answer one question for me afterwards."

"Fine, but can we sit down first?"

"You expecting a long session?"

"Yes." She pointed to a shady spot on the verandah.

And once they were seated, Martin said, "Go on then, what do you think I'm skirting round?"

"Nick wrote in his diary that you wanted to own the whole valley, his land, the Lander's land, the lot, and that you'd do anything to get it."

Martin looked shocked and bit his lip while he considered the accusation. "I'm gutted to think he had such a low opinion of me." He took a deep breath. "The only possible explanation I can think of is jealousy. All to do with Helen."

He stopped speaking and buried his face in his hands. Sandra stayed silent, waiting for him to continue.

"Before I went to Europe to work I fell madly in love with her. Yes, Helen Lander. Her old man was so damn strict she insisted we keep the relationship secret. I had even asked her to marry me. And she'd accepted, but begged me to keep our relationship secret until after her birthday, over three months away. I loved her so much, I agreed."

"So you never told Nick, or Simeon."

"No not a word. And being so close to each other it was really hard. Anyway I went to cover a story at the coast. Got the job done quickly and rushed back to spend time with her, only to find her and Nick together."

Sandra didn't need more details to understand he'd experienced the same betrayal she had.

"Nick had no idea about Helen and me. Her insistence on complete secrecy made me wonder if she'd been with him all along. I was shattered. At first I wanted to kill him, instead I walked away. Years before we had fallen out over a girl, and made a pact never to let a woman destroy our friendship. I figured exposing Helen would cost me a friend. She'd already destroyed the fragile pact she and I had."

He fiddled with his cuff. "Maybe I was a coward. I backed off and left the field clear for Nick. A job offer to work in Europe made the decision easier. A few weeks later I heard they had married, and soon afterwards they were to become parents. I stayed away for nearly two years, until I had to return for my mother's funeral."

Martin stopped and looked around. "Any chance of some coffee or something?"

Sandra called Juma and asked him to bring some out.

Martin might be finding it difficult talking about

his relationship with Nick and Helen. But she didn't intend letting him stop now.

"So what happened when you came back?"

"I discovered Helen was having an affair with Rory, without bothering to be discreet. I'm not sure why, I guess I still hurt and possibly sought revenge, but I had a duty to tell Nick. A bloody stupid thing to do, especially as he was cleaning his guns at the time. I never expected him to react the way he did. He stared at me for a moment then lifted one of guns off his desk and aimed at me. I laughed, never expecting him to pull the trigger. I'm certain he didn't intend to shoot."

Juma put down the tray of coffee. Sandra waited until he had left. She poured two cups, handed one to Martin, and waited.

"I saw Simeon in the doorway. Seconds later I heard a shot and felt it thud into my shoulder. Simeon threw himself at Nick. His second shot went wide and lodged in the wood panelling. I often wondered if the distraction of Simeon's arrival caused Nick to fire. I also wonder what might have happened if Simeon hadn't been there. Nick had been aiming at my heart."

"According to his diary, Nick wasn't sure either."

"Nick's hands were shaking as he put the gun down. He was more shocked than me." He reached forward and poured milk into his cup. "Simeon was brilliant. He took charge as soon as he'd locked the guns up and put the key in his pocket, he went to tell the staff the gun had gone off by accident and got the first aid kit. He dressed my wound and got me out of the house."

"You didn't call a doctor?"

"No, the bullet went right through my shoulder. Sure it was painful, but not life threatening by any means. All we wanted was to keep the incident quiet, and avoid contact with the police. Simeon drove me across the border to Uganda, and I caught the first plane out."

He spooned some sugar into his coffee and stirred vigorously. "Six weeks later Simeon called me to say Helen had taken an overdose of sleeping pills. I've always blamed myself. If I hadn't told Nick she would probably still be alive. No one understood why she'd want to kill herself. Everyone thought she was happily married. It worried me that Nick had made her life hell for those last six weeks."

Sandra realized he had to know the truth.

"You mustn't blame yourself. Nick discovered Rory was her half brother? He had to tell her to make her end the affair."

Martin nearly dropped his cup. "God, no wonder she killed herself." He regained his composure. "Are you sure about all this?"

"Yes, the papers are in Nick's safe. That's why he gave Rory the right to live on the Lander's land for the rest of his life."

"No wonder Rory thought that if Nick died, he would inherit the Lander's property,"

"He fixed the brakes."

Sandra nodded. "Yes, but he hadn't bargained on Nick leaving me in control of the children's interests."

"And when he said he wanted to get rid of the twins he didn't mean, drop them off at home?"

"No, he intended to kill them. He told me before he died. I was shocked because I thought they were his children."

"Why?"

"Helen told Nick he wasn't the twins' father."

"Are you serious?"

"Yes, I thought they might have been Rory's, so I asked him. He swore they weren't.

Martin said quietly, "I think I know why." He rummaged in his pocket then handed her the small silver oval photo frame. "I think you know too. I took this off my mother's dressing table last week."

Sandra held the faded photo, not sure what to say or do.

"Yesterday Sam saw this." Martin continued. "He spotted the resemblance to Emma immediately."

Sandra let him go on.

"There's every chance they're mine. It never occurred to me that Helen married Nick because she was pregnant."

"Don't blame yourself. The possibility never occurred to Nick either. Helen blurted out that the twins weren't his after he confronted her about Rory being her brother. He assumed Rory was their father. He wanted to protect them from the truth and told her he was willing to pretend they were his."

"So why did he shoot me."

"Helen being unfaithful was bad enough, but involvement with her brother created the problem of incest. Not something he wanted to hear or deal with. You were the unlucky messenger."

"Is that all?"

"Not quite, he bitterly regretted what he did. Apologizing to you meant telling the truth, and he didn't dare risk such a scandal becoming public knowledge. His biggest concern was protecting the children at all costs from the stigma of incest, and stopping them from ever finding out the truth."

She looked at the photo again. She remembered the other photos in the albums in his house. In her heart she was sure Martin was their father, but she was scared. Proving it was one thing, dealing with the fallout was another. She didn't relish trying to explain the situation to the twins, and she had no idea what, if any, role he would want or expect to play in their lives.

"Thanks for telling me. I'm glad to know he wanted to apologise."

"And now?" she asked.

"I'd like to acknowledge them as mine, but only if you agree. I'll get DNA testing done if you want. I trust you to decide what's best for them."

"And if I refuse?"

"I'll have to convince you that it's the right thing to do."

"Who for? You or them?" she asked, wishing she didn't have doubts.

"What do you mean?"

"Simply that we are back with the first question I asked you about Nick's diary entry. You stand to gain more than they do."

"I think this might prove otherwise. I drafted this after Sam pointed out the resemblance. I've had it checked by a lawyer. Hank and Simeon have witnessed my signature, and have instructions to lodge it with the solicitor when they get to town. Read it and tell me what you think."

Sandra took the folder of papers and started reading. The top one was a contract committing all his land to the Ol Essakut project but retaining the right to live in the family home. An additional clause stipulated all future building on the property had to be similar in size and construction to buildings his grandfather built. His final condition was that all the land be committed to the trust that was to be managed by the trustee of Sam and Emma's portion of the estate.

"Why?" she asked, completely taken aback by his actions.

"Because I love you, and want you to marry me. I want you to come and live with me and my children, and I want to remove any fences that might come between us."

"What about your work?"

"My work is here. You and the children are more important than any assignment. I'm home to stay, and I want you to be with me."

"You thought about the fences, but what about the rivers?"

"I thought I'd already proved by crossing the rope bridge that I wasn't going to let a flooding river come between us."

"The rope bridge crossing certainly proves a lot, but I don't think I'm ready to rush into anything. My question to you, is, how long are you prepared to hang around while I make up my mind?"

"For as long as it takes. I'll be here."

MHM photography

Caro Ayre

A childhood in Kenya provided lasting memories of hot sun filled days, vibrant coloured birds and flowers, armies of insects, roaming wildlife in vast expanses of open spaces and warm waves lapping on silvery sands.

I now live in rural Somerset where family, gardening, painting and writing keep boredom at bay.

For more information about my writing go to:-
http://caroayre.wordpress.com/
Twitter @AyreC
Facebook- Caro Ayre Author
www.CaroAyre.co.uk

A Kindle version is also available at:-.

http://www.amazon.co.uk/Feast-of-the-Antlion-ebook/dp/B006PZBXCI
and
http://www.amazon.com/Feast-of-the-Antlion-ebook/dp/B006PZBXCI

Reviews can be found on Amazon.com.

If you would like to leave a review please visit Amazon.com.

Clare has battled for sixteen years to keep Hannah healthy, while her husband, Mike, has never accepted that their daughter has Cystic Fibrosis.
The reappearance of an old flame and exciting challenges set by her children complicate Clare's bid for a fresh start. Repairing the fragile bond between her children and their father is an uphill struggle, but worth fighting for.

A reader's comment.

There is something extraordinarily authentic about this novel of a family in crisis. The characters are compelling and I got completely wrapped up in the dilemmas and challenges and relationships so beautifully portrayed of life married to a domineering, obsessive man who turns out to have secrets of his own. Her priority is her daughter Hannah, who has Cystic Fibrosis and while the condition is central to the novel it does not dominate in any way.

A donation will be made to the Cystic Fibrosis Trust for every copy sold.
Cystic Fibrosis is a lifelong challenge.

www.Amazon.com/dp/B00DOFT5VI
www.Amazon.co.uk/dp/B00DOFT5VI

ISBN 978-0-9572224-1-0

Lightning Source UK Ltd.
Milton Keynes UK
UKOW04f1033150913

217207UK00001B/2/P